THE UNICORN AND THE WHITE LION

GUARDIANS OF THE WILD: BOOK 1

ANNA BROMLEY

ISBN:
978-1-916529-66-3 (Paperback)
978-1-916529-68-7 (Hardback)
978-1-916529-67-0 (Ebook)

Cover design and illustrations by Lynda Mangoro.
Images of Fairstone School created from an original pen and ink of Bedstone School by J Hibbs.

The Unbound Press

www.theunboundpress.com

Hey unbound one!

Welcome to this magical book brought to you by The Unbound Press.

At The Unbound Press, we believe that when women write freely from the fullest expression of who they are, it can't help but activate a feeling of deep connection and transformation in others. When we come together, we become more and we're changing the world, one book at a time!

This book has been carefully crafted by both the author and publisher with the intention of inspiring you to move ever more deeply into who you truly are.

We hope that this book helps you to connect with your Unbound Self and that you feel called to pass it on to others who want to live a more fully expressed life.

With much love,

Nicola Humber

Founder of The Unbound Press
www.theunboundpress.com

Praise for
The Unicorn and the White Lion

"Anna has created a magical tale suffused with wisdom and wonder. The story combines mystery and myth in an adventure that has a little bit of something for everyone. A great achievement, with a rich tapestry of characters that represent each and every one of us, in an adventure for all ages."

Monty Halls, star of Channel 4's My Family and the Galapagos and BBC TV's Commando series

"A joyful insight into the world of spirituality and magic."

Isla Halls

"When I finished *The Unicorn and the White Lion*, I immediately began demanding the next instalment – that's how much I loved this book! I fell in love with these characters and loved watching them grow and learn what they're capable of. Heartwarming and hilarious, magical and mischievous, this story kept me riveted right to the end – I can't wait for the next one! I look forward to learning more with Nanny Watkins and having more adventures with Grace, Daisy, and Archie!"

Jesse Lynn Smart, Editor and Book Nerd, Bookstagram: @FaeryJessReads

"I so enjoyed tagging along on all the adventures of Grace, Daisy and Archie in *The Unicorn and the White Lion*. I love, love, love the way so much practical magic wisdom was interwoven with such ease and grace.

And I was so pleased that the ending of the book was so much deeper than just 'the good guys keep the bad guys from doing something horrible.'

I enjoyed the book as an adult and think it would have been a wonderful benefit to me as an adolescent. We should all be so fortunate to have accepting friends and mystical beings to share our journeys with. I'm anxiously awaiting Book II."

Jennifer Muldoon, Designer

"I loved the whole story – the storyline is beautiful. I found it very exciting. I loved how you included the shamanic and magical teachings through each of the characters, particularly Nanny and Grace. The reader will learn in a lovely open and receptive way. I learnt a lot too!

I love how they change the hunters' ways through magic. That's earth changing. And what happened to the big pants Grace bought in the beginning? That was so funny!

It felt like an alchemical fusion of Mallory Towers with the Magic Faraway Tree yet with so much more within and so much better."

Eimear Stassin, Founder of The Irish
Wisdom School and Seanchaí Storyteller

A magical romp!

"This is the kind of book you won't be able to put down – a sparkling, hilarious and utterly enchanting adventure. Grace, Daisy and Archie will steal your heart, as they discover the magic in their world. A story about friendship, courage and the gift of being different, this book is a must-read for anyone who believes in the extraordinary hiding just beneath the surface of the everyday."

Nicola Humber, Author of Heal Your Inner Good Girl and Unbound Writing, Founder of The Unbound Press and Transformational Writing Mentor

Dedication

To my beloved Mum, who always championed my writing and who, like Nanny Watkins, lost her son too soon.

To my darling daughter, Phoebe. Together, we came up with the idea for the book and her love of horses inspired the character of Ahbleza.

To all my friends and teachers from Bedstone College. You were the inspiration for this book. My memories of my time there are precious. I hope it stirs some good memories for you too.

And to my Younger Self, who would have loved to read of Grace's adventures. She would have learned so much from Grace's journey.

Contents

Preface

Meet Grace – she's a very magical and highly sensitive person. But at 15 years old, she doesn't yet realise this is what makes her unique. She just feels weird and different, unsure of herself, amongst the confident posh kids at the boarding school where she's just got a scholarship.

But magic seeks her out, and befriended by two kind hearts in her class, Archie and Daisy, she begins a great adventure. Out walking in the woods one day, the three amigos meet a wise old healer, Nanny Watkins, who is versed in the ancient ways of indigenous Britain. Under the wing of Nanny, the kids begin to learn about the magical practices that will help them step into their power and purpose. They learn how to work with their dreams. They learn about shamanic journeying and meet their guide, a magnificent White Lion. They time travel through magic portals and learn about ley lines and standing stones. And most magical of all, they meet a star-born horse with a spiral horn of healing light and find that his fate is entwined with theirs.

This is the story of how the kids set out on their mission to become 'Guardians of the Wild,' and all the adventures that unfold as a result. For Grace, it also includes learning to become a healer, and she comes to accept that what makes her different, makes her special.

I wove their tale with much humour, as they get into hilarious scrapes at their very quirky boarding school and come up with ingenious ways to solve them.

Once upon a time, I was Grace – that awkward teenager and young person who felt that she didn't fit in, especially when I started discovering my skills in shamanic journeying and dreamwork. I thought everyone was thinking, "What a weirdo!" – until I matured enough to start valuing my skills and talents as what makes me unique.

So I wrote this book to help all those feeling like outsiders and wanting to find their purpose. I also wrote it because like Grace, I went to a country boarding school. It turned out to be a huge adventure, where I made friends for life, and many of the hilarious scrapes in this book are based on real events that happened to me at school.

I started writing this book for teenagers, and in particular, my own daughter. But I soon came to realise that it's for people of all ages. If you love magical, mysterious adventure stories with plenty of humour, and have an interest in dreamwork, healing, shamanism, or want to learn about stepping into your power and owning your own unique skills and talents, I hope that you will love this book.

And there is another twist to this tale – the heartbreaking timing of the publication of this book coinciding with the closure of my school after more than 70 years of shaping young lives and providing them with the best education. So this is also my tribute to my beloved Bedstone College. I hope it brings back fond memories for all who knew and loved the school.

Hope you enjoy reading this book as much as I loved writing it.

.

With much love, Anna Bromley

PS This is Book One of a three part series, so hold tight while I bring to life more magical adventures for our three heroes.

Chapter 1:
The Birth of Ahbleza

A star fell to Earth that night. A star ended its life over the mountains. And in the dying embers of its light, a new life was born to the wild herd that roams the White Mountains.

On Cefn Hill, the herd of wild horses stamp and snort in a chill spring wind, as the sun begins its slow descent into the west and the light starts to fade from the sky. Glowing orange ribbons of cloud paint the luminescent blue above the sharp back of the Darren, and rose-coloured light outlines the edge of its scarp.

There is magic in the air over the White Mountains tonight, a portent of something momentous about to happen. Epona, the lead mare, is about to foal. She has taken herself off a little distance from the herd, into a copse of trees next to a bubbling spring that fills a bathing pool. The humans that remember know that this spring is sacred, a place of healing and fertility. Nearby is a circle of standing stones, also a sacred place, but most have forgotten its importance – a portal to the stars.

Her glossy black sides begin to heave as the first of the contractions start. Strong, fast, brave and wise, the herd relies on Epona to lead them out of danger. Tonight they are nervous. Who will do this for them while she is in labour?

Proud and haughty Rohan, their stallion, will have to be extra vigilant. He tosses his golden mane in the wind, lifting his nose and sniffing the air for signs of anything out of the ordinary. There is something, but it is not like anything he has experienced before. It's a sharp tang, like the smell of ozone when lightning splits the sky, yet he has no sense of an impending storm.

Two pairs of ravens wheel across the sky in a final fly past before night falls. Their otherworldly cry of, "Conk, conk," echoes off the hills. Blackness descends on the mountains and the first star of evening shines over the Darren. In the east, a faint glow appears behind the trees, as the moon slowly sails into the sky until she is in her full silver glory.

Epona is in the last throws of her labour now. The foal will soon be here, wobbling about on new legs. A few more deep breaths and a push should do it.

Suddenly, a blazing light illuminates the sky, like a falling star coming to Earth. The horses are terrified. Rohan stands his ground as the star descends slowly to Earth, coming to ground in the stone circle. This is like nothing he has ever known before, but something about it tells him he need not give the signal to flee. The light is so bright he can barely stand to look.

Epona's foal is born, but not yet up on its feet, a pure white colt. Out of the blazing light steps a radiant figure, a winged being, an angel of pure light. He makes his way into the copse and Epona stands mesmerised as the radiant being comes towards her newborn foal.

"His name is Ahbleza. He is a shining one of great power with an important purpose on Earth. He will face much danger in his young life as he brings his message to humankind to take care of the Earth and to take care of all God's creatures. You must guard him and protect him so that he can fulfil his mission." The angel touches the foal on his forehead just above his eyes, which leaves a glowing mark like a star. Then the angel steps back into the blaze of white light and is gone.

"So your name is Ahbleza. Welcome, little one," says Epona, blowing a soft greeting to her son. His eyes are the deep blue of the sky at twilight. Starlight entwines his mane and tail. Starlight is shining from his brilliant golden-white coat. Starlight shines from his forehead in a spiral cone that points towards the heavens.

Epona is overwhelmed by the beauty of her new son. She is proud of giving birth to this special being. She nudges him gently to encourage him to get his weight up on those long gangly legs. She is excited by his auspicious entrance into the world and a little nervous. How will she take care of this one and guard him from danger as he grows, as he shines out for all the world to see?

Summer Term

Image based on an original pen and ink of Bedstone College by J Hibbs

Chapter 2:
A New Girl at School

Grace settles herself on the back seat of the family Peugeot estate, as it purrs along the country roads. She looks out on rolling green hills, under a soft blue April sky, watching the miles slide by in this borderland between England and Wales. Her father is a good, safe driver, although rather fast, having first learned to ride a motorbike back in his youth. He always takes the corners faster than is comfortable for his passengers, expecting everyone to lean into them, just as he would have on a bike, so she is hanging onto the strap above the window.

Grace is already feeling uncomfortable, in her stiff and rather prickly new school uniform. It is grey, oh so grey, and made of wool – a pleated skirt, an itchy cardigan and a blazer with the Fairstone School badge carefully sewn on by her own hand. She has laid this beside her on the seat, it being too warm to wear on this mild day. The only saving grace is the blouse – a gold and white check in fine, soft cotton with a little rounded Peter Pan collar. She thinks it adds a touch of sunshine to an otherwise dismal outfit. She wiggles her toes in her new stiff brown leather shoes. "I mean, brown! Whoever thinks that brown shoes go with a grey uniform!" her thoughts are loud and outraged inside her head. Even worse are the knickers. And she giggles to herself as she recalls the trip to Rackhams Department Store in Birmingham. Her mother had read the items from the Fairstone uniform list to the very snooty woman behind the big glass counter in the Uniform Department.

"It says here, the next item is five pairs of grey briefs."

"What age?" snapped the woman, Mrs Primm, according to her name badge. The corners of her mouth are pulled taught by the tightness of her greying bun.

"Well, dear Grace here is 15, so we had better see the age 15 knickers," replied Mum. Grace had a sense of foreboding as the woman brought out a very large bundle of stiff, drab grey undergarments and held up an enormous pair for inspection. Grace saw her mother's jaw drop and her eyes bulge, as she inspected the proffered article. "Oh, nothing very brief about those!" muttered her Mum. They were made of such thick, stiff fabric that they practically stood up on their own. She had leaned close to Grace's ear and whispered, "Just like an elephant's backside!" Then she had tentatively stretched the very strong leg elastic, which recoiled with a resounding thwang, and said, "And this double thickness gusset which extends all the way up the back – that should keep out the draughts!" Grace would have laughed if she hadn't been so horrified. Her mother continued, "These must be the most unattractive garments I have ever seen."

"I think that is precisely the point. A young lady must preserve her modesty in a mixed school," said Mrs Primm.

"Oh, I see – they are deliberately ghastly!" Grace's Mum replied to an appalled-looking Mrs Primm.

Shifting uncomfortably in the unwieldy knickers, Grace wants to remind her Mum of the scene, as she sits in the front passenger seat, but thinks better of it, feeling too embarrassed to discuss undergarments in front of her Dad.

It's the start of the Summer Term. Grace is worried that it's a strange time to be starting at a new school, but Grace's Dad has just got a new job managing a big estate of farms and they have moved up from Somerset. Grace's Mum has tried to reassure her, saying it's perfect – a whole term to settle in to the new school before starting her 'O' level year.

"Nearly there, Love," says Dad. "We're just going over the railway bridge at Hopton Dando. It must be about a mile to Fairstone now. We should be able to see it soon. The house is quite a size. You must be excited about starting your new school?"

"Yes Dad, but a bit nervous too," Grace replies.

"You'll be fine, Gracie. You did so well in their entrance exam to get the scholarship, which means they really want you here and you're going to be top of the class," says Dad.

"Yes, that's what's worrying me. I don't think it's going to make me very popular with the other kids in the class. They'll think I'm a pauper and a swot."

"Oh, I'm sure it won't be that bad. I bet there are some really nice children in your class," says Dad. Grace winces at the word 'children'. At 15, she doesn't feel like a child anymore.

"Yes, I am sure you will make friends in no time at all," says her Mum.

Grace's Dad turns the Peugeot in through the big stone gate pillars and they set off up the driveway towards

Fairstone Court, the main school building. They pass the gatehouse on the right and Grace notices an athletic-looking man wearing tracksuit bottoms and a hoodie emblazoned with 'Fairstone School' in the garden of the gatehouse. He looks up as they pass and smiles at Grace. He has thick, dark hair, a luxurious moustache and warm, friendly eyes. Grace hopes that he is one of the staff. She thinks she might get on well with him. He is, in fact, Mr Aveen, the games teacher, and he will be her introduction to the delights of hockey, athletics, cross-country and trampolining, to name only a few of the sports on offer at Fairstone, where physical ability is highly rated.

They pass playing fields with a cricket pavilion on the left and tennis courts on the right. Above the playing fields and to the left of the school building is a field with a few sheep in it, kept out of the main school grounds by a ha-ha ditch. And then there is Fairstone Court itself. It is an impressive sight as they sweep up the drive, a black and white Tudor-style mansion with many doors, windows and chimneys.

They drive on past the main school building in search of Fairstone House, where she will be boarding with the other senior girls. Her Dad says, "I hope we're going the right way for the boarding house. I'm not sure we're supposed to drive across the playground. Hey, he looks like a helpful chap and about your age, I'll stop and ask." A tall, rangy boy with a shock of curly brown hair is walking towards them across the tarmac. Grace's father winds down the window. "Excuse me, young man, could you tell us the way to Fairstone House?"

"Yes Sir," says the boy, having a good look into the interior to see who the new girl is. "Straight ahead, keeping those tennis courts to your left. Fairstone House is just behind the laurel hedge on the right, but you have to drive round to the back to get to the car park." He gives Grace a winning smile and she feels a little flutter of nerves about getting to know all her new classmates.

"Well, he seemed very nice," says her Mum. "I hope he's in your class."

Dad negotiates the narrow gravel drive around the edge of the grounds of Fairstone House and parks in the car park. A man comes to greet them.

"Hello, you must be Mr and Mrs Bellaport? And is this Grace? Welcome, welcome! I'm Mr Chapeau, your Housemaster here at Fairstone House." He runs a hand through unruly auburn curls and extends the other to shake hands with Grace's Dad. He smiles warmly at them, as his brown eyes take everything in. "Let me help you with Grace's luggage and I'll show you her room."

Grace's Dad opens the boot and gets out the enormous trunk which she has filled with the beastly uniform, sports kit and all the other things she will need for her first term at Fairstone. "I can't make you carry this, Mr Chapeau. You've probably lugged 15 of them already," says Grace's Dad.

"You're right! Let me take this then," he says, picking up a small holdall with Grace's personal things. "This way," he says, opening the front door onto a black and white tiled hallway with a wide, gracious stairway leading to the upper floors.

Upstairs, he leads them down a corridor going round to the right and knocks at a door, before opening it onto a bedroom with three beds. "You'll be sharing with Charlie Rogers and Daisy Davies. They're not here yet, otherwise I would ask them to show you around. I'll leave you to settle in. Tea is at 6pm in the main building. I'll get someone to show you where it is if Charlie and Daisy aren't here by then. Loo and bathroom are back along this corridor on the right. My room is downstairs, across the hallway on the left, if you need anything. Any questions so far?"

"Yes Sir, could you tell me where my classroom is, please?" says Grace.

"It's down the long corridor to the right of the main school building. I'll get the girls to show you later." He left the family to say their farewells to each other.

"Well, this is a lovely room, dear, and with only two other girls, so not a great big dorm then. I'm sure Mr Chapeau will have put you in with someone nice. He seems like that sort – you know, thoughtful about that kind of thing," says Grace's Mum.

"So this is it then, my dear. We'd better leave you to get on with it. I'm sure you will have many adventures here. Can't wait to hear about them," says Grace's Dad.

"Make sure you call us tomorrow to let us know how you're getting on. I'll miss you, Poppet," says Grace's Mum, giving her a hug and kissing the top of her head.

"Me too," says Dad, hugging both of them together. "Come on then, parting is such sweet sorrow and all that. Let's get it over with."

Grace holds back her tears as her parents leave and waves to them out of the window as they get in the car. Then she sits on the bed and gets out her hanky as a few fat teardrops slide down her face.

"Come on, Gracie. Pull yourself together. This is going to be fun. I can feel it. This is going to be an amazing adventure," she tells herself. And with that she sets off back down to the playground where she had seen the tall, curly-haired boy who had smiled at her.

Chapter 3:
The Outcast

The months pass and Ahbleza grows in both size and mischief. Racing and playing with his fellow colts and fillies is his favourite pastime. Epona watches him closely, sure that he will become a stallion of fine stature. But she also worries for him. He has been marked out as different by the circumstances of his birth. Rohan is nervous around him and looks worriedly at the strange bump which is starting to form on his forehead, where the angel touched him. It glows with an eerie light, making him stand out even more from the other foals.

Rohan is frightened of this abnormality and nervous that this special starlit soul will draw too much attention to his herd. As soon as Ahbleza is independent of his mother and stands a chance of living on his own, Rohan resolves to drive him from the herd.

By the age of one year old, Ahbleza has developed the ability to send a spiral of light out of the bump on his forehead. Sometimes this seems to happen spontaneously when he is excited. At other times he seems to do it deliberately. When Rohan sees him projecting this spiralling horn of light and touching it to the leg of one of his playmates, injured through too much rough play, he decides that enough is enough. He will not tolerate any weirdness, and it is time for Ahbleza to go. What he doesn't realise is that Ahbleza's spiral of light is healing the injury and that this ability would be such an asset to the herd.

Rohan flies into a rage, screaming his disgust at Ahbleza, repeatedly charging at him, biting his rump and rearing up to drum his hooves on Ahbleza's back.

Shocked and frightened, the little white colt runs from the herd, fleeing the hillside, making for the shelter of the woods in the valley. He runs as fast as his hooves will carry him, far away from this raging beast he once thought of as father.

He is swift as the wind and has disappeared from view by the time Epona realises what has happened. Desperate to catch up with her son, Epona is dismayed to follow the trail of blood down off the hill. Eventually, she finds him, his sides heaving and his legs trembling, head down, by a stream at the edge of Farmer Morgan's land. He is not seriously injured, but is bleeding from superficial wounds where Rohan has nipped and kicked him.

In a few strides, she is by his side, nuzzling him with love, blowing soft kisses into his ears. "You cannot stay here, Son," she tells him telepathically. "It is not safe. You are on Morgan's land. He is no friend of horses. But I know of one who is. I will lead you there. She will know what to do."

Chapter 4:
A Strange Encounter

As she walks across the playground, Grace becomes aware of someone looking intensely at her. He is walking past what looks like the assembly hall and is heading for some steps that lead to a formal garden with a statue in the centre. When he notices that she has spotted him, he gives her a bright smile and makes his way towards her.

"Hello, you must be the new girl in Form 4? What's your name? I'm Jonnie, by the way, Jonnie Watkins. Pleased to meet you." He puts his head on one side, as his small bright eyes appraise her. He has a kind of wolfish smile, showing lots of teeth, which gives him the air of a faithful puppy. Grace tries to guess his age. Will he be in Form 4 with her too, or perhaps he's a bit older? There is something that doesn't quite add up about him. His school uniform looks kind of old-fashioned, with its big lapels, his wide kipper tie and outrageously flared trousers. His light brown hair is spiky on top and longer down the back, which reminds her of a seventies rock star.

"Perhaps he's just a rebel who likes to dress in vintage clothes," she thinks to herself, before saying out loud, "Yes, my name's Grace and I'm looking for Form 4."

"Come on then, I'll show you the classroom." He leads her down the steps where he had been heading, on a path past the formal garden and into a long corridor with classrooms along one side. "This first one is Form 4. The next one along is the Fifth Form classroom. Best to avoid them if you want to get any work done. They're a rowdy bunch – good fun – but a complete bunch of dossers. And I've heard that you're really bright. Rumour is you got a scholarship award. So my advice to you is – there are only two people in this class who are worth making friends with. They're both really smart, but not too boring. Oh, I think this one's your desk," he says, indicating a single desk in the middle of three rows of wooden desks, all neatly lined up to face the front.

"Oh yes, who are they?" she asks.

"Daisy Davies and Archie McBride," he says. "Daisy has the kindest heart of anyone I know. She is funny and sweet, a bit clumsy, always getting into scrapes. If you make friends with her, you will have a friend for life and you will always have fun and adventure. And Archie, well, he's just an all-round top banana. He's sickeningly good at everything, but he has a heart as big as a lion's. A really good person to have on your side. He's very clever and witty, but he can also be a bit of a dimwit at times – acts before he's got his brain engaged. He needs someone bright like you to keep him out of trouble."

"And how about you, Jonnie?" asks Grace. "Shouldn't I be friends with you too?"

"Oh gosh, no! I'm complicated. In fact, I'm a bit of a weirdo. Best not to get too attached to me, but I'll be around if you need me."

"Well, you seem like you've got a good heart too. I'm going to look forward to getting to know you better." Grace begins to put some books in her desk and then looks up to find that Jonnie has gone. "Oh, I wonder where he went? Hope I didn't say anything to offend him," she thinks.

Grace hears music coming from the classroom next door and wonders if that's where Jonnie went. She walks down the corridor, intrigued by what Jonnie has said about the dossers next door, and peeps nervously through the window. Three tall boys are singing and dancing to the haunting strains of 'Ghost Town', by the Specials, which is booming from a large cassette deck. The wind howls and eerie organ music is followed by melancholy flute and horns over a reggae beat. Two of the boys hold long-handled brooms like mics on a stand and sing into them, swaying in time to the music. The third croons into a board rubber microphone...

This town is coming like a ghost town.
All the clubs are being closed down.
This place is coming like a ghost town,
Bands won't play no more –
Too much fighting on the dance floor.
Aargh la la la la la la la lar... they wail the chorus like banshees.

A shiver goes up Grace's spine.

"You don't want to get involved with those reprobates," says a voice from just behind her. Grace jumps and spins round to see the boy with the mop of curls from earlier in the playground. "Shhh, come this way before they realise we've been watching," he says, beckoning her back to Form 4.

"Goodness, you gave me a fright then," says Grace.

"Sorry, couldn't resist," he says, with a mischievous twinkle in his blue eyes. "It's a spooky song, huh?! And they do it so well. Anyhow, I'm Archie and I'm in your form. Pleased to meet you. It's Grace, isn't it? I saw you in your car going up to Fairstone House."

"Oh, Archie McBride? I've just been hearing all about you!"

"Really? Who from?" says Archie.

"Jonnie Watkins. He showed me to the form room and told me about you and another girl, Daisy Davies."

"Huh? I think you must have got the name mixed up. There's no-one called Jonnie Watkins in this form, but the name is kind of familiar. Daisy Davies, on the other hand, is larger than life – very enthusiastic and funny. I call her Oopsy, because she's a bit clumsy and she's always falling over. But she's heaps of fun. And Daisy knows EVERYONE. Her family lives locally and she always has a cousin or an aunty or a friend who will know where to find that piece of information you need or the place to get something important. So definitely a good friend to have. I expect you'll meet her soon."

"Yes, she's in my dorm," says Grace.

"Oh, brilliant! You'll have a cracking time," says Archie. "Come on, it's almost tea time. I'll show you to the dining hall. I have to warn you, the food here is terrible, but you need to eat something, so let's brave it." He leads her back across the playground and through a side door into the main school building. "Girls' bogs on the right. Boys' bogs on the left. Down the corridor. The kitchen's on the right and Boss's dining room on the left (don't get caught going in there or you're in big trouble). Big wooden staircase to your right goes up to Boss's office and the junior boys' dorms. Door to the left goes to the Old Hall. Library straight ahead. Almost there now – the dining room's round to the right, but we'll probably have to start queuing from here ... and yes, here's the queue."

"Who is 'Boss'?" she asks.

"Oh that's what we call the Headmaster, Mr Williams."

"Oh yes, I met him when I came for the entrance exam," says Grace. She takes in the sights of her whistle-stop tour. Archie walks so fast with his long legs. The interior of the school is a strange mixture of scuffed corridors and badly painted plasterboard, contrasting with polished oak panelling and the gracious sweep of the elegant stairs to the first floor in the older part of the school building. Through the glass panels of the door to the Old Hall, she can see acres of polished wood, stained glass windows and walls decorated with photos of school teams and events, going back through the years.

A girl with hair as dark and glossy as a raven's wing joins the queue behind them and elbows Archie in the ribs. "Hey Arch, how was your Easter?"

"Oh hi, Daiz. It was great but I did miss all you lot. I know I'm a saddo, but it's actually nice to be back. Here, let me introduce you to Grace. This is Daisy Davies."

"Oh cool, you're the new girl! Pleased to meet you, Grace." She grins at Grace with perfect pearly white teeth and sparkling eyes as dark as her hair. "I think we're sharing a dorm. And this is Charlie. She's in our dorm too," says Daisy, standing aside to introduce a titan of a girl, almost as tall as Archie, with rosy cheeks and strawberry blonde, wavy hair.

"Wotcha, Grace! Pleased to meet you too," says Charlie

and grabs Grace's hand for an eye-wateringly firm handshake.

"Blimey, Charlie, have you been practising your arm wrestling over the Easter hols?" says Archie. "Grace's eyes nearly popped out there!" They all laugh and go into the dining room for the first of many appallingly bad suppers. The oak panelling of the dining room and beautiful old windows contrast with the rubbery green lino flooring and the stainless steel serving counter, designed for easy cleaning of food spills.

When they have finished eating, Archie says, "Hey girls, we'd better introduce Grace to the delights of the Rec."

"What's the Rec?" asks Grace.

"Well, it's that big ugly building next to the Gym. You must have seen it on your way down from Fairstone House. It's right on the corner there, as you come out of the grounds of your boarding house," says Archie.

"Oh, you are a dimwit sometimes, Archie," says Daisy. "I think Grace wants to know more about what happens there."

"Yes, please, I'd like to know more about that."

"Oh, I see, OK. Well, the Rec, short for the Recreation Centre, is the huge barn-like, ugly building where we young people are expected to conduct our social lives in the tiny amount of free time that we have from our studies. It is a place of gathering that is designed to keep us out of mischief, such as the temptation to go and snog each other or have a ciggie in one of Farmer Morgan's barns. It's filled with a couple of pool tables, a couple of ping pong tables, some extremely uncomfortable benches round the sides, a few nasty plastic chairs and large numbers of bored teenagers. Oh, but I'm forgetting to mention the legendary MaxPax machine, from which you may purchase a cup of the most mediocre hot chocolate, which doesn't live up to its name as it is always lukewarm and tastes more of the cardboard cup it's served in than of chocolate. Or if you're feeling adventurous, you could go for a Cup-a-Soup. But I don't recommend that because it's absolutely revolting. There, does that cover it, Daisy?" says Archie.

"Yes, I get the gist, thank you," says Grace.

"I thought it would be a good place for Grace to get to meet a few more of the kids in our class. And because, for a change, we don't have prep tonight, we've got some time to kill before we have to go to our boarding houses," says Archie.

"Don't let him spoil it for you, Grace. I really like the hot chocolate and I am looking forward to whupping you at pool, Archie," says Charlie.

"No chance, Charlie. I've been practising in the holidays," says Archie.

"What's Prep?" asks Grace. "So many new words I've never heard before!"

"Ah, you've got that delight to come tomorrow night. It's basically supervised homework time. We sit in our classrooms in silence for 45 minutes and a Prefect sits at the front and makes sure we don't talk or misbehave – it's very boring!" says Archie.

"Yes, but without it, you would never get any work done, Archie," says Daisy.

"That's true, but it's still boring. Anyhow, let's go," says Archie. "Any of you fellas want to come up the Rec?" he says to the three boys sitting further down the dining table, who had been surreptitiously staring at Grace and very obviously eavesdropping on their conversation.

"Yes, but aren't you going to introduce us, Archie?" says a tall, muscular boy with shiny golden-brown hair that flops into his twinkling hazel eyes.

"Want to keep the pretty new girl all to yourself, do you

McBride?" says another boy, shorter and stockier with thick, very straight fair hair, who winks at Grace.

The third boy, slighter in build than the first two, with shiny brown curls, slides up the bench towards Archie and whispers in his ear, "Ey up, Arch old mate, she's a corker."

"Grace, meet Tom," says Archie, indicating the first boy. "He's the best swimmer in school (after me, that is) and not bad at rugby. He's an all-round top bloke," and then leaning close to Grace's ear, he says in a stage whisper, "But between you and me, he's not very bright."

"Oy, you cheeky git!" says Tom, punching Archie on the arm. "Don't listen to him – just because he's an annoying brain box, who got the highest IQ marks in the entrance exam, doesn't mean he's got any common sense. Pleased to meet you Grace. I hope you'll be really happy here," says Tom.

"And this is Calum," says Archie, indicating the stocky, fair-haired boy, "Also a pretty good swimmer and the best rugby player in our year. But steer clear of his charms – he's a total cad."

Calum shook his head, saying, "See what I mean, Grace. He's just trying to put you off. You're welcome to come and hang out with us anytime you get bored with Mr McBride's company."

"And this is Dan, also known as Burnley, because of his Lancashire accent. Another all-round top bloke, and absolutely hilarious. He might look like a skinny little stripling, but once he's got the rugby ball under his arm, he's as fast as a whippet, and one of our best kickers."

"It's right nice to meet you, young lady," says Burnley, looking sincerely into Grace's eyes and taking her hand in a warm handshake, giving her the most sparkling smile. Grace makes a mental note to learn more about the rules of rugby. It looks as if she will need to understand it if she's going to be able to make conversation with the boys here.

"Right, formal introductions over – let's go!" says Archie.

They make their way back down the corridor, cross the playground and over to the Rec, for an evening of ping pong, pool and lukewarm hot chocolate.

At 8.30pm, Daisy says, "I hate to break up the fun, but we need to get up to Fairstone House. It's lights out at 9pm. See you guys tomorrow."

"Yep, see you tomorrow for another day of fun-filled adventure at Fairstone School," says Archie.

"Bye, Grace," Tom, Calum and Burnley say in unison.

Later that night when they're getting ready for bed, Charlie and Daisy notice that Grace is wearing her Big Girl's knickers.

"OMG, Grace, you're not really wearing the elephant's backside knickers are you?" says Charlie.

"Don't be mean, Charlie. Can't you see Grace is really embarrassed?" says Daisy.

"I'm not being mean. I just want her to know that nobody actually wears them, because she'll be even more embarrassed if anyone else finds out."

"I don't understand," says Grace, blushing bright red. "Why does it say you need five pairs on the uniform list if we're not supposed to wear them?"

"We only wear them for Games, under our gym skirts or under our cross-country running knickers, which by the way, are practically see-through. Other than that, hopefully no-one is going to know what you're wearing. Unless you fall over and flash everyone that is! And they're so bloomin uncomfortable with that thick knicker elastic – they give you terrible VPL."

"What's VPL?" asks Grace.

"Visible Panty Line," says Charlie.

"Euw! You're right, they are bloomin uncomfortable. They're cutting my circulation off. I feel like my legs are about to drop off! My goodness, I'm so relieved to hear we don't have to wear them all the time. But I'm going to have to ring my Mum and ask her to bring me some more regular knickers. I've only brought a couple of pairs for the weekend."

"I'm not offering to lend you any of mine!" says Charlie.

"They'd be massive on her anyway, Charlie!" says Daisy.

"Wouldn't it be terrible if they fell down when she was halfway across the playground?!"

"Cheeky!" says Charlie, giving Daisy a flip with her towel. The girls all laugh with relief that the topic is now out in the open.

Grace feels green, naïve and very new, but relieved that they can have a joke and that Daisy seems to be on her side. She feels nervous and worried. Will she ever fit in here? Everyone, although they seem to be very nice, is really confident and worldly-wise, and also wealthy and quite posh. She is acutely aware that she has come from mainstream school and wouldn't be here if she hadn't won the scholarship which pays for all her fees. Her father is a farm manager. She has that in common with Daisy and Charlie, who are both farmers' daughters, but unlike them, her family doesn't own their own land.

Chapter 5:
This Toast is Rubbery!

Breakfast at Fairstone

Grace wakes to the sound of Mrs Chapeau ringing a bell and calling out, "Morning girls, time to get up!" It's Monday morning and the start of the Summer Term.

She is still halfway in and halfway out of dream world. She's had a restless night after all the excitement of the day before, meeting all these new people. It took her a while to get off to sleep – with all the thoughts that whirled around her head. Everything is so strange and different to her old school in Somerset. Her dreams flit through her mind. In the fragments she can remember, strange mythical beasts – lions and unicorns – populated her dreamscape, along with many faces – the faces of all the new people she has just met, but particularly Archie and Daisy.

"Good morning, Grace. Good morning, Charlie," pipes the cheerful voice of Daisy. "How did you both sleep?"

"Like a flippin' log," grunts Charlie. "I wish I could sleep for a few more hours. But hey ho, time to get on with another day at Fairstone."

"And how about you, Grace? How was your first night at Fairstone House?" asks Daisy.

"A bit restless – so many new things whirling around my head. I had some crazy dreams which I can't quite remember. Oh, and these blankets are so itchy. I didn't realise we could bring our own duvets," says Grace.

"Yes, I had some mad dreams too – something about a unicorn and what else? Oh yes, a white lion. I mean a white lion. Do they even exist?' asks Daisy.

"Yes, I think they do. My Mum has a book called The White Lions of Timbavati. It's somewhere in South Africa."

"Oh, how interesting. I'd love to read that book. I adore lions," says Daisy.

"I'll ask Mum to bring it when she brings my duvet and knickers, so you can borrow it."

"Thanks! Oh yes, I'd forgotten about the knickers. I'll show you where you can have a private phone call. There's a phone we're allowed to use in the hallway here, but everyone can hear what you're saying – it echoes around on the tiled floor. And you don't want everyone hearing about your knickers, do you! There are some phone booths down at Main School. I'll show you later.

Anyhow, we need to get going, or all the showers will be taken. Grab your wash stuff and let's head down to the bathroom. Are you coming, Charlie?"

"No, I need another five minutes," she says sleepily. "I'll see you later."

After their showers, they dress in the itchy grey uniform and brown shoes. It all feels strange and stiff to Grace, but at least she's wearing more comfortable knickers. And the uniform helps her to feel like one of the crowd. She feels so desperate to fit in.

Charlie is ready too. She seems to have the knack of going from zero to top speed very quickly, once she is properly awake. The three of them make their way down to the main school building and join the queue in the dining room for breakfast. They are greeted by a warm blast of air that smells of burnt toast and the sulphurous smell of boiled eggs.

"Hi Gorgeous Daisy, how were your Easter holidays?" An older boy with big brown eyes, full of mischief, and the most luxuriously thick eyelashes, puts his arm round Daisy's shoulder and gives her a big squeeze. Grace recognises him as the boy crooning into the board rubber in the 5th Form classroom. "And who is your lovely new friend?" he asks.

"Oh, hi Darius! I had a lovely time seeing lots of cousins, and the farm is full of beautiful little lambs now. This is Grace, she's just started in our form."

"Pleased to meet you, Grace," says Darius, taking her hand and bowing over it. "Welcome to Fairstone. You've chosen well for your first friend." And he winks at Daisy with a mischievous grin.

As he saunters away with as much young swagger as he can muster, Grace whispers, "Who's that? What a lovely accent he has!"

"That's Darius Darvesh. He's in 5th Form, very sweet, but a bit of a numpty. You'll get to find out what I mean by that very soon, I'm sure. He's always playing pranks. He's Persian, so that's where his accent comes from. His Dad's a journalist and they were chucked out of Iran because he was telling too much truth. I think that's the gist of the story anyway."

"Stop ogling the 5th Formers, Grace!" says a voice from behind. Grace spins round, blushing crimson. It's Archie and Tom, who've just joined the breakfast queue behind them.

"Oh, I was just getting to know the local characters," says Grace, trying to sound casual.

"Morning ladies," says Tom. "How's things this morning?" he says, looking directly at Grace.

"Oh, fine, thank you," she says, relieved that the subject has changed. "I'm slowly getting used to everything."

"Well, this morning, you're in for a treat – a gourmet breakfast of soggy toast that smells like old socks, hard-boiled eggs and congealed beans," says Archie.

"Oh yummy, it sounds great. My mouth's watering! But how come the toast is soggy?" says Grace.

"Well, they have this ingenious way of toasting the cheapest, rubberiest white bread, buttering it, or should I say margarineing it, while it's still hot, and then stacking it in huge piles on a ginormous baking tray – enough to serve 200 people. By the time we get to eat it, it's been sitting there steaming and soaking in melted marg for ages. The piece right on the top of the pile might have a bit of crunch left around the edges, but the rest is about as soggy as Tom's socks after a hectic game of rugby and smell about the same.

"Oy, speak for yourself, McBride. My socks smell lovely," says Tom.

Archie is right. The weird-smelling, rubbery toast is a whole new experience for Grace, and served by the most stony-faced woman in a blue flowery overall and hairnet.

"We call her Rhino Woman," whispers Archie to Grace, "Because she's so charming."

"But Ethel, down the end there, serving tea, is much nicer. She always saves me the best toasted buns after rugby matches – she's so sweet," says Tom.

"That's because you're a big charmer, Tom. You bat those twinkling eyes at her and she's putty in your hands," says Archie.

"Well, it doesn't cost anything to be nice," says Tom, looking at Grace and giving her a winning smile.

"I think she's a bit saucy too. We're only allowed half a bun – top or bottom. I've heard her saying, "I've saved you a bottom, young Tom. I know you likes bottoms!'" says Charlie. They all laugh as Tom blushes.

"The other thing you need to know about Ethel, Grace, is that she runs the local taxi service, so if you ever need a lift to the train station, or you're thinking of running away (which I very much hope you won't), she's your woman," says Archie.

Chapter 6:
Getting to Know the Fairstone Routine

The Welcome Assembly

After breakfast, it's time for the Welcome Assembly. They make their way back down the corridor, out of the old school building and into the main school hall, a modern extension with a stage at the opposite end and a parquet-floored seating area big enough to house the whole school.

Grace sees that the seats are arranged in three blocks, with aisles leading to the front and the stage. "Does it matter where we sit?" says Grace.

"We all sit in our houses," says Daisy. "And it's younger ones at the front and older ones further back. Do you know which house you're in?"

"Oh, I think Mr Chapeau said I'm in Clifford," says Grace.

"Splendid!" says Archie. "You're in the same house as me and Daiz. It's the best house to be in – the best and brightest people are all in Clifford."

"I beg to differ," says Tom. "Long Town people are all good eggs, aren't they, Charlie?"

"Yes, definitely the best sports people too," says Charlie.

"And what about the other house?" asks Grace.

"That'll be Snodhill," says Archie.

"Oh, what a funny name!" says Grace. "And what are the Snodhillers like?"

"I guess it is a funny name. I never really thought about that before," says Daisy. "All the houses are named after local castles."

"The Snodhillers are like the name sounds – a bit snooty-tooty. You've got the likes of Anne Smith and Portia Jenkins in Snodhill," says Charlie.

"Oh, Portia Jenkins is alright," says Archie.

"Just 'cos you fancy her, McBride," says Tom.

"Well, don't we all?" says Archie, with a dreamy look on his face. "She's magnificent – runs like a gazelle!"

"OK, enough of the chit chat, we better get to our seats, guys," says Daisy. "Clifford is on the left, Long Town in the middle and Snodhill is on the right. Come and sit by me, Grace. See you guys later."

They make their way to their seats. Grace can't quite believe that some of the youngest children are only seven years old. "Poor little mites – they're so young to be away from home," she whispers to Daisy.

"I know! But a lot of them are day schoolers, living locally. And Mrs Henn, the Prep School head, is very sweet with all of them."

A small, rotund man with a shiny bald head, little gold-rimmed glasses, and kind, friendly eyes, stands at the front of the stage and addresses the children. "That's Mr Williams, the Boss," whispers Daisy.

"Oh yes, I recognise him," whispers Grace.

"Welcome everyone, to the Summer Term here at Fairstone. Welcome back to all the familiar faces, and only one new one this term. We welcome Grace Bellaport to Form 4. Stand up please, Grace, so we can see who you are."

"Oh, how mortifying!" thinks Grace, as she stands to receive the curious gazes and mainly welcoming smiles of the whole school.

"Grace is the winner of the scholarship award, a very bright young lady, so we are looking forward to seeing her brilliant work this year. Thank you, Grace, you can sit down now – I've embarrassed you enough!" says Mr Williams.

Grace gratefully sits and Daisy gives her hand a little squeeze of reassurance.

"So we have a packed final term of the year. The 5th Form and the Upper 6th will of course be taking their 'O' level and 'A' level exams. But we'll make sure there's time for recreation and, as always, plenty of sporting events to keep the mind and body sharp. In particular, we have the Inter-House Endurance Race, which is an opportunity to earn big points for your house. There's also the Independent Schools Athletics Meet in Birmingham. We always do well as a school in that one, so keep up with your athletics training towards that. And this year, Fairstone has the honour of hosting the Inter-Schools Swimming Gala, which I'm sure you'll all train hard for and do us proud.

On the recreational side, we have a trip to watch the Shakespearean play at Ludlow Castle to look forward to and many field trips to be organised by your form tutors and subject teachers.

The summer term at Fairstone is perhaps the most glorious time to be here – enjoying her grounds and the surrounding countryside. So I hope you will all work hard, train hard and have a very enjoyable final term this year.

Now please stand to sing our school hymn, 'Jerusalem'. Mr Parsons, if you would kindly accompany us on the piano."

The school sings a rousing rendition of the hymn and the assembly finishes with the Lord's Prayer. Then it is time for all the children to go to their classes for the day.

The First Night in Prep

All is very quiet in the 4th Form classroom, where the kids are diligently doing their evening's prep for tomorrow's lessons. Alexander McGregor, a tall, stern-looking Upper Sixth Prefect, is supervising from the teacher's desk at the front of the class.

He quietly turns the page of his book, when suddenly "FRAAAP!!!" – a thunderous farting sound breaks the silence. Grace is startled into looking up. The sound seemed to come from the desk in front of her, where Tina Brewer is sitting, head still bowed over her book, getting on with her work.

To Grace's horror, everyone (including Tina) looks up and turns in the direction of the sound, to see Grace's rapidly reddening face, as she realises that they all think that she's the one who farted. Alexander is staring directly at her. He shakes his head and mutters, "Dirty, filthy pig!" and then continues with his work. There is much suppressed sniggering and giggling, but soon everyone returns to their work. Grace is mortified and squirms with embarrassment until the end of Prep. Finally, after what seems like an age, the bell for the end of Prep goes. Everyone heads for the door. Grace races up to the boarding house, hoping not to speak to anyone about the humiliating incident. But a voice calls out from behind her.

"Bad luck, old girl, for taking the blame for Tina Fartypants' disgusting bottom." Grace stops and looks behind to see Archie and Daisy hurrying after her. "We know it wasn't really you. She has previous form on that front. I think it must have been the beans on toast she ate at teatime. Mind you, Daisy's almost as bad – she can be a right old windypops! You'll notice that they serve a lot of baked beans here. It's a cheap form of protein. I sometimes think there must be a green haze of methane hovering above the school. It's a wonder none of the 6th Formers have blown themselves up when they sneak out the back of their studies for a quick ciggie!" says Archie.

"Archie McBride, you are a big fat liar. I am NOT a windypops!" says Daisy, elbowing him in the side. "But yes, Grace, we know it wasn't you because he's right about Tina having a windy bottom."

Archie turns towards Grace and out of sight of Daisy, he mouths, "She IS a windypops!" Out loud he says, "Well, I guess Grace will find out in the dorm tonight whether you're a windypops or not. The giveaway will be that her duvet will be hovering six inches above her bed!" Archie clutches his sides laughing, as Daisy thumps his arm to make him stop.

Chapter 7:
A Mother's Love for Her Son

A Year and a Half Ago…

Nanny Watkins is walking in the woods, gathering mushrooms and foraging for herbs and greens for her supper. It's a beautiful early September day. The light has that golden quality, as it shines from a crisp blue sky. The air is fresh but mild – her favourite kind of day. She delights in the beams of sunlight filtering through the trees and the glimpses of that lovely velvet sky that she can see through the canopy.

"Ooh, that'll be lovely fried up with a bit of garlic butter," she says as she picks a large horse mushroom and places it in her basket. "That's it now, I can't fit anymore in. Better be off home." She hums a little ditty to herself as she returns home, feeling pleased with her haul of foraged food.

She's almost home when she senses something – the presence of a being, an animal she's not familiar with. She knows all the forest creatures from her walks in the woods and the way their energy feels. But this is different – something big that she has not sensed here before. And there's a certain tangy smell of a large animal's sweat. And there is emotion with it too. Whoever or whatever it is feels sad and anxious, and needs her help.

She stops to quietly tune in with this being, putting down her basket. She sends a message from her heart to tell them that she is a loving soul, and not to be afraid of her. As she does this, she hears a snort – a blowing of air through large nostrils. Out from the tree cover steps the most magnificent glossy black mare. It's Epona.

"Well, hello, me Beauty," says Nanny. "What brings you to these parts?" She holds out a hand for Epona to sniff, to show her that she means no harm.

Epona edges forward and sniffs Nanny's hand. She already knows that Nanny is a good woman – she senses it with the keen instincts of the Lead Mare, and she has seen it in her dreams – that is why she has come here with her precious son.

The two mothers recognise kindred souls in each other. Both know what it is to fear the loss of your son.

"Where is he then, this son of yours?" says Nanny, reading Epona's mind, "And how can I help him?"

Epona whinnies and nods her head towards the trees. Ahbleza steps shyly towards his mother. Nanny gasps as the most beautiful horse with a gleaming white-gold coat steps out. There is a radiance that glows from his every cell.

"Well, my goodness, you're a handsome one, aren't you?"

Nanny says to Ahbleza, and then to Epona she says, "You must be so proud of him!"

Epona nods her head towards Ahbleza. It's then that Nanny notices the wounds – the torn skin, the dried blood, where Rohan has bitten and kicked him.

"Oh, I see, someone in your herd didn't like your son – he's too beautiful by half. Maybe a bit threatening to a lesser horse who's trying to hold onto his power, eh? Am I near the mark?" Epona nods her head up and down again, her beautiful, glossy mane waving in the breeze.

Nanny holds out her hand for Ahbleza to sniff. He comes forward more boldly now. He sees that this woman has a kind and loving heart, and presents no danger to him. Yet more than that, he senses a wise but wounded soul. In that moment, he knows why he is here. They can both help each other.

"What's your name, me lovely?" asks Nanny, and in her heart, she hears his words.

"I am Ahbleza. I am here to help you heal your broken heart."

"Well, that's as maybe," says Nanny, taken aback by this. How did he know? And how can he help her heal?

"Epona, you can leave your boy here and go back to your herd. They need your leadership and protection. He will be quite safe with me, I promise. I can do something to heal those wounds of his. I have some magic salve that heals things almost instantly. It's got beeswax from my wonderful bees, calendula from my garden and a big sprinkle of magic from me. And you can come back and visit him anytime."

Epona sees the change in her son as he speaks with Nanny. He is beginning to step into his power. She knows that he is safe here, and so she takes the chance to slip away as Nanny tends to his wounds.

Chapter 8:
Meanwhile, Life Goes on at Fairstone

Bitter-Sweet Memories in the Old Hall

The bell goes for breaktime. Grace excuses herself to go to the loo, but taking a wrong turning, finds herself alone in the Old Hall. The smell of wood polish soaks her senses. Sunshine pours in through the stained glass window and a thousand dancing orbs of coloured light reflect off the polished wood of the shiny parquet floor and the oak panelling of the walls. There is a staircase leading to a great gallery above and rooms leading off it, including Boss's office.

She has a feeling that she shouldn't linger here, that it's not her place. Echoes of the past are all around her. This would have been the place of celebration and dances when the original owners, the Ripleys, lived in the house. She can almost hear the buzz of conversation and glimpse the finely dressed ladies and elegant men out of the corner of her eye.

She is drawn to look at a set of black and white photos from twenty years ago. The more recent past is recorded in the many photos of school activity. Photos of special events, whole school photos going back through the years, and team photos of muscular boys and athletic girls – the heroes of their sports, the victors of many an epic rugby or hockey battle, or swimming, cross-country, tennis, cricket. Many of the pupils here at Fairstone excel at these physical events, which are so lauded by the teachers and headmaster.

It makes Grace feel uneasy. Sport wasn't emphasised at her previous school. She loves to run and isn't bad at cross-country, but all these team games make her nervous.

Her eyes zoom in on the description of one of the photos. It says, 'Senior Boys' Cross-Country Team, 1972.' Ah, that's more like her kind of thing. Four very fit-looking, sinewy boys grin out of the photo. She recognises the wolfish grin of one of them and looks down to see his name, 'Jonnie Watkins.' Her heart gives a little jolt and the hairs on her arms stand up. "How can that be?" she thinks. "I met Jonnie Watkins looking the same age as this just the other day, but the caption says 1972." She gives a little shiver as a cold breeze ruffles her hair.

She nearly jumps out of her skin, as a voice behind her says, "Yes, that was me. I was a pretty darn good runner. I loved it – steaming through the fields and the woods. I felt at one with nature, like a wolf running after a deer." Grace spins around to see Jonnie Watkins standing there, looking the same age as he was in the photo. "I was an excellent swimmer too – best in the school. There are some photos of me in the swimming team somewhere."

"Oh, Jonnie, it's you! You startled me."

"Sorry about that. Didn't mean to scare you. How are you

getting on? Have you made friends with Archie and Daisy yet?"

"Yes, I have. But why those two? There are lots of nice kids in school."

"They're special, those two – friends for life. And I have a sense, a hunch, that there's some important mission for the three of you together."

"Oh, that's interesting. What do you mean exactly? What sort of mission?"

"I don't know yet. Just a feeling I get."

A loud bell rings and Grace looks towards the door. "I'd better get to my next lesson. That's the bell for the end of break. She looks back to where he had been standing, but just like the first time she saw him, he has gone. Grace shudders, "Wow, how weird! Did I just imagine that conversation?" She is determined to get to the bottom of this mystery. And what on earth is this 'important mission' he talked about? Life had just taken a turn for the weird, and who could she trust to talk to about this? Gosh, she'd only just met everyone. "I don't want to start off my time at Fairstone with everyone thinking I'm a weirdo – 'Grace Bellaport (whisper, whisper), she's the one who sees people who aren't actually there. What a nutter!'"

Hockey Practice

"To you, Grace!" yells Charlie, seeing that she is in the perfect position to have a shot at goal and wanting her to get some glory. Charlie gives the hockey ball a mighty thwack in Grace's direction. The ball is coming so fast and high at Grace that she fails to get her stick up to stop it in time. Instead, it drives into her forearm, which is tensed in anticipation of the ball hitting her stick at top speed.

"You're supposed to stop it with your stick, not your arm, you numpty!" shouts Charlie.

Everyone is laughing. Searing pain from the impact is throbbing up her arm. It feels as if it might be broken. Hot tears are prickling her eyes. "Don't cry, don't cry..." Grace is saying over and over in her head. "My first hockey practice, a chance to show I'm good enough to get into the team and then I go and do this. What an idiot!" Grace is thinking to herself.

The Games Teacher, Mr Aveen, blasts the whistle to stop play, but he needn't have, because all the girls have stopped and are staring at Grace. Most are wondering how badly hurt she is and whether she is going to cry.

"Are you OK, chook?" says Mr Aveen in his soft Scottish accent. "Let's have a wee peep at that. Can ya still move it? Flex ya hand for me. It all seems to be in working order – nothing broken. Are ya OK to carry on, or do ya want to tek a wee break?"

Grace has been looking down at the inside of her forearm with growing horror as she follows Mr Aveen's instructions. A bright white circle forms, the shape of the hockey ball, and edged with crimson. The force of the hockey ball, hitting her arm, unleashed by the might of Charlie's ample muscles, has blasted all the blood from that part of her arm to the outer regions of hyperspace, leaving a white fleshy void. And now it is beginning to swell with the lymph fluid that her body is rapidly pumping into the area to try and repair it. A lump the size of half a grapefruit rises from her arm, taking on a life of its own.

One by one, the girls come round to inspect the damage. Most are visibly wincing, with mutterings of, "Ooh!" "Yuck!" "Ouch – nasty!" "Going to be a heck of a bruise!"

Grace is now in panic mode. "I need to be brave," she

thinks, "But I don't know how the heck I'm going to hold my stick, let alone run up and down the pitch."

"I'm fine to carry on," she says unconvincingly.

"Are ye sure?" Mr Aveen looks doubtful.

"Yes, yes – it's just a little bump," she says.

"OK then, if you're sure. Tek your positions, girls."

Charlie sidles up to Grace, "I'm really sorry, Grace. That looks as if it hurts like hell. I wouldn't think less of you for sitting this one out."

"Don't worry, Charlie. Really, I'm fine," says Grace and she trots towards her position on the right wing.

Charlie watches as Grace slowly buckles at the knees and face plants into the mud. Grace has fainted – she's out cold. With a wry shake of the head, Charlie looks at Mr Aveen. "I saw that one coming, Sir. Shall I take her up to the boarding house?"

"Better take her to be checked out by Nurse Bernie first."

"Nah, that mad old woman – she'll only try and rub Bonjela on it. She thinks it's a cure for everything, but it's really not. I'll pop her in her bed and get Mrs Chapeau to check in on her later."

Charlie picks up Grace and wraps her good arm around her shoulder. Daisy rushes to support her on the other side. Grace is beginning to groggily come round.

"You poor love," says Daisy. "Are you back in the land of the living yet?"

Grace mumbles a weak, "Yes, I'm fine."

"Do you think you can walk, if we support you?" asks Charlie.

"Absoo-lutely!" slurs Grace like a teenager who's drunk too much cider at a party. Slung between Daisy and Charlie, she zig-zags and wibble-wobbles her way back to the boarding house. Daisy and Charlie get her out of her muddy clothes and into her pyjamas, then put her to bed.

Grace is mumbling, "Oh, I won't get picked for the hockey team, now."

"You were doing really well till you tried to stop the ball with your arm, you dufus – a good little runner on the wing. And you were reading the game well, getting in the right positions. But you've got some practice to do on your ball control!"

"She's not going to remember any of that!" says Daisy.

They watch as Grace rolls her head from side to side, saying, "I'm fine. I'm absolutely fine!"

"We'd better tell Mrs Chapeau to keep an eye on her!" says Daisy.

A Trip to Ludlow

It's Friday afternoon and a new delight awaits Grace – a trip to Ludlow on the school bus. She's feeling heaps better after her mishap on the hockey pitch, but she has the most startling coloured bruise on her arm and it aches a lot.

"Come on Grace, you don't want to miss this. You don't have to go, but it's great fun," says Daisy. "Grab your purse, there are some really nice shops in Ludlow. You know – crafts, nice clothes, handmade bath stuff, and some lovely cafés. You not coming, Charlie?"

"Nah, don't fancy it this time."

They make their way to the school playground and spot Archie waiting to get on the bus. "Hi girls, I'm glad you're coming. Mind if I tag along? None of my mates are coming. Boring swots, they're already revising for the mocks."

"Oh my goodness, already?" says Grace with a pang of guilt that she's not doing the same.

"Yeah, they're worried about the November 'O' levels," says Archie.

"Oh gosh, I hadn't even thought about those yet," says Daisy.

"Are you doing any 'O' Levels in November, Grace?" says Archie.

"Well, I suppose so, but I need to talk to Boss about my choices," she says.

"He's sure to want to put you in for a bunch, knowing what a brain box you are, Miss Scholarship Girl," says Archie.

"Ooh, can we change the subject, please, Arch? It's giving me the collywobbles just thinking about it," says Daisy.

"Yes, sure. Sorry Daiz. Oh look, here comes the bus. You're in for a real treat, Grace – your first trip to Ludlow on the school bus. It's a momentous occasion!"

As he is saying this, the most ancient old jalopy of a bus steams and puffs its way up the driveway and onto the playground.

"Wow, that really is vintage. Is it steam-powered?" laughs Grace.

"Probably. You wait till we have to go to Birmingham for the athletics meets in it – it's a real adventure!" says Archie.

"All aboard," says Mr Aveen, their driver for the day.

They climb aboard the ancient relic of a bus and set off for Ludlow, the bus backfiring like a flatulent cow all the way. After half an hour's drive through the glorious Shropshire countryside with all the spring flowers and trees in blossom, the bus pulls up in the car park next to the ruins of a castle. "Wow, look at that!" says Grace.

"Impressive, isn't it?" says Archie. "In the summer, they hold an outdoor Shakespearean play here and the school always has a trip to one of the performances."

"Oh, I really want to go to that!" says Grace.

"Yes, let's all go," says Daisy. "They're always very dramatic – it's such an amazing setting, especially for something like the 'Scottish Play', but it's definitely a bit creepy. But I think this year it's *A Midsummer Night's Dream* and it's on our 'O' Level syllabus."

Grace gazes at the castle and a cold shudder goes up her spine. "Oh, yes, I can still feel it – very creepy even now! I wonder what terrible things happened there to leave that feeling?"

"Plenty, I'm sure," says Archie. "Let's do something a bit more cheerful. Shall we introduce Grace to the delights of De Greys Tea Room, Daiz?"

"Ooh yes, let's," says Daisy. "They do the best cream buns."

"I bloody love cream buns!" says Archie.

"I bet you do," giggles Grace, as they set off for De Greys oldy-worldy tea shop, a black and white timber-framed building. An overhead bell rings loudly as they push open the ancient, thickly painted door. Inside, Grace is greeted by the smell of freshly baked scones and warm soup. Black painted oak beams contrast with the white of the ceiling. There is oak panelling around the walls and polished wooden chairs at tables covered with red and white tablecloths. They find a table and sit down. An ancient old lady, dressed in a smart grey uniform, with a frilly white apron and hat, wobbles towards their table to take their order.

"Hello dears, what can I get you today?" she asks.

"Hello Doris, so good to see you. How are you doing today?" says Archie.

"Oh mustn't grumble!"

"Well done! We'll have three of your finest cream buns and a pot of tea for three, thanks, Doris," says Archie.

"Jolly good. You'll enjoy those, young lady," she says to Grace. "Are you new at Fairstone? I haven't seen you before."

"Yes, my name's Grace. Pleased to meet you, Doris."

Doris reappears with the buns and tea, managing not to

spill too much of it on her wobbly way to their table.

"Oh my goodness, these buns are divine!" says Grace, taking a huge bite.

"Told you," says Daisy.

There's time for a spot of shopping before they re-board the bus to school – all three together on the back row. Content and replete from the tea and buns, and lulled by the rhythmic chugging of the bus, Grace falls asleep. To her huge embarrassment, she is woken gently by Daisy as they arrive back at school, to find that she has been dozing with her head on Archie's shoulder and gently dribbling onto his blazer.

"Oh, I'm so sorry, Archie," she says, dabbing it with her hanky.

"No worries," says Archie. "It's nice to see you feeling a bit more relaxed now, and you look so sweet when you're asleep!" Graces blushes.

Chapter 9:
Meeting Nanny Watkins

The Old Man of the Forest

It's a beautiful spring afternoon and Grace has cabin fever. It's Saturday and school is almost finished for the week – Grace's first full week at Fairstone and what an eventful time it's been already. Her Mum is coming to pick her up later and she'll spend Saturday night and Sunday at home with her parents. She's so looking forward to it. She's really missed them. She's especially close to her Mum – they're like best friends, and she's got so much to tell her.

She is gazing out of the classroom window thinking about all this, as the Geography teacher, Mr Lipton, brings the lesson on Market Gardening in the Vale of Evesham to a close. Finally, the bell for the end of lessons and lunchtime goes – she's relieved that it's the start of the weekend break now.

Daisy and Archie walk alongside Grace as they head for the lunch queue. "So how was your first week at Fairstone, Miss Bellaport?" asks Archie. "Did it make you want to run away, or are you eager for more?"

"Well, it's been pretty jam-packed, hasn't it? And it's had its ups and downs, but on the whole, it's been great. And you two have been so kind to me. I can't thank you enough," says Grace.

"You are so welcome! We've really enjoyed getting to know you," says Daisy. "What time are your parents picking you up today?"

"Oh, not till 6pm," says Grace. "They thought we'd have some sort of match and that I wouldn't be free until then."

"Yes, mine too," says Daisy. "They forgot there isn't usually anything on the first Saturday of term."

"So what are you going to do this afternoon?" says Archie. "My buddies are all going home straight after lunch, so I'm going to be at a loose end too. Do you fancy going for a walk? We could walk down the back road and show Grace Paradise Wood – the bluebells should be out by now."

"Yes, great idea," says Daisy. "Do you fancy it, Grace?"

"I think that sounds lovely. I love bluebells and it's such a beautiful day," says Grace.

"Getting there on the back road takes a bit longer, but it avoids crossing Farmer Morgan's land. And we'll have plenty of time if we set out soon," says Archie.

"Yes, why don't we just grab some cheese, Ryvita and salad from the dining room and take it with us? We could have a picnic when we get there," says Daisy.

"Sounds perfect. Let's go!" says Archie.

After grabbing some food for their picnic, the three kids head off past Fairstone House and turn left onto the back road. It's a pretty country lane, which, after half a mile, leads them over a little stone humpbacked bridge crossing a brook, which babbles and sings as it swirls over the stones of its bed.

The sun is shining brightly, the air has that clarity of a warm spring day and the hedgerows are full of flowers and humming bees. Grace takes a deep breath of the fresh spring air and has one of those moments when all feels right with the world. In spite of the hockey incident and taking the rap for Tina farting in prep, she feels that coming to Fairstone was the right decision. "Here I am with two new friends in the most beautiful part of the world. How lucky am I?" she thinks to herself.

"You're very quiet, Miss Bellaport – a penny for your thoughts?" says Archie.

"Oh, I was just having one of those moments – you know, thinking how lucky I am to be here with you two lovely people."

"Well, the feeling's mutual," says Archie, giving her a wide grin.

"Yes, me too," says Daisy.

"The wood's not far now. I think you'll love it. There are some amazing trees there," says Archie.

"I always think it's very magical in there," says Daisy.

They come to a gate with a stile next to it and a footpath sign pointing across a meadow towards the woodland beyond. They head across the meadow and soon they enter Paradise Wood. The woodland feels spacious, with its elegant beeches, their smooth silvery bark and bright green spring leaves. The sunlight filtering through the canopy of new leaves dances and sparkles on the forest floor. The woodland floor is covered with the gorgeous purple of bluebells, whose subtle scent, warmed by the sunlight, wafts in waves upon their nostrils. A path, worn by the feet of many animals, weaves its way among the trees.

"Wow, the trees look like people!" says Grace. "Look at that one, it looks as if it has a face, with even a nose and a mouth."

"I told you it's magical in here," says Daisy.

"You wait till I show you my favourite tree. I call him the Old Man of the Forest. And there's a surprise waiting for you there," says Archie. They walk for a couple of minutes more before they come to a bit of a clearing, and in the centre of the clearing is the most giant tree of the whole woodland.

"Here he is, the Old Man of the Forest. Isn't he magnificent?" says Archie. The Old Man is a huge gnarly old oak tree, its bark wrinkled into the contours of a face. There are two shapes where limbs have fallen off, like two beady eyes which Grace feels are trained on her, complete with wrinkles in the bark forming the Old Man's eyebrows. A drooping, bulbous bit of the trunk forms his nose and a scar in the bark looks like a smiling mouth. On either side of the Old Man, two low limbs grow out, looking like his arms.

"He looks like a real character!" says Grace.

"He is!" says Archie. "Come on, let's climb him. We can sit on one of these low branches. I think he must have been coppiced at one time."

"What does that mean?" says Daisy.

"Oh, the woodsmen used to cut the trees right back to use for firewood or making things. And then they would grow back faster, with extra branches growing out from lower down," says Archie.

"Ooh, I can practice some gymnastics – it's just like a balance beam," says Daisy. She takes a run up and a flying leap onto the Old Man's arm, landing with her belly across the branch. Lifting one leg to the side and bending her knee, she manages to straddle the branch. "Let's see if I can remember any of my standing moves."

"Are you sure, Daiz? It's a long time since you did gymnastics and there's no crash mat here," says Archie.

"Oh, don't be a killjoy, Arch. I'll be fine," says Daisy.

"What could possibly go wrong?" says Archie, giving Grace a wide-eyed look, with eyebrows raised, that said he feared the worst.

Daisy gets to her feet and walks along the branch with arms outstretched. "It's all coming back to me now. Jump and turn."

"No Daiz, not a good idea!" says Archie. Ignoring him, she jumps and spins around, but she hasn't anticipated how much springier the branch is than a balance beam. Grace watches with her heart in her mouth. As Daisy pirouettes in the air and her feet descend towards the branch, the back spring of the branch comes up to meet her and … boof! … it sprongs her off, launching her back up into the air. She sails in a graceful arc, letting out a startled, "Whaa…" as she flies through the air and lands in a crumpled heap several feet away from where she started.

Archie and Grace rush over to her. "Wow! That was spectacular!" says Archie, trying to suppress a laugh until he finds out whether she's badly hurt.

"Oh my goodness! Daisy, are you OK? Have you hurt yourself?" says Grace.

"I'm fine, I'm fine," says Daisy, struggling to her feet and brushing leaves and soil from her clothes. She looks OK, apart from a gash on her knee, which is rapidly swelling up.

"Oh, you've hurt your knee," says Grace.

"Oh, it's nothing. I'll be fine," she says, taking a step forward and trying to put weight on it. "Idiot!" she mutters to herself, as a grimace of pain contorts her face.

Nanny's Cottage

"Oh dear, that looks painful. Can I be of any help?" says an unfamiliar voice. The kids turn to see an old woman with a basket full of herbs standing there. A beam of sunlight pours over her, shining with a soft gleam on the silver of her curls, giving the impression of a halo of light around her. Kindly blue eyes twinkle from an ageless face of such warmth and charm that the kids are immediately put at ease. "The Old Man been playing his tricks again, has he?" she asks, indicating the tree from which Daisy has been recently spronged with a nod of her head.

"Oh, I don't think it was his fault," says Daisy. "I was being an idiot."

"Oh, my dear, don't put yourself down – just being young and lively, I expect. But he does like people to ask permission before you go climbing on him," says the old woman. "Would you like me to have a look at your knee, dear? I have some skills in healing. Otherwise it's going to be difficult to walk back to Fairstone like that. My name is Nanny Watkins, by the way, because it would be weird to have a complete stranger doing healing on you. I live just over there," she says, pointing further into the woods.

"Oh, Nanny Watkins! I've heard my Aunty Sarah talk about you," says Daisy.

"Would that be Sarah Evans? She's a very fine woman."

"Yes, that's right. And I'm Daisy Davies – very pleased to meet you. And this is Grace and Archie."

"Great to meet you, Nanny," says Archie, sticking out his hand to shake Nanny's. "You've arrived just in the nick of time."

"Lovely to meet you, Nanny," says Grace. "I feel as if we've met before, but I can't think when or how."

Nanny gives her a penetrating look and says cryptically, "Perhaps in our dreams."

"I'd love you to have a look at my knee, Nanny. You're right, I am going to struggle to get back to school like this," says Daisy.

"Alright dear, why don't you come and sit on this log. Lucky for you, I've got some yarrow in my basket – it's just the job for stemming the bleeding." She takes a green feathery herb out of her basket, crushes it between her hands and places it over the wound, speaking some words under her breath that Daisy can't quite hear. "Now, let's see what we can do for the swelling." She scans her hand over the wound, about four inches above Daisy's knee. "Is this the most painful bit, right here?" and she points to an area of Daisy's knee.

"Ouch, yes, that's it!" says Daisy.

"Yes, I thought so," says Nanny. "Keep still while I take the shock and pain out. It might feel a bit worse for a moment, as it leaves, but better out than in, eh?" She points a knobbly finger at the painful spot and extends the thumb and forefinger of her other hand to form a triangle with the first finger. A look of intense concentration comes over her face.

Daisy gives a little shudder and tears form in her eyes as she cries out.

"There it is, may it be transmuted and transformed. May Daisy be well. May Daisy be happy and healthy," says Nanny in a little sing-song incantation. Archie and Grace watch in disbelief, as they see the swelling on Daisy's knee go down and disappear altogether. And by now the bleeding has stopped too.

"Wow, that was amazing, Nanny!" says Grace.

"Very cool," says Archie.

"Thank you SO much," says Daisy. "That feels much better. I think I can probably walk on it now."

"Would you kids like to come and have a cuppa and a bite to eat before you head back? My cottage isn't far and I think it would do Daisy good to have a bit longer to rest before you set off back. She's had a bit of a shock, though she's bearing it well."

The kids all look at each other and then Grace answers for them. "That would be lovely, if it's not too much trouble."

"No trouble at all. I was planning to put the kettle on anyway."

She leads them down a path through the forest amongst the bluebells and a sea of white wild garlic flowers. The smell of sun-warmed garlic wafts to their nostrils on a gentle breeze, and the subtle scent of the bluebells in the background intoxicates them into a dream-like state. Daisy seems to be walking miraculously well after her tumble.

Soon they come to Nanny Watkins' little stone cottage, looking like something out of a fairy tale, with its front garden full of colourful spring flowers. Grace has a momentary flash of apprehension, remembering the story of Hansel and Gretel – what if Nanny is secretly a wicked witch, who wants to boil them in her pot and eat them? But she quickly dismisses the thought because Nanny Watkins seems wholly good and kind, with a reassuring presence.

"Here we are then," says Nanny. "I'll get the kettle on. And would you like something to eat? Don't look so worried, dear. I'm not going to entice you with sweeties and then eat you!" she says, giving Grace a knowing look, with a rascally chuckle. Grace blushes – "She read my thoughts!" she thinks to herself.

"Well, we don't mean to be any trouble. We brought a few things from school to have a picnic in the woods, before I was daft enough to fall out of the tree," says Daisy. "We could just have that. But I'd love a cup of tea." Archie gets their food out and puts it on the table.

"No disrespect meant, kids, but you don't want to be eating that rubbish out of packets, when I've got lovely homegrown and homemade food to give you. How about some oat cakes with goats' cheese from my goats and some sauerkraut? I was going to make a bit of pesto out of this wild garlic I've just collected too. It won't take a minute to rustle up while we're waiting for the kettle to boil. Grace and Archie, can you lay the table while Daisy has a sit down to rest that knee? We could eat in the back garden if you like, as it's such a lovely day."

"Ooh, yes, in the garden, please Nanny. I'll take everything out for you," says Archie. "I found these fold-out chairs and table in your back porch, Nanny. Hope you don't mind. I spotted them earlier and thought how nice they would be for a picnic." In no time at all, Grace, Archie and Nanny have set up the table, full of delicious food and cups of tea on the stone patio nearest the cottage.

From the patio, a path leads to a little gate at the bottom, which opens into the paddock where she keeps her goats. On either side of the path, herbs, flowers, fruits and vegetables of all kinds grow in abundance. Nanny is a woman who isn't going to go hungry in a crisis and her medicine chest is also stocked with all manner of dried herbs, tinctures, creams and syrups that will treat all of the common ailments and a few that are not so common.

The sun is out and the bees hum busily amongst the flowers and herbs, collecting nectar and pollen. In a sunny spot at the bottom of the garden are their hives, where they work their magic, turning the nectar of the flowers into honey.

Nanny sees Grace watching the bees at work, "I love my bees and I treat them like my friends," she says. "I go to see them every day and I make sure I tell them all the latest news. The old ones used to say you must always tell it to the bees, because if you don't, the hive will die and it will bring ill fortune on your house."

"That's fascinating, Nanny. One day, I would love to keep bees," says Grace. She is so delighted to be eating real, healthy food instead of the terrible school meals. She misses her Mum's cooking and her garden at home.

"Wow, Nanny. This food is amazing! I hadn't realised how hungry I was," says Archie.

"You're very welcome to take some back with you to school," says Nanny. "Right, me dears, time you were heading back. You know the quickest way back is along the footpath over Farmer Morgan's land. It's much shorter than going back along the road, so it'll be easier for Daisy. But don't get caught. He gets really cross about seeing kids on his land and he'll be straight down to the school to complain. It's been lovely meeting you and I hope you'll come again. You're welcome anytime."

"Thank you SO much, Nanny, for everything, for healing Daisy's knee and all the lovely food," says Archie.

"Yes, thank you, thank you," say Daisy and Grace together.

"You're very welcome. It's been lovely having your company. Oh, before you go, have this little pot of healing balm to put on your knee, Daisy. It's got herbs to heal and soothe in it, if it starts to hurt again. Put some on when you get back to school and some at bedtime. See you again soon, I hope." And she hands Archie a little parcel of food to take back.

The kids head home along the footpath that crosses Farmer Morgan's land, looking carefully around to make sure no-one sees them and are quickly back in the school grounds.

"Wow, what an adventure!" says Archie. "I know you weren't intending for the accident to happen, Daiz, but you did us all a favour, because we got to meet Nanny Watkins – what a character she is!"

"Yes, there's more to that old woman than meets the eye," says Grace.

"Well, according to Aunty Sarah, Nanny has a reputation for being an amazing healer. She's known as 'Betty the Bone Setter' round here, because she can even heal broken bones," says Daisy. "Oh, here's my Mum to give me a lift home. You keep all the food, Archie. Grace and I will eat well at home. See you on Monday," says Daisy.

"Bye, Daisy. Hope your knee heals quickly. Don't forget to put the healing balm on it. Oh, here's my Mum too. Bye, Archie," says Grace.

"Bye, Daiz, bye, Grace – well, what a first week you've had! See you Monday," says Archie.

Chapter 10:
Dreaming of White Lions
and Unicorns

On Monday morning, Archie is having breakfast with the boys from his form. "Bye, lads, I'll catch up with you later. I've got something I need to tell Daisy and Grace," says Archie.

"Stop flirting with the girls, Archie, you old dog," says Calum, giving him a shove in the back as he gets up to put his breakfast tray away.

Ignoring him, Archie slides up the bench towards Grace and Daisy. "Morning ladies. Flip me, I had some mad dreams last night!" says Archie. He's been sitting with Tom, Burnley and Calum, but he knows that they'll think he's a bit soft if he starts telling them what he dreamed about.

"Ooh, did you?" says Daisy. "So did I, but I want to hear

yours first."

"Yes, me too," says Grace.

"Well, I dreamed that there were white lions roaming all around school. And there was one huge male lion with a big thick mane, whose face was right in front of me, talking to me, as real as if he was in this room with me. He was telling me something really important, but now that I'm awake, I can't remember what he said – so frustrating! Then the scene changed and I saw this incredible white horse, standing tall and proud under the moonlight on a hilltop with a spiral horn of light shining from his forehead. It reared up on its hind legs and I could see that it was next to a huge standing stone. And lightning seemed to strike it and merge with the light shining from its forehead. Then there was an ear-splitting sound, like a needle scratching over a vinyl record and Nanny Watkins came into view. And she was saying, 'You must come and see me, my boy. It's REALLY IMPORTANT to find the meaning of this dream.' I wonder what it all means?"

"Oh my gosh, Archie, that is almost scene by scene exactly the same as I dreamed last night. How spooky!" says Daisy.

"You're not going to believe this but I dreamed exactly the same too!" says Grace. "But I do remember a bit of what the lion was saying."

"Yes, brilliant!! Come on, what did he say?" says Archie.

Grace felt a little embarrassed to put it into words – "First he told me his name is Regulus and that he is a guide for us. And I know this is going to sound a bit farfetched, but he said that we have an important mission together to become Guardians of the Wild."

"Oh, now I remember – you were mumbling in your sleep last night and Charlie said, "Shut up, Grace, or I'm going to have to chuck my pillow at you. After that, I went back to sleep and had my dream. It's got to be something really important, if we all dreamt it," says Daisy.

"An important mission, eh? That sounds intriguing. Hey, isn't Regulus the name of the heart star in the Leo constellation?" says Archie.

"Wow, Archie, you're such a fountain of interesting facts! I'm sure you're right. I want to know more about the white horse and the white lion, and how exactly can we become 'Guardians of the Wild'?" says Grace.

"I feel another visit to Nanny Watkins coming on!" says Archie. "I'm sure she can help us unravel this mystery."

The Meaning of Dreams

The kids walk up the garden path to Nanny Watkins' cottage, calling out to her as they arrive. "Nanny, where are you? We need to talk to you!"

They hear her call back, "Come in, come in. I'm in the back garden. I'll be with you in a sec." She comes into the cottage through the back door that leads into the kitchen from the garden. Bright sunlight silhouettes her against the backdrop of the green garden. Dazzling colours of gold and green and violet around the door seem to dance about her. The sunlight on her silver-white hair makes her look like a radiant angel. She has a trug filled with fruits and vegetables over her arm.

"Oh hello, dears, you're just in time for lunch, if you have time to stay?" she says. It's as if she was expecting them.

"Yes please, Nanny, if it's not too much trouble. We've got so much that we want to tell you!" says Archie.

"And so much we need to ask you too!" says Daisy, catching her breath.

"How about you, Grace? What are you here for?" asks Nanny with a twinkle in her eye.

"Well, Nanny, we've all had some amazing dreams we need to ask you about," replies Grace.

"Come on, help me make this lunch and when we've done that, you can tell me all about your dreams," says Nanny. They begin to rinse and chop the vegetables. Soon they are tucking into their lunch of steamed vegetables and poached eggs from Nanny's happy chickens, followed by pudding of compote of berry fruits from Nanny's garden, sweetened with honey from her bees and homemade yogurt made from Nanny's goat's milk.

"Oh, Nanny, this food is gorgeous!" says Daisy with a look of rapture on her face.

"Yes, it is. And it's so much healthier than the rubbish they give us in the school canteen," says Grace.

"It'll put hairs on your chest, Archie," Nanny says with a saucy grin, winking at the girls as Archie blushes a shade of deep crimson. "But hopefully not on yours, girls, though I dare say all this fresh goodness will make your skin glow and your eyes shine."

"Well, come on then kids, I'm dying to hear about these dreams?" says Nanny. "Starting with Archie, tell me as if you're telling a really good story." So the kids tell her what they remember, the words tumbling out in a breathless jumble.

"Those are what I call Big Dreams. And the fact that you all dreamed the same goes to show how important they are. You need to learn how to work with them. If they were my dreams, I would be wondering how much of them might come true in the future?" says Nanny. "I would also be thinking that these animals – the unicorn and the white lion – are quite mythical. I'd go and read up all I could find about the myths and stories about white lions and unicorns, and see what messages spring out at me.

These animals could also be what I would call your power animals – beings that have chosen to come to you to act as guides. The lion comes with a big message for you – a message to speak up about injustice. You will need to have the heart of a lion and the courage to let your voice roar out your message. When the lion roars, everyone listens!"

"One day, I will show you how to connect with these animals, so you can hear their guidance more clearly. So my dears, I hope that has helped."

"That's so cool, Nanny!" says Archie. "I love the idea of having power animal guides. And I love myths and stories. We've got plenty of research to do now."

Mr Chapeau and the White Lions

The wind is whirling across the playground and squally showers threaten to soak anyone who ventures out without a raincoat, as the kids make their way to the biology lab. Although they all love Mr Chapeau's lessons, the mood is one of general restlessness. Rowdy chatter, prolonged scuffling about with bags and books, and a reluctance to settle down ready for the lesson tell Mr Chapeau that they are not in the mood to get much work done today. It's a shame. He had planned a lengthy introduction to a key topic that they need for the 'O' level syllabus and he can see that he will be wasting his time by trying to get them to focus on this new subject. "In common parlance, they have the wind up 'em," he thinks.

"OK, you 'orrible lot, I can see that I won't get much work out of you at the moment. You are all far too antsy. So, change of plan. Is there anything you would really like to talk about? Keep it clean and preferably biology related."

A hand goes up at the back, "Mr Chapeau, can you tell us

anything about white lions? Where do they come from and how are they different from ordinary lions?" asks Archie.

"Well, that's a great question, Mr McBride and one of my favourite subjects. I think white lions are simply magnificent creatures and that the whole world should know about them. Bear in mind that it's going to take me a while to tell you and that it will mean you doing some extra homework to catch up on what we should have been talking about today for the 'O' level syllabus. If that's OK with everyone else, I'd be happy to tell you what I know about white lions and it may even be helpful for the genetics part of the syllabus. What does everyone think?"

He has Form 4's attention now. They are all sitting forward on their chairs and waiting to hear what he has to say next. There is a general chorus of, "Yes, Sir. That sounds really interesting."

"OK then, settle down, and I will begin," he says in his best storytelling voice. "White lions at this present time exist in only one place in the wild – a place called Timbavati in South Africa and in the Kruger National Park, which is the region next to it. They are a subspecies of the Southern African Lion and their white fur is caused by a rare mutation in the gene that codes for the pigment in their coats. White cubs can be born in the same litter as tawny cubs to tawny parents, if the mum and dad both carry the recessive gene.

"White lions aren't albinos (who have no pigment at all), as they have pigment in their eyes, paw pads and lips. Their coat colour can vary from blonde to pure white and their eye colour can be hazel, blue, or green. The males have pale manes and tail tips instead of the usual dark tawny or black.

"Some people have suggested that being white would put them at a disadvantage when hunting, but scientific studies have not found this and they seem to be as successful as tawny lions when hunting. In fact, white lions often seem to be significantly bigger than tawny lions.

"White lions are thought to have been indigenous to the Timbavati region of South Africa for centuries, although the earliest recorded sighting in this region was in 1938. And they first became known to the wider world in 1977 through a book called The White Lions of Timbavati."

"Yes, that's the book where I read about them, Sir. There's a copy in the library," interrupts Archie.

"That's a great place to start, Mr McBride. You might also want to look at the work of Linda Tucker, who has set up a reserve to protect white lions. I believe she's written several books about them. She goes into detail about the mythology and the sacred nature of the white lion."

"That's the author of the book my Mum has," whispers Grace to Daisy.

"They are thought of as special and sacred by the indigenous African cultures and there is a legend which describes the appearance of white lions around 400 years ago during the reign of Queen Numbi of Timbavati. The story tells that a shining star was seen to fall to the ground, but when Queen Numbi and her people approached, they discovered that it was a shining ball of metal, brighter than the sun. Queen Numbi, who was elderly and sick, was beckoned into the light by strange beings. When she emerged again, she had been restored to health and youth. The fallen star stayed there for several days and then rose back into the sky.

"After this occurrence, strange animals began to be born –white impala and green-eyed white leopards and lions. To this day, white animals are born in Timbavati, including a blue-eyed white elephant. Some believe that the legend of unicorns started here, as one-horned white elands began to appear. Whether or not you believe in visiting spaceships, it is now known that radiation can cause these mutations. So folks, that in a nutshell is what I know about white lions. It's my dream to go and see them in the wild one day. I hope I've answered your question, Mr McBride."

"Wow, thank you, Sir. That was so interesting. I'm definitely going to look up those books. And you're right – it's a really good example if we need to write about recessive genes in the 'O' level paper," says Archie.

"Yes, I loved that, Sir! And maybe you could tell us all about unicorns another time," says Daisy.

"Well, that would be a bit trickier, Daisy, because no-one's ever done a scientific study on unicorns! Oh, that sounds like the bell. Perhaps as Mr McBride suggests, for your homework, you could write about how the appearance of white lions amongst tawny lions demonstrates how recessive genes work."

On the way out of class, Archie says to Grace and Daisy, "Well the plot thickens. The whole white lion and unicorn topic just got even more intriguing. Can't wait to ask Nanny Watkins about it."

Chapter 11:
Matron

Matron and Mr P

Grace is looking out of the Art Room window, deep in thought about her painting, when the statuesque figure of Matron comes into view. She strides across the school playground like a galleon in full sail, her prominent chin held high and her neatly permed and sprayed hair moving not an inch in the breeze. Her winged glasses are a tribute to the film stars of her favourite era, the 1950s. Her magnificent bosom thrusts at the world like the prow of a ship cutting through the water, clad as it is in an outrageously pointy bra from the same era.

On this windy day, the general atmosphere in class has not improved since double biology with Mr Chapeau.

Everyone is fidgeting and in high spirits. Not much work is getting done and Grace is finding it hard to concentrate. She is working on a painting of the white lion from her dreams, but can't get him to look as magnificent as he is in her mind. She glances over at Mr Parsons, the Art Teacher. Matron's appearance has not been lost on Mr P, who is watching her in a distracted way. Grace could swear that she hears him whisper the word, "Glorious!" under his breath. Out loud he says, "Stop tittering, you lot, and get on with your work." Unfortunately, this results in everyone else noticing Matron and the tittering only grows worse.

On their way out of class, as soon as they are out of earshot of Mr Parsons, Archie nudges Grace. "I reckon Mr P has a bit of a crush on Matron, don't you think?"

"Yes, I think you're right," Grace replies.

"Definitely!" chimes in Daisy. "She's a funny old stick, but I guess there is someone for everyone. And it must be lonely being a teacher out in the wilds of nowhere like this."

Darius Serves Supper

The three kids make a dash through the rain, heading for supper after Prep. "Oh, it's my favourite tonight – hot chocolate!" says Daisy, leaning on the oak panelling of the dining room as they wait in the queue.

Supper is served in a rota by the 5th Form and Lower 6th Form Monitors. Tonight it is being served by Darius, the Persian boy with the huge dark eyes. There is some kind of commotion going on at the front of the queue and cries of, "Urgh, Darius, you're disgusting! That's not funny at all." But they can't see what's happening.

"Don't know what he's talking about!" says Darius. It's now Archie's turn in the queue and he holds out his mug over the cauldron of hot chocolate for Darius to ladle some in. As he does, there's a ceramic plonk sound, as something large and brown lands in Archie's mug. "Oh, whoops, my friend Richard seems to have made another appearance!" Darius says, stifling a laugh.

Daisy lets out a shriek, "Aargh, it's a poo! Archie, there's a poo in your chocolate."

"Don't be silly, Daiz, it's a fake one. Very funny, Darius. By the way, what do you mean by your friend Richard?" says Archie.

"Richard the Turd, of course," says Darius, and they all burst out laughing.

Just at that moment, Matron comes round the corner to investigate what all the commotion is about.

"Oh, I'm appalled at your behaviour, Mr Darvesh!" says Matron in her Irish brogue. "I'm taking you to see the Headmaster at once." With that, she grabs him by the ear and marches him up the stairs to see the Boss. The kids decide to follow at a safe distance and ear-wig outside the door, trying not to snigger and give themselves away. They can hear the Boss saying, "And why have you brought Mr Darvesh to see me, Matron?"

"Well, Headmaster, he did something really disgusting at supper and I want you to punish him."

"Tell me, what exactly did he do, so that I can make the punishment fit the crime?"

"He, he … Oh, it's too disgusting. I can't bring myself to tell you."

"Well, how can I punish him if you won't tell me what he's done, Matron?" says Boss.

"Well, maybe I could write it down." At this point, the laughter is bubbling up inside the kids who are all fit to burst. Archie is biting his hand to keep the laugh in. Daisy's eyes are streaming with silent tears of laughter, Grace is clutching her sides – so they beat a hasty retreat back downstairs before they get caught. They lurk around the bottom of the stairs waiting for Darius to find out what his punishment is. Finally he appears, looking suitably chastised for the benefit of Matron, but gives them a wink as he passes. They follow him to the door of the 5th Form classroom, as Matron has now gone back to her room.

"What did you get?" asks Archie. "Was it worth it?"

"Oh, I've only got to clean the boys' bogs for a few days. I think the Boss secretly thought it was pretty funny, especially the fact that Matron was so flustered. I could tell he was trying not to laugh!"

"Good one, man. I'm sure you can manage that!" says Archie.

Chapter 12:
More About Dreams

The Lightning Dreamwork Technique

"So Grace has had another big dream about the white horse then? I think it could be time to teach you the Lightning Dreamwork technique. It will help you to understand how to work with your dreams when I'm not around. Would that be useful?" says Nanny. The kids have made their way back to Nanny's cottage for more help in deciphering dreams.

"Oh, yes please, Nanny," they all chorus together.

"OK then, this was taught to me by a lovely fella. Known him for years. Right handsome he was in his younger days. A big bear of a man. Always had a twinkle in his eyes." Nanny's great bosom heaves as she gives a big sigh and a faraway look comes over her. "Robert, his name was..."

"Go on, Nanny. How does it work then?" asks Archie, who's dying to find out more about how to work with dreams.

"Where was I – oh yes – Lightning Dreamwork," says Nanny, coming back from her reverie. "He's got a mane of silver hair now, just like that white lion you saw in your dreams. A lion and a bear in one man... Hmmm."

"Who does, Nanny?" says Grace, getting impatient to hear the technique.

"Robert, the fella who taught me the Lightning Dreamwork, of course," says Nanny. "Anyhow, enough of my reminiscences. It goes like this... As soon as you wake up from a dream, make sure you write it all down in your journal. I mean every detail you can remember, even if it doesn't make sense to you at the time. Just get it all down, before it starts fading away. So it's a good idea to have your journal and a pen right next to your bed – probably need a torch in your cases too, so you don't need to disturb the other kids in the dorm.

"When you've got it all down, think of a title and write that at the top – helps your brain to start sorting it out. Then write down how you feel. Did you wake up feeling scared or happy, or excited? Now you write down everything you know about this subject in your everyday life. So if it was a dream about horses, you write down what you know about horses and if you have met a horse lately. Then you think about what else you would like to know about this dream. And write the question down.

"Now you need a partner for the next bit. You three could do it together. So you tell each other your dreams when you meet up. Make it into a really good story. Then one of the others asks you the questions – how do you feel about the dream? What do you know about it in this reality?

What else would you like to know from the dream? And is there anything in this dream that could happen in real life? Because dreams can often tell you something that is going to happen in the future.

"Now you get to tell each other what you know about the subject of the dream. Don't try to tell each other what the dream means. That's for the person who had the dream to work out. Just say something like, 'If it was my dream, it would remind me of the time that I rode a horse … and this is what happened to me…' Then you can work out an action plan of what to do to about what you've learnt from the dream."

"That sounds great, Nanny. I definitely want to try that. In fact, I have a dream I would like to try it with now. But can you tell me why it's important to write about your feelings, Nanny?" says Grace.

"It's because it gives you a clue about what action you might need to take. You know, if it was something that you really didn't like or put you in danger, you might want to do something to avoid it happening in real life. Or it might be showing you something you need to face up to. Or if you really enjoyed it, you might want to go to that place and do the thing that you enjoyed from your dream in your waking life."

"Oh, I see," said Grace. "So can I tell you about my dream now? And can we practice doing the Lightning Dreamwork on it?"

"Ooh, go on then, dear. I'm looking forward to hearing this one! Tell it to us like a good story."

Grace's Dream – Meeting the Radiant White Horse

Grace begins, "I've heard a rumour that a radiant white horse has been seen near the school, but I can't find him. He appears to me in my dreams and someone has shown me a photo taken by a pupil some time ago, but I still don't know where to find him.

"There are signs of horses everywhere – piles of horse poo, the smell of horses on the breeze and some darker horses in the field behind my room, but none of them are the pure white horse I have seen in my dreams.

"I decide to go for a walk, to clear my head, and I follow a path into the woodland. There are apples on the path, falling leaves of gold and russet, and that fresh smell of soil that comes after rain as the earth begins to cool. I step carefully on the narrow path which leads through the ancient woodland of beech and oak trees.

"A scene comes into my head of the birth of this pure white horse. I see that he came down from the stars, and he will be discovered by you, Nanny.

"I see images of the wild herd he was born to. I hear the thunder of galloping hooves across the valley, not once, but three times. I strain my eyes through the trees to the opposite side of the valley, waiting to see the horse who is making this sound, but none appears.

"I walk a little further along the path, and the smell of horse sweat and horse poo is so strong, but there is still no sign of the horse that made them. I begin to think I will never find this horse.

"It is almost time to go back to school, so I turn and walk back along the forest path. When I get near school, I see a mysterious doorway in an ancient wall that surrounds a farmhouse and it leads to the back, where there are stables.

"I feel like this is my last chance to find the real starlight horse. I look up from the path into the distance to see two horses – one pure black and one pure white. There he is at last!

"My heart is beating fast as I make my way towards him. The huge black horse that is with him looks up from her grazing, staring straight at me and gives a loud whinny of greeting. My heart pounds as she gallops across the field to meet me, her black coat is shining in the sun like a raven's wing.

"I walk up to the fence where I can get closest to her, and she leads her pure white colt to meet me. And there he is, the horse I've been looking for. His mother tells me his name is Ahbleza.

"'Hello my beauties, we meet at last,' I say, holding out my hand for them to sniff. 'I will come again to meet you tomorrow and promise to bring you a juicy apple.'

"'Yes, yes,' says the mother horse as Ahbleza peeps shyly from behind his mother.

"I go home with a glow in my heart, knowing something magical happened today."

"Well, my dear," says Nanny. "What a lovely dream and a lovely story. What's the title of your dream?"

"Um, I think it should be *Meeting the Radiant White Horse.*"

"Yes, I like it. And how did you feel after this dream?" asks Nanny.

"I was really excited and pleased to meet the radiant white horse. But there was also a little niggle for me. I felt responsible for this horse – kind of like I have to take care of him."

"Hmmm, interesting," muses Nanny. "Is there anything like this in your life at the moment? I mean do you recognise this horse or is it something that could happen in the future?"

"I love horses, but I don't know one that looks anything like the one in my dream. But we have all dreamed about a white horse recently. I suppose it's possible that it could happen in the future."

"Yes, my dear. It has that feel. I remember you coming to tell me about your dreams about white horses and white lions, if I recall. If it were my dream, I would write all the details down carefully in my journal and look out for it happening in the future. Especially as this is the second dream you've had about this white horse. I would also do some research to see if I can find the meaning of his name – Ahbleza. It's quite unusual. It's another Big Dream and you always need to make an action plan from a Big Dream. I also have to tell you, it's a sign for me about your powers. This is a very special dream, because you have actually dreamed something that happened to me."

"Gosh, thank you, Nanny. That's really interesting and helpful. I'd love to know more about what happened to you."

"I can't tell you right now. I have to check up on something. Perhaps you could come back another time and I will tell you more. But just for now, do your research, keep pondering on the meaning of the dream and trust that all will be revealed in exactly the right time for you to know it.

"Well, goodness, look at the time. I think you'd better be getting back to school for your tea, before anyone notices you're gone. I don't want you to get into trouble, because I want you to be able to come back whenever you need to. For now, you will have to go back over Farmer Morgan's land. Make sure he doesn't see you." Nanny pauses and ponders for a moment, then says, "Are you good at keeping a secret?"

"I am, and Grace keeps her cards pretty close to her chest, but I'm afraid Daisy can be a bit of a blabbermouth at times," says Archie, winking at Grace and nudging Daisy in the ribs.

"That's not fair! I only pipe up when I think someone needs to know the truth," says Daisy. "If keeping a secret means protecting someone, then I won't breathe a word."

Nanny continues, "There is another way here, you know, a secret way which you will need to learn how to use if you're going to come here often – which I hope you do. I'm worried that you've been pushing your luck so far." With that, she stands up and ushers them towards the door.

"Hold on a minute, Nanny, what do you mean about a secret way? Where do we find that and why can't we use it now?" asks Archie.

"Because the way will only open to those who understand it. I'm afraid you're going to have to find out for yourselves. It involves some detective work, a good heap of intuition and showing that you can keep a secret, because blabbing about this could put someone in grave danger, and I'm not going to let that happen. There is someone special I want you to meet, when the time is right." She had their full attention now. They were listening hard to every word.

"Please go on, Nanny. We're dying to know more," says Grace.

"My dears, you're not the first ones from your school to find their way to me. I've lived here a very long time and over the years I've met many Fairstonians. Since Farmer Morgan the younger took over, he's made sure most of them have got into trouble for coming to see me. It wasn't like that in his Dad's time. He was a good man, and tolerant. As long as people stuck to the footpaths, he didn't mind them crossing his land. Which is as it should be.

"So what I am going to tell you now will make it easier for you to come and visit, and no-one will know you've been here. You won't have to cross Farmer Morgan's land, so you won't get into trouble."

"Oh, how exciting!" squeaks Daisy.

"I will tell you a bit more, but a good deal of it is for you to work out for yourselves. All I can tell you is this – you know that your main school building is known as a Calendar House? Do some research on that. I believe there's a book about it in the Top Library," says Nanny.

"That Top Library is really spooky, Nanny. Some people say it's haunted," says Daisy.

"That's as maybe," says Nanny. "But there's nothing dangerous there. Nothing for you to worry about. Have a look at the windows in the Old Hall. They're very interesting. There is a way of leaving Fairstone Court and arriving here in the blink of an eye. No-one will see you leave and you will arrive back almost as soon as you have gone. It's as if Old Father Time turns a blind eye to your visit. The rest you will need to find out for yourselves. It will be a test of what you're made of. Now, it is time for you to return back the regular way. Bye for now then, young 'uns. Good luck. I have faith in you. Hurry back now and perhaps I'll see you next Saturday."

She waves them off and disappears back inside the cottage, reappearing 30 seconds later and calling out, "Oh, kids, seeing as how the food is so terrible at school, maybe you'd like to take some of my homemade bread and strawberry jam back with you. At least you can make yourselves a decent piece of toast. And here is some of my bees' honey. This is very precious, you know. It's magic stuff, see – because those clever little bees have managed to capture the special essence of each flower and herb and capture it in their honey. It's like medicine. Use it wisely."

With that, she waves them away at the door.

Chapter 13:
In Trouble

The Wrath of Mr P

"Guys, I'm really not keen on that Top Library. I'm sure it is haunted," says Daisy, giving a shudder. "I can feel it every time I go in there."

"Yes, but like Nanny said, I don't think it's a bad ghost. Just someone who had something unfortunate happen to them. Maybe a kid like us," says Archie. This sets Grace's mind racing with possibilities.

"Oh my goodness, look at the time!" says Grace. "We're going to have to run to get back in time." They quicken their strides and go into their best cross-country running pace. But running like this, they are perhaps less careful not to be seen than normal.

"Phew, we made it," says Daisy, as they near the dining hall and hear the bell for tea. Most of the other kids are already queueing and they rush to join the line. But just as they enter the corridor that leads to the dining hall, Mr Parsons stops them.

"Umm, you smell of strawberry jam and honey. You didn't get that from the school kitchen, did you?" he says, putting his hand on the wall just above Grace's shoulder and leaning his face far too close to hers. "And you're all out of breath. Where have you been? You haven't been pinching things from the Boss's dining room, have you?"

"Nowhere very interesting, Sir. We were just up the top of the playing fields. It's probably my strawberry and honey lip balm you can smell. We just lost track of time because we were nattering away and so we had to run back down to get a good place in the queue for tea. I love the toasted teacakes they serve on Saturday. They're my favourite and I'd be so disappointed if they ran out."

"Hmmm, a likely story. I will find out, you know. I do hope you're not going to get into trouble about this. I would hate for it to distract you from the excellent artwork you are creating in class, Grace."

"No, Sir. I'm loving my artwork at the moment. In fact, that's one of the things we were talking about. I was asking advice from Daisy and Archie about how to get my white lion to look more realistic and Daisy was telling me to model him on the photos of white lions in a book my Mum has. They are fascinating, you know, Sir."

"Well, I'm so glad you're so dedicated to your art, my dear," he says a touch sarcastically, removing his hand from the wall behind Grace. "On you go now and get your tea."

Charlie Rogers and the Full Moon

The girls are settling down in their beds for the night. Daisy and Grace are both still feeling wide awake and talk over the day's events. Charlie is soon asleep and making loud snoring noises. The full moon shines through the thin curtains, illuminating her bed.

"Hey, Grace, doesn't Charlie look weird with the full moon shining on her like that?" says Daisy.

"Oh yes, she does look a bit strange, doesn't she? I hope she's not going to turn into a werewolf or anything!" jokes Grace.

"No! Don't say things like that, Grace. It really gives me the creeps. I'm terrified of all that stuff. You know it will give me nightmares."

"Sorry, Daisy, I was only joking. I don't believe werewolves really exist. Let's go to sleep now. Night, night. Sweet dreams." They both turn over and try to get to sleep. But the thought of werewolves has unsettled them both.

Suddenly, there is a whooshing, rustling sound as Charlie sits bolt upright in bed and her covers fall to the side. Both girls turn over and stare at her. "Oh my goodness, Charlie, are you OK?" says Grace. There is no answer as Charlie, with a strange look on her face, stares out of the window and up at the moon, its eerie light bathing her face in a blue glow. Then, arms stretched out in front of her, a zombie-like look on her face, she swings her legs around and onto the floor. She gets up out of bed and starts to move towards the door, making a low moaning sound, her arms still outstretched in front.

"Charlie, can you hear me?" asks Daisy. There is still no answer. "She must be sleepwalking," says Daisy. "I've heard you're not supposed to wake them." Charlie opens the bedroom door and starts off down the corridor towards the bathroom.

"We'd better follow her to make sure she doesn't fall down the stairs or anything," says Grace.

"Good idea," says Daisy. They follow the softly moaning Charlie till she reaches the toilet, which is halfway along the corridor to the bathroom. Charlie goes in and sits on the loo. As the light is left on at night, they can just see her outline through the frosted glass panel in the door. She looks as if she is slumped over. "Do you think we should call Mr Chapeau? Maybe she's ill?" says Daisy.

"Let's give it a couple more minutes and see what happens," says Grace. The girls from the next dormitory have heard voices and come out to see what is going on.

"What's happening?" they ask. Grace and Daisy explain.

"Oh, how spooky!" says Eve Minton.

"Shouldn't we get Mr Chapeau?" asks Portia Jenkins. But before anyone can answer, Charlie is moving again.

She bursts open the toilet door, shouting, "Raargh!!!" Most of the girls scream, except Grace and Portia, who stand looking very puzzled. Charlie has now doubled over again, but the giveaway is that her shoulders are shaking with laughter.

"Oh, you cow. You had us all going then and it was just a wind-up!" says Eve, giving Charlie's shoulder a little shove. She stands up, grinning all over her rosy face.

"Gotcha!" she says triumphantly.

Called to the Boss's Office

"I am very disappointed in you three. I have high hopes for you all. You have such potential, but behaviour like this cannot be tolerated, both for the sake of good relationships with our neighbours and for your own safety. You know that it is a school rule not to trespass on Farmer Morgan's land. What were you doing there anyway?"

The three kids are standing in the Headmaster's office, trying to look suitably sorry for their wrongdoing. All three have their hands clasped behind their backs and heads slightly bowed. It is the best way with Boss. Archie has told Grace that if you show remorse, he will usually be lenient, but if you're cocky and defiant, he gets riled up and is likely to give you some horrendous punishment.

They look at each other, none of them wanting to own up to the real reason they had been on Farmer Morgan's land. As far as they know, it is the fastest way to get to Nanny Watkins' cottage and besides, everyone did it at one time or other. It was a bit of a dare, like a rite of passage. But they couldn't say that to Boss.

"Well? I'm waiting for an answer!" he says. Daisy is squirming. She is rubbish at keeping secrets. Grace shoots her a look, begging her with her eyes not to tell him, but it is too late, and she can't help but blurt it out.

"We were visiting Nanny Watkins, Sir. The only way to get to her cottage is across Farmer Morgan's land. We didn't mess about there, Sir, and we used the footpath."

"Nanny Watkins? What did you want with her? I hear she's as mad as a fruit cake."

Archie cuts in, "We heard she'd had a fall and we wanted to see if she needed any help. She's not mad, Sir – a bit eccentric, but very kind when you get to know her. Daisy and I met her in the holidays when we were staying with Daisy's aunt, Sarah Evans. They are practically neighbours. And you've always taught us to be socially responsible. It seemed the right thing to do. We need to look after our elders. We're very sorry that it meant we broke a school rule, but we weren't breaking the law."

Grace can't quite believe that Archie has told such a whopper, but it seems to have the right effect on Boss, who is softening right up.

"I see, McBride. Well, those were very noble intentions, even if you did break the rules. So I am prepared to be lenient this time and let you off with a warning. But you must promise never to go onto Farmer Morgan's land again, not even the footpath. I have given him my word that you won't, and I'm a man of my word. And next time something like that happens, perhaps you could call Sarah Evans and ask her to visit Nanny Watkins, or tell a member of staff."

"We promise, Sir," they all say in unison. But Boss can't see that they all have their fingers crossed behind their backs. The kids are not about to stop going to see Nanny Watkins. They find her far too interesting and they are having so much fun learning all the quirky things she has to teach.

With a huge sense of relief that they pretty much got away with it, they make their way out of Boss's office and down the oak staircase to the Old Hall. Grace's eye is caught by a stained-glass window, which forms a bay with a desk in it. "That's an unusual window," says Grace. "Do either of you know anything about it?"

Archie replies, "It's called the Calendar Window. My Dad is a bit of a history bore. He's researched the whole history of Fairstone Court. It was built back in Victorian times for the Ripley family. It's known as a Calendar House because it has a chimney for every month, a window for every day, seven entrances and fifty-two rooms. There is a legend that these facts must never be checked, because something really bad will happen to anyone who tries."

"Oh, that's interesting. I wonder if it's true?" says Grace

"Well, I'm not risking bad luck to find out. I think we're

in enough trouble for one day," says Archie. "And maybe best to get out of earshot of anyone who might be keeping an eye on us!" he whispers.

They make their way out of the school building and head back to their form room. Grace has been deep in thought since seeing the window. "Guys, remember what Nanny said about the secret way to get to her house? I think it's really important now to find that way before we get in more trouble. She was dropping huge hints about looking at the windows and I think a major clue was what she said about 'Old Father Time.' I think we need to get up to the Top Library as soon as possible."

"You're right, Grace, I just didn't want to hang around there after our telling off," says Archie.

"I know you're right, Grace, but I'm going to have to brave up to go in that library," says Daisy.

Chapter 14:
The Calendar House

The Old Library

The door of the Old Library opens with a screeching creak. The sun is shining brightly through the upper-floor windows, illuminating motes of dust that have been disturbed by the movement of air as the door opens.

It's Monday lunch break. Archie, Daisy and Grace have finally decided to brave the Top Library on their quest to follow up on Nanny's hints about using the secret way to get to her cottage. They're looking for a book on Fairstone Court that has anything about it being a Calendar House, to try and get some information about where to find the secret way. But they've been reluctant to come to the Top Library because of its reputation of being haunted. Daisy is especially terrified of it, so she is being really brave to come here.

"Gosh, there's a lot of wood in here," says Grace, surveying the oak panelling, the oak flooring, the row upon row of wooden bookshelves with their hundreds of books, and the wooden desks in the centre of the room. Large windows look out over the lawn, past the ha-ha and onto the sheep field that leads to the woods.

"Shall we open a window – it's very stuffy in here?" says Daisy. "And can anyone else feel the creepy atmosphere?"

"Sure, Daisy, I'll open the windows, but I can't feel anything creepy. It's just a bit musty and old in here," says Archie.

Daisy looks at Grace. "Yes, there is a bit of a strange atmosphere in here, I agree," says Grace.

"The question is, where do we start looking for this book?" says Archie.

"I'm hoping they'll be arranged in subject headings – we could start looking under headings like History," says Grace.

"Good plan," says Archie. They begin to search along the shelves.

"Here we are," says Daisy. "Here's the section on History. But we don't know the title or the author of the book."

"Let's just split up and scan different shelves," says Archie.

"OK, I'll start here. Daisy, you do those ones and Archie, you take the next shelves along," says Grace.

"Great, let's get to it!" says Archie. Grace starts scanning along her section of books. She is beginning to get frustrated. Nothing looks very promising so far. All the titles are on dull, dry topics and nothing vaguely relating to their quest. Titles such as *The History of the Thermometer* by Prof W E Knowles, and Knitted Historical Figures by Jean Messent swim past Grace's eyes in a monotonous list.

She thinks she hears a boy chuckle and looks round at Archie to see if he has found something. Archie is still intently scanning his titles, but Daisy is looking over at her. "Did you just hear someone chuckle? Who was that? Archie, was it you?" says Daisy.

"Yes, I heard it too. I don't think it was Archie, though," says Grace.

"Hey, what?" says Archie. "I'm not having much luck here," going back to his title scanning.

"There it is again," says Daisy. "Ooh gosh, all the hairs on my arms have goosed." They hear a dry scraping sound and a very old, fat book falls out at Grace's feet. As she bends to pick it up, she glimpses a face through the gap in the shelf, smiling at her.

Startled, she says, "Who's there?" She hears footsteps coming around the bookshelves and then, appearing from behind Daisy, is the familiar figure of Jonnie Watkins with a cheeky grin on his face.

"I couldn't bear to see you wasting your time looking at all those boring books. I think you'll find that's the one you want," says Jonnie, indicating the book in Grace's hand.

"Oh, it's you, Jonnie! Thanks for this," says Grace, and she looks at the book in her hands.

"Whoa, who're you talking to Grace – who's Jonnie?" says Daisy.

"It's Jonnie Watkins. He's right there behind you," says Grace.

Daisy spins around, "Where, I can't see anyone?"

"Right there," says Grace. "Jonnie, say hello to Daisy."

"She can't see me, Grace. Only you can."

"What? Why? Archie, you can see him, can't you?" says Grace.

"See who?" says Archie, who has been concentrating on the books and so far not noticed the unfolding mystery.

"No, I'm afraid Archie can't see me either. I'm from another time. Only you are sensitive enough to perceive me, Grace. I'm going to go now, because I'm freaking your friends out. But you've got the right book. Bye, see you again soon." And with that, he fades from Grace's sight.

"Oh my goodness, Grace. You've seen the ghost, haven't you? Either that or you're going stark raving mad, or I am, or both. That's why I got the goose bumps. I told you it's haunted in here. Come on, let's get out of here!" says Daisy, starting to panic.

"Calm down, Daisy. You're perfectly safe. It was just my friend Jonnie, and he's gone now. He doesn't mean any harm. He was trying to help."

By now, Archie's paying attention. "Whoa, you've seen the ghost, Grace! Is this the guy, Jonnie Watkins, that you were talking about on your first day?" says Archie. "So many questions, Grace… Do you think he's someone who used to go to the school?"

"Yes, he definitely is. There are photos of him in the Old Hall. He was in the 1972 Cross-Country Team. And I think he was in the swimming team too," says Grace.

"Did you suspect that he was a ghost, Grace?" says Daisy.

"Well, there was something that didn't add up, like the date on the photo. But he seemed so real. I didn't want to believe that he wasn't."

"Oh gosh, I wonder what happened to him? And why is he still hanging around here?" says Daisy.

"I'll ask my Dad about it. He's in the Old Boys' Club. He might have heard the story of what happened to him. And I'm dying to see the photos. What's that book you've got there?"

Grace turns the book over and reads the title, "*The Calendar House: A Brief History of Fairstone Court*," she says.

"Well, that looks promising, but not very brief, by the size of it! Let's get out in the fresh air and have a proper look," says Archie.

"Yes, let's get out of here," says Daisy. "But one more thing, guys – the name, Jonnie Watkins. You don't think he's any relation to our Nanny Watkins, do you? She seems to know a lot about Fairstone. Didn't you wonder about that?"

"Very good point, Daisy. It is quite a common surname round here though, and she does live locally. But I guess we'll just have to ask her when we go back to tell her what we've found out about the secret way," says Archie.

"Uh, maybe we should be a bit cautious about asking her. If he is a relative, there's going to be sadness about him dying young and we don't want to upset her," says Grace.

"Oh, you're right, Grace. What a moron I am – totally insensitive to ask her about him! We'll have to let her tell us in her own time, if she wants to."

The Window of Old Father Time

At afternoon break, the three amigos gather to have a look at the book. Grace remembers noticing the stained-glass window in the Old Hall as they left Main School after their telling off by the Boss. "If I remember right, Nanny told us that Main School is called a Calendar House and she also told us to pay attention to the windows in the Old Hall," she says. "Hey Archie, didn't you say that the stained-glass window in the Old Hall is called the Calendar Window?"

"Yes, that's what my Dad told me. I've always been fascinated by that window and wondered what it really means," says Archie.

"OK, let's see what the book says about it," says Daisy.

Archie flicks through the book until he comes to a passage that reads, "'Fairstone is known as a Calendar House because it has a chimney for every month, a window for every day, seven entrances and fifty-two rooms...' See, isn't that what I told you!" says Archie. He continues reading,

"'The Calendar Window can be found alongside the main staircase in the Old Hall. It is thirty feet wide and ten feet high. Divided by heavy mullions into 13 sections, one for each month of the year, and one central section.

"'The image in the central section of the Calendar Window takes the form of "Father Time" surrounded by the seasons of the year. The episodes are arranged in three tiers, like a frieze. In the upper row, the sphere of mythology, each month and its planet is paralleled by the ancient god which represents that planet. The middle row shows the signs of the zodiac, while below depicts events related to that particular time of the year. The window was designed and constructed by the London firm Campbell, Smith & Campbell.' Wow, fascinating!" says Archie.

"And there's our clue!" says Grace. "Did you notice that it says the central image is of 'Father Time'? Remember, Nanny told us there's a way of leaving Fairstone and arriving at her cottage in the blink of an eye without anyone noticing you're gone? She said it's as if Old Father Time turns a blind eye to your visit. Do you think there is some way of using it to time travel?"

"Oh gosh, yes – I think you're onto something, Grace!" says Archie.

"But how on earth are we going to figure out how to use it safely?" says Daisy.

"Hmm, that's the big question, isn't it?" says Grace with a faraway gaze.

The Boss's Wife

Prep has finished for the evening. "Hey girls, do you fancy going up to the Rec for the last half hour before curfew? Better get your raincoats though – looks like the rain's getting heavier." Thunderous clouds had been gathering all afternoon. There had been that heavy, soupy feeling in the air that precedes a good downpour. Halfway to the Rec, the heavens really open. It starts with big, fat, heavy drops and then turns into a general hosing down in rods of water.

"Think I'm going to turn straight in, now that we've got this close to Fairstone House – sorry Archie," says Grace. "Daisy, are you coming or staying?"

"Yes, I'm coming too. See you tomorrow, Arch." And the girls hurry towards the shelter of Fairstone House.

"Maybe I'll call it a day too then," says Archie, mostly to himself and the drumming rain. And he runs back to school.

Once a week, Mrs Williams, the Boss's wife, does the girls' Lights Out so that Mr and Mrs Chapeau can have a night off. She sways slightly as she makes her way up the corridor and almost misses when she goes to lean on the door frame.

"Whoopsy!" she says. There is a strong smell of sherry trifle. Mrs Williams is famous for her sherry trifles, which must contain a whole bottle of the stuff.

Charlie is in one of her mischievous moods. Winking at Grace, she says, "Mrs W, I need your advice. I have an embarrassing itch."

"Oh, I'm sorry to hear that, my dear," she says in her perfect Scottish brogue. "Where exactly is this itch?"

"Well, it's kind of all-around and up, if you get my meaning, Mrs W."

"Now my advice to you is, dear Charlotte, and to all you girls for that matter, to never wear your knickers in bed. You simply must let the air get to your end." Charlie's eyes are wide as saucers as she tries not to laugh. Grace has stuffed her duvet in her mouth to stop herself from giggling and Daisy has disappeared under the covers in embarrassment.

"Thank you so much for the advice, Mrs W," says Charlie.

"Oh, well, if it doesn't clear up soon, you'd better go to see Nurse Bernie. I'm sure she can give you something for it." She switches off the lights, seeming not to notice the stifled mirth. "Goodnight girls." She starts to walk away and then adds, "I've heard that yogurt is good too. Sleep well."

Nurse Bernie's Jollop

"Where's Archie this morning, guys?" Daisy is trying to make it sound like a casual remark, and failing dismally. A warm fug of eggy toast, hot tea and congealed beans cocoons the kids in the dining room. Archie hasn't turned up for breakfast and the girls want to talk to him urgently about finding the secret way to help them get to Nanny Watkins' place quickly without having to cross Farmer Morgan's land.

"You haven't heard then?" says Tom. "Half the boys are in Sick Bay with the shits. Archie's got it bad – he's a delicate flower! Calum's there too."

"Ah, he's got a pooey bum then?" says Daisy.

"Oh, poor Archie," says Grace. "He must be feeling really bad if he's had to go to bed with it."

"Aye, they reckon it's because Stinky Morgan spread pig shit on 'is land and it got washed down't hill by the 'eavy rain and contaminated the water supply to Main School," says Burnley. "Nurse Bernie's busy dosing them all with't special jollop. I overheard 'er speakin' to Matron this mornin'. She were sayin, 'I can't let them into assembly – they'll be shittin' all over the place!'"

Daisy looks shocked and puts her hand over her mouth to stop herself laughing at this awful scenario.

"So what's in this special jollop of Nurse Bernie's? Does it actually work?" says Grace.

"I think it's 'er version of kaolin and morphine, but she's put 'er own extras in it. She gev it me once, when I 'ad a poorly tummy. I'm not sure it 'elped and it made me go a bit funny in the 'ed. Gev me reet weird dreams," says Burnley. They're all laughing now at the thought of Burnley going 'a bit funny in the 'ed.'

"So be careful – only drink the bottled water. Wouldn't want any of you girlies pooing your pants!" says Tom with a cheeky smile.

"How come you two got away with it?" says Grace.

"Not sure – I've spent a lot of time on my uncle's farm, so I'm probably immune to it," says Tom.

"Me old Mam always says, 'A bit of dirt don't hurt,' so I'm probably immune too," says Burnley.

"Can we visit Archie to cheer him up?" asks Grace.

"No, Sick Bay is strictly out of bounds. Matron says it's really contagious, so no visitors allowed," says Tom.

"Oh damn, that's a blow," says Grace quietly under her breath, giving Daisy a 'What do we do now?' kind of look.

Chapter 15:
On the Trail of the Secret Way

Finding a Way Out

It's first break. Grace manages to get Daisy on her own. "We have to find a way to get to see Archie. That Nurse Bernie's jollop stuff sounds absolutely poisonous. I've got a jar of Nanny Watkins' special honey. Do you remember she said it's powerful medicine? I know honey is anti-bacterial too. Is there any way we can sneak in and give some to him?"

"I'm not sure. It would have to be at night, when no-one else is around, but the problem is getting out of the boarding house and getting into Main School. The doors are all locked and there are alarms on the fire exits," says Daisy.

Charlie sidles up. "What are you two plotting?" she says.

"Oh, nothing. We were just saying how terrible it is that the boys are all sick," says Daisy.

"Yes, I can read you like a book, Daisy Davies – you're worried about Archie and plotting to go and see him, aren't you?"

Daisy squirms and gives Grace a sideways look, as Charlie fixes her with a ruthless 'take no prisoners' kind of stare. "Oh damn, you've rumbled us, Charlie. But you mustn't breathe a word to anyone."

"Course not. I don't dob in me mates," says Charlie. "Now you're probably wondering how to get out of the boarding house without setting off the fire alarms, aren't you? I'll let you into a little secret – I know a way out. I've never bothered to use it because I like my sleep too much and can't be mithered to go gallivanting about at night. But I'm happy to show you."

"Oh my gosh, Charlie, that would be brilliant! Tell us more – where is it and how did you find it?" says Grace.

"It's easier to show you than to tell you. I'll meet you after lunch in the dorm at Fairstone House. We'll need to get our torches and wear trackie bottoms 'cos you might get pretty mucky."

"Ooh, how exciting! Thanks, Charlie," says Daisy.

"Before you get too excited, Daisy, you're gonna need to find a way to get into the Main School building as well – it'll all be locked up at night. Maybe you could get someone on the inside to let you in? Let me have a think a minute," says Charlie. All three of them search around, thinking who would be best to let them in.

"Got it – Daisy, you're always flirting with that Darius guy and he's got a massive soft spot for you. He's a bit of a rebel – he might be up for it."

"Correction, he's always flirting with me, not the other

way round," protests Daisy.

"Harumph," says Charlie, giving Grace a knowing look.

"But I guess I could take it for the team and use my charms on him!" Daisy practises flashing her best smile and doing the coy thing with her eyes.

"Yes, perfect. But you'll have to play down being so concerned about Archie, because he might get jealous. So you make out it's Grace who has a crush on Archie and is desperate to see her fallen hero (not so far from the truth anyway!) and you're just tagging along to give your friend moral support." Charlie is enjoying making Grace squirm now.

"Wow, Charlie – I never had you pegged for being so devious before!" says Daisy.

"Ah, well, you always need a strategy – that's why I'm so good at hockey – got the game planned three steps ahead in me mind all the time," says Charlie. "So Grace, are you up for this? Because if you get caught, you're in big trouble. I don't think Boss would be very happy about his little scholarship girl getting up to no good. And you've already been in trouble once about walking on Farmer Morgan's land."

"Oh, I'm definitely up for it. But I'll let you guys sort out the details, because you know how everything works at Fairstone better than I do. So next step after finding the route out of here is for Daisy to get flirting with Darius and pray that he hasn't got the pooey bum too."

"Yep, you got it!" says Charlie.

* * *

It's Friday afternoon – many of the kids have gone to Ludlow on the bus to spend their pocket money and to have tea and cream buns in De Greys. It's quiet around school and the girls have a couple of hours to kill before the afternoon lessons start. Daisy, Grace and Charlie are in their dorm room, changing into their navy tracksuit bottoms and Fairstone hoodies.

"If anyone asks, we're going for a run, right? We're getting in some extra training for the Inter-House Endurance Race," says Charlie.

"Good job it's not that warm today after the thunderstorms, or we'd look like a bunch of nanas wearing so many clothes," says Daisy.

"Yes! Come on now, Charlie, I'm dying to know where we're going and why we need to put this lot on," says Grace."

"Well – and we'll have to keep our voices down – last term I was kicking around on me own one afternoon. I'd sprained me wrist and couldn't play in the hockey match – they were playing away that day. I decided to go for a walk along the back road to cheer meself up. So as I was walking past the back of Fairstone House, I noticed the coal scuttle going into the house. It just got my curiosity going and I thought to meself, 'I wonder where that goes and how they got the coal out on the other side and into the house?' So I decided to investigate. I got me torch. Then I climbed over the little wooden railings and slid down the coal chute. And that's all I'm going to tell you for now – the rest can be a surprise."

"Ooh, what an adventure!" squeaks Daisy. Grace just grins and her tummy does a little flip in anticipation.

"Right, let's go – act casual like we're not up to something suspicious," says Charlie. They make their way out of the garden and round to the lane at the back of the house. Luckily, no-one is around and all is quiet. "Here it is. Who's going first?"

"I will," says Grace, already with one leg cocked over the

wooden railings, painted a jaunty shade of blue. "Just slide down the chute on your bum and then get out of the way so we can come down," says Charlie in a hoarse whisper.

"Will do," says Grace, a little nervous of plunging down into the dark, but eager to prove her courage to Charlie. Whoosh – and she is down, just like a slide in a children's playground. She gets to her feet and steps to one side. "I'm clear," she whispers up the chute and Daisy soon comes flying down.

"Wee, that was fun!" Daisy tries to say quietly.

"Quick, move out the way so Charlie can come down, or you'll get launched into orbit if she crashes into you," Grace says to Daisy. "She's clear," Grace whispers up the chute. And then the larger bulk of Charlie comes hurtling down and slides out a distance along the floor.

"I love doing that!" says Charlie, as quietly as she can. "Right, get your torches on and follow me."

Grace flashes her torch around and sees that they are in a large room with shelves and storage cupboards around the walls. The coal has long since been taken away, but there is still some coal dust, which now covers their bottoms from sliding down the chute. The rest of the room is relatively clean and bare, except for a few cobwebs and a layer of dust. Someone has obviously cleared it out.

"This way," says Charlie. "Follow me." She walks to the far side of the room and round to the right, where they find a staircase going up."

"Oh my goodness – that must go up into Fairstone House," says Grace. "Where does it come out?"

"Let's see, shall we?" says Charlie. They climb the stairs to the top, where a chink of light shines around the edge of a door that leads into Fairstone House. The girls stand quietly, breathlessly listening. They hear footsteps and voices, then a door opening and closing. Charlie motions for them to retreat back down the stairs, so they can't be heard.

"That sounded like Catherine and Yasmin from the 3rd Form going into their dormitory," says Daisy.

"Bingo!" says Charlie. "Have you never wondered where the door between their dorm and the shower room goes? It's always locked – I've tried it a few times."

"So how are we going to use it to get out then?" says Grace.

"Aha," says Charlie. "It's only bolted from this side – they must have got someone to put bolts on when they converted it into a boarding house, to stop us getting out, because they don't use the cellars anymore. And they didn't think any of us would go rummaging around in a dirty old coal scuttle."

"So you mean if we just undo the bolts on this side, then we'll be able to open it from the inside of Fairstone House?"

"Yes, bingo again – you've got it, Miss Smartypants!" says Charlie.

"Let's do it then!" says Daisy and slides back the rusting bolts. "Oh, I hope no-one heard that. Shall we open it and take a peek?"

"Just listen first to check the coast is clear," says Grace.

"All quiet in there. One, two, three, Open Sesame!" says Daisy, opening the door just wide enough for all three to peep out. They can see the shower room door to the right and know the 3rd Form dormitory door is on the left, but hidden from their view.

"Quick, better close it again in case anyone comes," says Charlie. "And you need to pray that the catch is strong enough to keep it shut if anyone leans on it from the other side."

Back in the dorm, changing out of their dirty sports gear, the girls fall about with giggles of relief after the tension of having to be quiet and stealthy.

"Oh, that was so much fun!" says Daisy.

"OK, now for Operation Flirty Pants. Where do you reckon Darius will be?" says Grace.

"Probably hanging out at the Rec or in the 5th Form classroom in this damp weather," says Daisy.

Operation Flirty Pants

Strains of Queen echo down the corridor emanating from the 5th Form classroom. They find Darius and two other boys – Phil and James – playing loud music on their boom box. Grace recognises the three of them from her first day, when they did the haunting rendition of 'Ghost Town' by The Specials. This time, they are singing to Queen's 'We Will Rock You'. Phil and James are using their brooms as air guitars and Darius is taking the part of Freddie Mercury, singing loudly into the board rubber. They are re-enacting Queen's epic set at Band Aid. Darius has Freddie Mercury's moves just right as he struts up and down his pretend stage.

The track comes to an end and the girls clap and cheer. "Did you enjoy that, girls?" says Darius, delighted for once that he has a real audience.

Daisy says, "Oh my gosh, Darius, you've got such a great voice – you should be on one of those TV talent shows! Can I sing something with you? What have you got on that cassette deck? Anything suitable for a duet?" Daisy is all smiles, perfect teeth and flashing eyes. Darius doesn't stand a chance.

"How about Cyndi Lauper's 'Time After Time'?" says Darius.

"Oh yes – I LOVE that song!" says Daisy, clapping her hands together in excitement.

"Cool, let's do it! Anyone got another board rubber?" says Darius.

"No, but I can use my hairbrush!" says Daisy.

"Perfect! You sing the first line, then I'll sing the alternate lines and we'll both sing the chorus together," says Darius. "You ready?"

"Yes," says Daisy, and Phil presses the play button on the cassette player.

As they finish, the room erupts into applause. "Flippin' brilliant, you two! I loved that," says Charlie.

"Me too," says Grace, wiping tears from her eyes. Phil and James are lost for words, not wanting to appear too soft.

The bell goes for afternoon lessons. "Oh, what a shame. I was really enjoying myself then," says Daisy.

"Hey Daiz, can I walk you to tea after lessons and maybe we could sing some more songs afterwards?" says Darius quietly, hoping the other boys don't hear.

"Yes, I'd really like that!" says Daisy.

Charlie is grinning from ear to ear and nudging Grace in the side. "Bingo!" she whispers, winking at Daisy.

As the girls leave to go to their lessons, they overhear James saying, "Whey hey, Darius, you're in there!"

"Yeah, she's a cutie, alright," says Phil.

"Shut up, guys! Keep your voices down – don't ruin it for me," says Darius.

Daisy is sitting next to Darius at teatime. Charlie and Grace hover nearby. They overhear Daisy saying to him, "Darius, there's something important I want to talk to you about. Can we go somewhere private after tea?"

A dreamy look comes over Darius – he can't quite believe his luck. Charlie thumps the side of Grace's leg. Grace looks down with a grimace of pain to see Charlie's fist giving her the thumbs up.

"Ouch, no need for that!" whispers Grace.

Daisy rejoins the girls on their way to Prep. "Well, how did it go?" says Grace.

"You're right in there," says Charlie. "You had him eating right out of your little pink handy wandies!"

"Yes, he's up for it," says Daisy looking a little worried.

"Oh, I bet he is," says Charlie. "Nudge, nudge, wink, wink!"

"Oh, don't rub it in, Charlie. I'm going to have trouble letting him down afterwards – I feel bad for using him like this. He says there's a window with a dodgy catch at the back of the 6th Form studies and he'll let us in. It's not far to Sick Bay from there. His dorm is next to Sick Bay, so he's going to sneak in before Lights Out and warn Archie that we're coming, so it's not too much of a shock for him," says Daisy. "Lucky for us, he's really fond of Archie. They're buddies from the rugby team, otherwise I think he might have been a bit warier."

"Brilliant!" says Charlie.

"What time are we meeting him?" says Grace.

"Midnight. All the staff have long gone to bed by then. He says they're all early birds. Lights out for the boys is 9pm, so there won't be anyone else around and it'll be dark too."

"Do you want to come, Charlie?" says Grace.

"No thanks, love. I'd feel a bit of a gooseberry with you and your boyfriends. And probably best to have fewer people. Plus, quite frankly, I can't be arsed. I like my sleep too much. But don't worry. I'll cover for you. You're in luck tonight – it's Mr and Mrs Chapeau's night off and Mrs Williams is doing Lights Out. She'll probably have too much 'sherry trifle' and fall asleep in the armchair in the sitting room. So she won't notice you've gone."

The Raid on Sick Bay

The alarm clock goes off, muffled under Grace's pillow.

"Psst, Daisy, it's time," whispers Grace.

"I'm awake," says Daisy. "Too excited to sleep much anyway."

"Keep it down, you two," grunts Charlie. "But good luck and don't get caught."

Daisy and Grace are already fully dressed under their pyjamas. They swap their pyjamas for their trackie bottoms and hoodies, to keep the coal dust off their clothes.

"Don't forget the honey, Grace," says Daisy.

"No, I've got a teaspoon too. I nicked it from tea earlier. It's all wrapped up in my hoodie pocket."

Earlier that evening, Grace had said, "We can ditch the trackies and hide them before we go into school, because we don't want to be leaving a trail of soot all over Sick Bay. That would be good, wouldn't it – a trail of sooty footprints that leads right back to the culprits!" – Grace and Daisy had had a good giggle at the thought of that and decided to go barefoot once they were in school and leave their sooty trainers to clean up later.

"Good job we can take our kit home, and clean it tomorrow," Daisy had said, and offered to take Charlie's home too.

They open the door quietly and listen for any signs of life. All is quiet, except for the loud ticking of the grandfather clock, which echoes around the marble-tiled hallway below and comes to them up the stairwell. There is no need for torches yet – they use the light from the plug-in night lights to find their way. They creep down the back stairs towards the shower room and there it is – the door to the cellars. There's no sound coming from the 3rd Form dormitory. So they open the door as quietly as they can, softly closing it behind them.

The cellars smell dusty and dry. They put their torches on and make their way down the stairs and through the cellars to the coal chute. Unsettling scuttling noises of tiny feet scrabble away from them.

"Euw, I think there might be mice or rats down here," says Daisy.

"Don't worry, they're not going to hurt us," says Grace. "I'll go first up the chute. Can you shine your torch on it so I can see what I'm doing? Then I'll do the same for you from the top.

"Righto," says Daisy.

Grace takes a bit of a run-up and grabs the railings to pull herself up the last bit. "I'm up," she whispers to Daisy. "Your turn." Daisy tries the same as Grace, but halfway up, her feet slip and she slides back down the chute.

"You nana," says Grace, stifling a giggle. Daisy is a giggling heap at the bottom of the chute. "You have to grab the railing to pull yourself up the last bit. Or I could lean down, and you could grab my arm," says Grace.

"I'll grab the railing. Otherwise I'll probably pull us both down."

"OK, I'll get out of the way."

With a bit more of a run-up, Daisy makes it this time. "Phew, made it! Right, let's get to it. Darius will be waiting," she says.

They step into the chill of the night air. The thunderstorms have passed and it's a clear sky full of stars. In the distance, an owl hoots from the trees behind the school. The moon is not quite full, but bright enough to light their way, so they decide to switch off their torches. They hurry, as quietly as they can, hugging the bushes to hide their shadows. They sneak round the back of school, avoiding crossing the playground, which seems too exposed.

They get to the back of the 6th Form studies without being seen and then a stern voice says, "Halt! Who goes there?"

The two girls freeze and try to melt back into the bushes. "It's only me, don't worry," says Darius, stepping out from the shadows. "Had you going there, didn't I?!"

"Oh my goodness, Darius, you scared the wotsits out of me!" says Daisy.

"I'm sorry," he says, patting Daisy on the arm. "Come on then, ladies. Welcome to Main School. I'll be your tour guide for the night. This way, please. You'll need to climb up onto this wall, and the window is just above it. Do you need a bunk up, Daisy?"

"Don't be cheeky, Darius," says Daisy.

"She probably will after our incident with the coal chute," says Grace. "But we better take our sooty clothes off first."

"Don't tell him about that!" says Daisy.

"Ooh err!" says Darius.

"Don't get too excited, we're fully clothed underneath," says Grace.

"Oh how disappointing," says Darius. "But I don't blame you – it's a cold night. Right, Grace, you go first. And then stand on the ledge to the side of the window. Joking aside, it is going to be easier if I give you a bit of a push from below. I can do it on my own, but I'm taller than you and I've had more practice."

"How do you know about it?" says Daisy.

"Oh, I've got some buddies in the Lower 6th who showed me it – it goes into their study."

"Right, let's give it a go," says Grace. She jumps and grabs the top of the wall, as Darius deftly pushes her bottom to give her the momentum to scrabble up the wall. "Thanks, Darius," she says, safely on the ledge now.

"You're welcome!" he replies. "Your turn, Daisy – do exactly what Grace did and I'll support you." Daisy takes a flying leap at the wall, gets halfway up and then wobbles and almost falls back down. Luckily for Daisy, Darius manages to get his shoulder under her bottom and Grace grabs her arm at the top. "Up you go," he says, giving her a good shove.

"I'm up!" says Daisy triumphantly, as she manages to scrabble onto the wall. "Thank you, Darius."

"The pleasure's all mine," he says with a chuckle. "Right, stand back, I'm coming up." He takes a run up, leaps, grabs the top of the wall and scales it like a spider monkey. "OK, I'll go in the window first, so I can help you down the other side. Daisy, you next, so Grace can help you."

Getting in the window is easier than up the wall and they all manage it without incident, landing on someone's desk, just below the window. They are in a study with three desks, which smells of coffee and toast, and the slightly musky smell of teenage boys.

"You'll be glad to know that's the trickiest bit over. We'll just have to be really quiet now," says Darius.

"It's really good that we're barefoot then. It'll be much quieter than wearing shoes," says Grace.

"Good point. I'm going to take mine off too," says Darius. "Archie's expecting us. I sneaked into Sick Bay earlier to warn him, so he's not too startled by two gorgeous girlies arriving in his bedroom. Right, this way. Follow me and be really careful with the doors."

They are in a pre-fab building, which has been tacked onto the back of the main house to give the 6th Formers a quiet place to study. They leave the study they're in, pass into a hallway and then through another door, passing under a stone archway and up three steps into Main School, coming out in the corridor just along from the dining hall.

"Tread really quietly now. Everything is a bit echoey here, and torches off. We'll just have to use the night-lights to see. Here, hold my hand, Daisy, and Grace, hold Daisy's," whispers Darius.

Linked together like this, they creep along the corridor, up the main staircase and along the gallery above the Old Hall. One more creaky door on a heavy spring, and they are in another corridor with doors to boys' dormitories on either side. They can hear the occasional sound of snoring and farting, and passing one dormitory, a mumble of someone talking in their sleep.

At the end of this corridor is another heavily sprung doorway onto a landing. "Almost there, whispers Darius. "Sick Bay is just in here. Archie's in the first room." He softly opens the door and they slip in. "Arch, are you awake? I've brought the girls to see you."

"Hey, what?" mumbles Archie, turning over. "Oh, it's you guys! Thanks for coming to see me. I apologise if it smells a bit fruity in here. My tummy is very poorly."

"Yes, sorry to hear you've got a pooey bum!" says Daisy.

"Hi Archie, you poor sausage," says Grace. "We've brought you some of Nanny Watkins' special honey to make you better."

"Oh, that's so kind of you. It's got to be better than Nurse Bernie's jollop. I swear it gives me hallucinations," says Archie.

"Yes, we've been hearing about it from Burnley. He says it made him go funny in the 'ed." says Grace.

"Yes, it does! But it also gave me some very interesting

visions. I'll tell you all about that another time."

Grace sits on the bed next to Archie and gets the honey and spoon out of her pocket. "Archie sit up and shade your eyes. Daiz, can you shine your torch on this so I can see what I'm doing? I think two teaspoons would be good as a starting dose." She scoops out a spoonful and gives it to Archie.

"Oh my goodness, that is SO delicious. I haven't been able to eat anything and that feels like it's feeding all my cells!" says Archie.

"Here, have another one then," says Grace, giving him another spoonful. "We'll leave it with you and you can take it whenever you need it, but best to hide it from Nurse Bernie. She might confiscate it, thinking it's bad for you."

"You can put it in my wash bag in the locker next to the bed."

As Grace bends to put the honey away, Archie whispers in her ear, "I know the secret way, Grace – it's a portal. I've seen a vision of it. When I'm better, I'll show you." Grace gives Archie's arm an excited little squeeze to show she's heard him.

"Right guys, we better get going – we can't push our luck for too long," says Darius.

"Thanks for coming and thanks so much for the medicine. I'm feeling better already," says Archie.

"Hope you get well soon," says Grace.

"Yes, hope your pooey bum clears up soon!" says Daisy, giggling.

"Get well, mate. We need you back on the cricket team. Got a big match coming up on Wednesday against the Uptonians," says Darius. "And you can't wear white cricket trousers in the state you're in – far too risky!"

"I think that honey's done the magic trick," says Archie. "See you soon."

Darius checks the coast is clear and they retrace their steps through the main building. Darius goes first out of the window and down the wall with a flying leap. He lands like a cat.

"Daisy, turn around and go backwards. I'll help you down," he says. She does as he suggests, but her hands slip and she lands heavily on him, bringing them both to the floor in a giggling heap. "Are you OK, Daisy?" says Darius.

"Yes, but sorry for squashing you," she says.

"Oh, I kind of liked it," he says, getting up and helping her up.

Grace is down in one piece now. "You two look like you're having fun!" she says.

"Yeah guys, that is the most fun I've had in ages – a real adventure! But you better get back now before anyone misses you," says Darius. He gives Daisy's hand a little squeeze and says, "See you tomorrow, Gorgeous." Then he climbs back up the wall and into the studies. With a last wave out of the window, he is gone.

Daisy and Grace put their sooty clothes and trainers back on and head back to Fairstone House.

"Mission accomplished," says Grace as, back in their pyjamas, they slide into bed. The slumbering form of Charlie barely stirs, as she dreams of hockey triumphs over her arch rivals.

"Yes, but oh my goodness, Grace, I am in trouble now. How am I going to let that poor boy down?" says Daisy.

"I don't know. Do you have to let him down? I think you make a sweet couple, especially when you sing together," says Grace.

"Hmmm, maybe I'll sleep on it and see how I feel in the morning."

Archie's Vision

It's Monday morning. Archie is back from Sick Bay, tucking into a hearty breakfast and chatting to Tom, Burnley and Calum. Grace and Daisy are back in school, sports kit cleaned, after a weekend at their homes.

"Hey, Arch, good to see you looking so well," says Daisy.

"Yes, I'm feeling great now," says Archie.

Calum still looks a little green around the gills and is eating dry toast. "Are you OK, Calum?" says Daisy.

"Getting there," he says, not very convincingly.

"We want to hear all about it, especially about Nurse Bernie's jollop – well, not all the gory details, but you know what I mean," says Daisy.

"Gosh, that stuff's lethal, isn't it, Calum?" says Archie.

"Sure is," says Calum morosely.

"It somehow got out how alcoholic and hallucinogenic it is, and there were boys pretending to be sick just so they could get a dose!" says Archie.

"Didn't know what they were letting themselves in for," says Calum, going even greener at the thought of it. "I'm never taking that stuff again, even if I'm at death's door – eurgh!" and he gives a little shudder.

After breakfast, Archie is putting his tray away and out of earshot of the others, Grace says, "Come on Archie, walk with us up to Fairstone House. I'm dying to hear what really happened when you took Nurse Bernie's jollop."

"Yes, sure," he says.

As they walk across the school yard, "I'm really dying to hear about you finding the portal to the secret way. How did the jollop help you do that?" says Grace.

"It gave me visions. I'd been reading that book about the history of Fairstone Court. I was fascinated by what it said about it being a Calendar House and the Calendar Window. I was sure there was more to it than the book was saying, so I suppose that's why I found myself thinking about it a lot. Nurse Bernie gave me a dose of the old jollop and within a few minutes, all the images from the book began to swim in front of my eyes. One image really caught my attention. I had this strange vision – I was standing in front of the Calendar Window, looking at the picture of Old Father Time, with the images of the four seasons around him. He came to life –¬ he was smiling at me and beckoning – and told me he would show me the portal to the secret way. Then the white lion I saw in my dreams appeared – the one you called Regulus. His huge white face was right in my head and he said, 'I will show you how to use the portal,'" says Archie.

"Wow, so it looks as if the portal to the secret way is in the stained-glass window and the key to using it is to call Regulus in?" says Grace.

"Yes, that's right. But we also need to speak to Old Father Time and to somehow get him to come alive," says Archie.

"Guys, I'm a bit scared. Are we sure we want to do this?" says Daisy.

"Oh gosh, I can't think of anything more exciting! It was so clear to me. What could possibly go wrong?!" says Archie with a wry smile. "Grace, are you up for it?"

"Yes, I definitely want to have a go," she says.

"Well, I guess if you two are going to do it, I'd better come along – got to have someone sensible with you! And I suppose I've got to trust Regulus to keep us safe."

"That's decided then. When shall we go?" says Archie.

"How about teatime today?" says Grace. Everyone will be busy in the dining room and I'm sure Nanny will give us something to eat – she always does."

"OK, sooner rather than later is good," says Archie.

"Agreed, Daisy?"

"Yes, let's do it before I lose my nerve," she says.

Finding the Secret Portal

The three kids stand in front of the window in the Old Hall. No-one else is around – they are all at tea. The kids know they need to call Regulus for help. Grace says, "Shall I say it?" The others nod, knowing that Grace seems to have a knack for things of a magical nature. Grace thinks hard to bring up words of importance to bring Regulus here. She doesn't want anything bad to happen, or the wrong kind of beings to arrive instead of Regulus. She holds a strong image of Regulus in her mind and asks the others to do the same. She begins, "I call on our guide, the White Star Lion, Regulus, to be our protector for this journey."

In a blaze of white light, Regulus stands before them. He is immense, infinite, a being of great power and goodness. His great white presence seems to fill the whole room. The star on his forehead blazes with a diamond brilliance. He bows to them and says, "How can I be of service on your quest, children of the stars?" his deep voice resonating down the hallway. The kids are nervous that they will be discovered. "Do not fear, only you can see and hear me," he says.

"We wish to open the portal in the Calendar Window so that we can visit Nanny Watkins," says Archie.

"Then you must summon the Gatekeeper. Choose your words carefully, for words have power. Even more important than your words, is your intention. Remember that energy follows intention. Whatever you hold as a strong enough intention will happen, whether it is a good intention or not such a good intention."

"You got that, Daisy? Hold a strong intention that it will

all work out really well," says Archie.

"Yes, I'm on it," says Daisy.

Words are welling up inside Grace and she speaks again. "I summon the Gatekeeper of this Calendar Portal to open the way for us, as we journey to the cottage of Nanny Watkins. And as we journey there and back, I ask that we are protected from harm and that only good will come of this."

"Don't forget to say the bit about us going there and back in the blink of time before anyone has time to miss us," prompts Daisy.

"Oh, yes, thanks, Daiz," Grace whispers. "And we humbly ask that we go there and back in a wink of time before anyone misses us here. May it be so," adds Grace.

The window begins to shimmer. Old Father Time begins to move. He stands up from his seat, holding his staff in front of him. "Greetings, young journeyers. I hear you wish to travel to the cottage of Nanny Watkins and back again without anyone noticing you are gone? If I understand your request correctly, hmmm?"

"Yes, that's exactly right, Grandfather," says Grace.

"Then you may pass," he says. A shimmering door forms, which opens onto a light-filled corridor.

"Let's hold hands, so we all go together," says Grace.

"I will escort you," says Regulus and they all step into the tunnel. There is a great whooshing sound and a feeling of speed, and suddenly they are at the other end of the tunnel and they can see Nanny's garden through another shimmering door. Regulus tells them to make note of where this door is so that they can find their way back and that he will wait for them there. They step through and find themselves in Nanny's back garden next door to her outside privy. She is just coming out as she catches sight of them.

"Oh, hello you lot. You startled me. I was just taking the evening air, and a woman doesn't expect to find three kids in her back garden out of the blue!"

Grace didn't think Nanny looked startled at all. "It was almost as if she had been expecting us," she thinks.

"We found the Calendar Window portal, Nanny!" says Daisy excitedly.

"Oh, have you now? Well done, well done. That didn't take you long. Come on in, will you? I'll make us all a nice cup of tea." They head for the back door and the warmth of Nanny's kitchen.

"No, it didn't take us long, Nanny, thanks to your hints and some thanks to Nurse Bernie's jollop." They are sitting at Nanny's kitchen table, as she bustles about making tea. The smell of her fire is comforting and familiar. "It was Archie who figured it all out," says Grace.

"Oh, well done, Archie. You are clever! But what do you mean – Nurse Bernie's jollop?" asks Nanny.

"I had a really poorly tummy after Farmer Morgan contaminated the school water supply with his slurry. So I was in Sick Bay and Nurse Bernie gave me some of her jollop for my tummy. It gave me funny daydreams about the Calendar Window and Old Father Time. He came to life and showed me where the portal is. Then Regulus the white lion came and said he would help us."

"Did he now? Well, that was very clever of you, Archie. Shame on that Morgan for poisoning all you kids. And you want to be careful of old Bernie's jollop. I hear it's very addictive and it messes with your mind. You don't want to be taking things that mess with your mind. Especially at your age, when you're still developing. There are safer ways to do what you did."

"How do you mean?" asks Archie.

"I mean, did the jollop actually get your tummy better,

Archie? Or did it just give you funny daydreams?" asks Nanny.

"No, Nanny. It didn't work on my tummy at all. But Gracie brought some of your magic honey and that set my tummy right straight away," says Archie.

"Very good, Gracie. That was exactly the right thing to do," says Nanny. "And the safer way to find out about things like the Calendar Window portal is to do a journey with the drum and ask Regulus to show you. Now that I've shown you how to work with your dreams, I think it might be time for us to have a little go at journeying with the drum. You could also ask for a dream about it – you know – write out your question on a piece of paper and read it out at bedtime, then put it under your pillow and see what happens in your dreams."

"Oh yes, thanks, Nanny – that sounds like a great idea. I'm definitely going to try that out," says Daisy.

"We look forward to hearing what Daisy's been dreaming about. Every morning, when we meet up before assembly, she tells us her latest adventure from the night. They are always very entertaining," says Archie.

"That's really good, Daisy – I'm really pleased to hear you have lots of dreams. Keep telling them to your friends here and practice the Lightning Dreamwork on them.

I'm guessing you kids are hungry? I reckon you're missing your tea to come here. I can rustle up some food for you if you like?" says Nanny.

"Yes please, Nanny," they all chorus together.

As they sit and eat their food, Nanny poses them a new mystery to solve. "Now that you were so quick to find the secret way here, I have another question for you. Does anyone know why your school is called 'Fairstone'?"

"Ooh, good question, Nanny! But no – I have no idea. Never really thought about it till now," says Archie. Daisy and

Grace have no idea either.

"Well, think about it – Fair and Stone. What is the Fair Stone? Or the Fairy Stone? I'm going to give you a clue and tell you that it's somewhere in the grounds of your school. Not many people know about it – it's well hidden. I believe there may be something about it in that book I told you about in the Top Library.

"I'm going to set you a bit of research to find out all about the Fairy Stone and see if you can find where it is. Then come back and tell me what you've found out."

"Ooh yes, I love a challenge! Especially a mysterious one!" says Archie.

Grace looks at Nanny through narrowed eyes. "How do you know about all this, Nanny?" she says.

Nanny taps the side of her nose and winks at Archie, "Ah, that's for me to know and you to find out," she says with a little chuckle.

After a delicious meal with Nanny, they go out to find Regulus and ask him to help them get back to school via the portal next to Nanny's privy. They call to the Gatekeeper and ask him to take them back to school in the wink of time, with no-one noticing that they've been gone. True to his word, they arrive back with school teatime still going on, but with tums full of Nanny's lovely food, none of them fancy it.

Darius Proclaims His Love for Daisy

"You girls have to come with me. You're the ones who got me into this mess. Now you have to help get me out of this," says Daisy. They are just leaving the dining hall after lunch.

"What on earth are you talking about, love?" says Charlie.

"I think I've got an idea," says Grace. "Did Darius just ask you out?"

"Not exactly, but I think it's coming," says Daisy. "He says he wants me to meet him at the back of the 6th Form Studies in 10 minutes, because he's got something important to show me. What on earth am I going to say to him?"

"Ooh, intriguing. He said, 'Show you,' not 'Ask you,' – I like his style," says Charlie. "In any case, you could do worse. I think he's quite a funny guy."

"No, it's just corny like, 'I want to show you my etchings.' I can't take him seriously," says Daisy.

"What do you reckon, Grace?" says Charlie.

"I think he's sweet and funny and you'd make a lovely couple. He absolutely adores you, Daisy," says Grace.

"Oh, you're no help, Grace. Whah!! What am I gonna do?" says Daisy.

"Ah, now I've got it – you've got your eye on someone else! Come on, spill, who is it?" says Charlie.

"No, that's not it," says Daisy. "I'm just happy being single. There's just too much going on in my life right now without getting it any more complicated."

"Wow, listen to her. You'd think she was 35, not 15 years old. Anyhow, come on, let's go and see what all this is about. I'm dying to know what he's going to show you! We'll hide in the bushes, giving you moral support without being seen – it's going to be hilarious!" says Charlie.

They make their way to The Spares and round to the back of the 6th Form Studies. It's a beautiful sunny day and the sunshine seems to sparkle on the daisies which sprinkle the lawn at the back of the Studies. Charlie and Grace hang back in the bushes that surround the lawn and Charlie shoves Daisy forward.

A tall figure with luxuriant dark curls is standing on the wall next to the window that Daisy and Grace so recently used to gain access to Main School on their visit to Archie in Sick Bay. It is Ramesh Chandra, a friend of Darius from the Lower 6th. Causally exhaling a cloud of smoke from his cigarette, he shouts in the window, "Darius, she's here, your beloved is here!" He saunters along the wall and stands round the corner, where he can still watch what's going on, but is out of the way. "Don't come too close, Daisy. Wouldn't want you to get hurt." Then he engrosses himself in finishing his cigarette.

From inside the study, a lovely tenor voice begins to sing,

> *"Baby, look at me*
> *And tell me what you see.*
> *You ain't seen the best of me yet.*
> *Give me time, I'll make you forget the rest."*

And then suddenly Darius is taking a flying leap out of the window singing at the top of his voice,

> *"Fame – I'm going to live forever! I'm going to learn how*
> *to fly – High!*
> *People will see me and cry.*
> *Fame!*
> *I'm gonna make it to heaven,*
> *Light up the sky like a flame.*
> *Fame!*
> *I'm gonna live forever.*
> *Baby, remember my name..."*

He sails in a huge arc through the air to land on one knee in front of Daisy, still singing,

"Daisy Davies, I LOVE YOU…
…I got more in me
And you can set it free.
I can catch the moon in my hands,
Don't you know who I am?
Remember my name!"

Half laughing, half shocked, Daisy replies, "You're a nutter, Darius Darvesh – an absolute nutter," and walks away shaking her head in disbelief. From round the corner, guffaws of laughter come from Ramesh, "She ain't wrong there, my friend."

"Well, I think that went well, don't you, Ramesh?" says Darius. But Ramesh can't speak because he's laughing too much.

More laughter comes from the bushes where Charlie and Grace are hiding. Daisy joins the girls and they beat a hasty retreat.

Chapter 16:
A Journey to Find Guidance

"OK, kids, how much time do you have before you need to get back to school?" Nanny asks. "Oh, I forgot – silly question now that you're using the portal and can come and go in the wink of an eye. So would you like to stop for a spot of lunch?"

"Well we've got all afternoon now anyway. We don't have to be back until 6pm for tea. So yes, Nanny, lunch would be great, thank you!" says Archie.

"Good, good," says Nanny, "Because I think with all these Big Dreams and talk of important missions, it's time to teach you how to connect to your guidance so that you can ask for help whenever you need it. What do you reckon? As it's such a lovely day, I think we'll do it out in the garden. But first, come and help me pick some veggies for lunch." And the kids follow her out into the back garden.

After lunch, Nanny shows them the circle she has laid out underneath the apple tree, with four large stones marking each of the four compass directions and smaller white stones forming the edge of the circle.

"Come and find yourself a place in the circle," says Nanny. "Feel which direction you're drawn to most and sit there without thinking about it too much. It doesn't pay to use your head – the heart gets things right a lot more often than your head. Remember that. I'm just going to get me drum. I'll see you in a mo." They watch as she saunters back to the house in that purposeful but unhurried way of hers.

"What on earth is she talking about?" says Archie.

"I've got a feeling we're about to find out in the most dramatic way," says Grace.

"I'm a bit scared," says Daisy. "I've got a weird feeling in my tummy."

"Oh, that'll be because you ate too much raw veg when we were making lunch. I hope it hasn't given you a farty bum!" says Archie.

"Rude!" says Daisy, throwing a handful of grass at Archie.

"Settle down now, children. She's coming back," says Grace. So they look around the circle and choose their places to sit. The bright sun forms dappled patterns on the lush grass as it shines through the gently swaying leaves of the gnarly old apple tree. The blossom has gone over and the little apples are starting to form. Nanny's garden is full of scented flowers, and the bees from her hives hum busily amongst them. The humming of the bees, the warmth of the sun and the scent of the flowers begin to lull the kids into a contented drowsiness.

Nanny comes down the garden carrying two bags and a candle. "What's all this, Nanny?" asks Archie.

"Well, son, you lot keep coming to me for answers and

I think it's high time you found a way to answer your own questions. Then I might get a bit of peace on a Saturday afternoon," says Nanny.

"Oh, have we been bothering you too much, Nanny?" asks Daisy.

"No, my dear, I enjoy your company, but you do need a way to find your own guidance. You're growing up fast and I won't always be around to guide you, so this is really important. I'd like to take you on a journey to meet your Guides. How about it then?" says Nanny.

"Well, that sounds intriguing, Nanny. So how does it work then?" asks Grace.

"You just need to experience it for yourself – that's much better than me explaining the hows and the whys of it, dear," says Nanny. "You're going to have to trust me, Gracie, and let yourself just see what happens."

"OK, I'll give it a try," says Grace.

"Not so much 'trying' is needed, my dear. Let's just go with the flow, shall we? And what about you two?"

"I'm happy to go with the flow," says Archie.

"I'm a bit scared," says Daisy.

"Good, Archie. Nothing to worry about, Daisy. I've a feeling you'll be really good at this," says Nanny. "Bear with me while I do a bit of setting up," she says, unpacking the two bags. In one bag is a round skin drum with a painting of a winged white horse on it. Out of the second, she pulls a brightly painted rattle made from a large gourd with a wooden handle. A series of hares leaps around the circumference of this rattle. She places them on a flat stone in the centre of the circle. She lights a candle, saying, "Great Creator, God, Source of the Universe, I ask your blessing on our circle. May we travel safely between the worlds. May only good come of this. May it be so." She takes the rattle and proceeds to shake it around the circle, stopping to call in the Powers of each of the four directions – east, south, west and north – saying words that they can't quite hear, bringing in help and protection from her own guides. Then she goes back to the centre and shakes the rattle to the Earth and up to the heavens, asking for help and protection from the Earth and from God.

As the kids watch, something seems to be happening to Time. They are no longer sitting in Nanny Watkins' garden on a sunny afternoon. They are in a timeless place where anything could happen. Nanny looks different too. She looks like some ancient sage who has stepped out of the pages of a storybook. She seems bigger and an unexplainable power seems to be shining from her.

"Right then, you lot, here comes the good bit," she says, bringing them back to the present. "I'm going to play my drum for you and take you on a bit of a journey. The drumming is important because it calms your brain down so you can go into that quiet place where you can receive information from the magical realms. Follow my words as I lead you to meet someone who can give you guidance and connect you with your inner wisdom.

"Breathe into your hearts, and trust what you are being shown. And if your mind tells you you're making it all up, just agree with it and carry on.

"Alright then, are we all ready?" The kids nod to her, not seeming able to speak for now. "Good, get yourselves comfy then. You can lie down or sit – however you feel most comfy. Now close your eyes. Take some deep breaths and relax. Picture yourself in your favourite place in nature – somewhere you feel really safe and at home. This bit's really important, so listen up – you're going to say your intention in your mind that you, 'Wish to meet a loving and trusted guide who can help give you direction and answer your important questions.'"

Images begin to form in Grace's mind. She finds herself on a high plateau, underneath a tree and looking out over a wide, grassy valley. Next to the tree stands a magnificent brown and white horse, glowing with a radiant light. She approaches the horse and asks, "Are you my guide?"

The horse looks at her and says, "I am here to take you to meet your guide. Please get on my back." The horse has beautiful, friendly eyes. Grace feels that she can trust him, so she mounts onto his back. The horse sets off and runs towards the edge of the plateau. Grace's heart lurches as, just before they reach the edge, the horse sprouts wings and takes off, flying into the sky. Up, up, up they fly through the sky, heading towards the stars.

Finally, they land on the surface of a planet. In front of them is a vast palace of crystal, shining with iridescent light. Horse asks her to dismount and walk up the path towards the palace. Coming towards her is a magnificent white lion, huge and shining with golden light. His noble face has eyes of the brightest sky blue, and on his brow is a shining star. He speaks to her with a deep, booming voice. "Dear daughter, you are aptly named. Grace is your greatest quality. I am Regulus and I am your guide. Yes, I am the same white lion you have seen in your dreams and the one who came to help you navigate the portal of Old Father Time. You have an important task ahead of you. As I told you in your dream, your mission is to be guardians of the land and guardians of the wild creatures, including the white horse, known as Ahbleza. But I must warn you that, like all things from the light, the shadows are attracted to this beautiful horse. Do not fear – you have my protection. You three must bring your message to the world."

Staring deep into her eyes, he says, "Your mission is intertwined with mine. All three of you will need to work together and trust each other. The task may at times seem difficult and dangerous, but I want you to deeply know that I have been with you since the beginning of time and I will protect you to the ends of the Earth. You may come back and visit me whenever you like. You only have to call on me, and I will be there. Put your questions to your dreams as you go to sleep. I will come to you in your dreams and answer your questions. You can also come back here and ask Nanny Watkins to drum for you and meet me like this again. In time, you will learn to drum for yourself. Now it is time for you to return, but you can come back any time. Know that you are loved and you are blessed. For now, farewell." He stands on his hind legs and folds her into an embrace, hugging her to his furry white chest. She feels her heart light up and fill with love, as if he is transmitting love to her from his own great lion heart. It feels so wonderful that it makes her cry. He leads her back to Horse and she remounts, flying back down through the stars, back into the Earth's sky and landing once more on the high plateau.

Grace hears Nanny's voice again. "You are back home now – all of you is back. Feel the Earth underneath you. You are here in Nanny's garden. Have a little stretch, wiggle your toes and fingers, then come back and tell me all about your adventure, as soon as you are ready." She opens her eyes and sees Archie and Daisy stirring and looking a bit sleepy in the sunny garden.

"Well, how was that? Anyone got anything to tell us?"

"That was AMAZING, Nanny!" says Daisy, her eyes wide with wonder.

"Was it, love? Care to tell us what happened then?" says Nanny.

"As soon as I asked to meet a guide, it was as if I felt myself flying through the air. I was looking down on Earth from space as I crossed Europe and headed for Africa. Then when I was above South Africa, I started to come down to Earth. I was in a wilderness place. It was dry and hot with scrubby bushes all around. I felt as if I was standing at the edge of a dry riverbed. I started wondering if I was doing this right and where my guide was. Then an amazing thing happened."

"Go on, what was it? Tell us, Daiz," says Archie, leaning forward in his excitement to hear the rest of her tale.

"Well, you'll never guess! A huge male white lion steps out through the bushes and stands right in front of me. I should have been scared, but I wasn't. I just instantly knew. This is him. This is my guide. He looked just like the lion from my dream and the one who helped us with the portal."

"Oh, lovely," says Nanny. "Did he say anything to you, dear?"

"Yes, he did, Nanny. He told me that he is my guide and not to be afraid. He told me his name is Regulus and when he lived on Earth, this was the place where he was born. He called it something like Timbavati – the place where the star lions came down. I think that's the place our biology teacher was telling us about – where the real white lions live. He told me it is a very special place. I think he said it was a sacred place, and that one day I would visit the white lions that live there because it is part of my life's path. He said the three of us have an important task together and that I need to find my lion-heart, I mean, my courage. He told me that he loves me and will protect me forever, then he gave me a big hug, which was so lovely and made me feel all warm inside. Then I heard you saying it was time to come back. He told me to come and visit him again soon. And then I was back here in the garden."

"And how do you feel now, Miss Daisy?" asks Nanny.

"I feel really happy to meet him. He made me feel so safe – like I have someone really strong on my side. And I think I'm going to need that when we get to do this task together, whatever it is," says Daisy.

"Lovely, dear. You did really well. There, you see, it wasn't anything to be scared of after all, was it?" says Nanny.

Grace and Archie are both looking astonished at what Daisy has said and Nanny is eager to find out why, though she has a good idea.

"And how about you, Archie? Did you get to go on an adventure too?" she asks.

"Well, yes, I did. I met the same guide – Regulus the White Lion. He told me I could call him Reg for short. And he also told me we have an important task together and that he will help me. But I didn't go to Timbavati, I went to Egypt. I found myself standing in front of the Sphinx. I have always been fascinated by it. To me, it looks as if it used to have a lion's head and some big-headed pharaoh had it re-carved with his face on it. So I figure it must be really, really old because it must have been built a long time before that pharaoh came along. So I asked Regulus about it and he said I was right. So I asked him what it was for and he told me that there's a library of information underneath it, which holds the keys to the mystery of the whole universe. He took me in and gave me a look at the books. It was as if there were huge doors in the chest of the Sphinx and we walked right in. There were rows and rows of books, but they aren't like paper books that we have in our libraries. They're like virtual books. He told me to take one of the books down and have a look. So I slid one out and opened it up. It started playing like a video in front of me. At the time, it all made sense, but now I can't quite remember any of it. Regulus told me that there are some things I need to learn before I can understand the books in there and learn how to use them properly. I asked him what he meant and he told me that it would all unfold in the fullness of time as we complete our task together. Then it was time to come back, so he clapped me on the back, told me that I had his guidance and protection and that I will need to be like one of the action heroes that you see in the movies."

"Ooh well, I think you have the perfect qualities to be an action hero. How do you feel about all that?" asks Nanny.

"I'm excited, but it's a bit confusing and frustrating to not be able to read the books yet or to know what this important task is."

"Yes, so you are going to have to be patient for a while then, Archie. Keep pondering on the meaning of the book – it will have gone in on some level and you might have some flashes of what it means later. Grace, what about you? I think we're all dying to hear what happened to you."

And Grace told them about her journey. "So we all met Regulus the White Lion and he told us all that we have an important task together. But he didn't tell any of us what we need to do next. Nanny, what do you think?"

Nanny looks out across the garden. Grace notices how her shrewd eyes take in the scene – the changing light, the flowers, the bees, the weather – as she ponders her reply.

"I think you all have a lot to mull over. I have an idea what it might all be about, but I can't be sure yet. I think it will all become clear very soon. 'Guardians of the Wild,' didn't you say Grace? I think that is an important message for all you young people. Lord knows, we need people to take better care of the animals and nature!

"Right, me dears, your lesson in journeying for guidance is over for today. You best be heading on back to school. Come back soon."

Chapter 17:
The Fair Stone

Finding the Fair Stone

Grace stands at the edge of The Spares, her eyes scanning for clues to the location of the Fair Stone.

Grace, Archie and Daisy have read the chapter in the old book about the History of Fairstone, but it is not very specific about the location of the stone. It only says that it is somewhere in what the kids call The Spares – a piece of scrubby woodland that used to be part of the landscaped garden in the heyday of Fairstone Court, which has now largely been reclaimed by Nature. Amongst the trees are great sprawling tangles of rhododendron bushes with a profusion of magenta and purple flowers.

"Come on, magical stone, show me where you are," she whispers.

It's Wednesday afternoon. Archie and Daisy are away at cricket and netball matches. As Grace didn't make the team, she has a free afternoon. She's feeling a bit sorry for herself, but determined to do something useful. To be the first to find the Fair Stone would be so cool.

She's trudging back and forth, not having much luck, except for collecting nettle stings and bramble scratches. She thinks, "What would Nanny Watkins tell me to do? Maybe to tune in to Nature and see if the animals can give me some sort of clue."

She becomes aware of the sweet song of birds and follows it deeper into The Spares. A cloud of bright blue butterflies dance and swirl in front of her. She is mesmerised by the iridescent shine of their wings, shimmering in the sunlight. She follows them to a patch of sunlit grass and sits down to rethink what the book said about the stone.

The warmth of the sun makes her feel drowsy. She's exhausted from all this sporting activity – she's not used to doing so much physical activity and all her muscles ache. Before long, she has curled up and fallen asleep. She dreams that a wolf has come to see her. A wet nose nudges her, as if to say, "Wake up, Grace!" She begins to awaken, wondering if she should be scared of the wolf. When she comes to properly, she realises that it's not a wolf, but Jonnie Watkins trying to wake her.

"You got this far, don't give up now. If you only knew that you are just a whisker away from it," he says.

"Oh, is that you, Jonnie?"

"Yes it is."

"I have to ask, are you Nanny Watkins' son?"

"My mother is called Betty Watkins, and I believe people

know her as Nanny now that she is older," says Jonnie.

"Oh, Jonnie, how terribly sad. Can you tell me what happened to you?"

"Sorry Grace, but I don't like to talk about it – it's a bit of a sore point. Anyhow, back to the Fair Stone. You are very close. Want me to tell you how to find it?"

"Oh, I'm really sorry to be insensitive. And yes please, I would love you to show me how to find the Fair Stone!"

"See that big rhododendron bush there? It's actually a ring of bushes and the Fair Stone is inside it. If you walk round to the far side, you'll find the tiniest gap in the bushes where you can squeeze through. The stone is right at the centre."

"Wow, thank you so much for telling me, Jonnie..." But before she has finished speaking, he is gone. She walks around the bush, and just as he has said, at the far side from school, there is a tiny gap that leads diagonally through the bushes so that you cannot see from the outside, what is on the inside.

She emerges from the bushes to see an enormous golden-coloured stone, the sunlight pouring onto it. There is something welcoming about the stone and the air seems to shimmer and buzz around it. As Grace approaches it, she is convinced that it is shaped like the profile of a male lion's head, complete with a recess for its eye and the shape of a mane at the back.

As she approaches the stone, she feels a palpable sense of electricity around it. She is compelled to touch it, and as she does, she feels a buzz go right up her arms – not painful, but strong. Visions start to form in her mind. She sees Druids in long white robes chanting and levitating the stone into place. She sees Roman soldiers tearing down the circle of stones that once surrounded the Fair Stone. And she sees many gatherings of people through the ages – people coming here to celebrate weddings, or the equinoxes and the solstices, and also having lively discussions to settle disputes.

And then, as fast as the visions came, they stop, and the stone seems to push her hand away. She hears a voice in her head say, "That's enough for now, little human. Too much and your nervous system will be damaged. I don't want to fry you."

"Thank you, thank you," whispers Grace. She feels refreshed. Her tiredness and aches have gone. "Can't wait to tell Archie and Daisy about finding the stone," she thinks to herself as she returns to school.

Telling Nanny About the Fair Stone

Nanny is having a big cuddle with Ahbleza in the paddock at the back of her cottage. He likes to rub his big furry head up and down on her, which makes her chuckle, and she loves to stroke his neck. The only drawback is that she gets covered in white hairs. She hears laughter and realises the kids are on their way. "Better go, me 'ansome! Those kiddos aren't quite ready for you yet. They've been dreaming about you though, and I think it won't be long before you meet them – just got to prepare them a bit more first. I've got to be sure that they won't blab about you to anyone who doesn't need to know you're here." She looks down at her dress and brushes it off as best she can – she doesn't want to give away his presence – and she hurries back towards the house.

Ahbleza is an adept at the skills of camouflage. He lets himself out of the paddock, using his teeth and lips to undo the latch of the gate and carefully closing it again behind him, so as not to let Nanny's goats out. His shimmering white form becomes translucent as he blends in with the trees around him, hidden in plain sight.

The kids find Nanny looking at her herb patch. "Hiya kiddos, how are you all? Nice to see you back so soon. Did you manage to find the Fairy Stone yet?"

"Yes we did, Nanny. Well, Grace did actually. Then Daiz and I had a look too," says Archie.

"And what did you think of it?" says Nanny.

"Very impressive," says Archie. "I had no idea it was hidden there in The Spares amongst the rhododendrons!" says Archie.

"Oh, what did you think of it, then, Grace?" says Nanny, staring at her.

"It's a powerful stone, Nanny. It seems to kind of buzz when you touch it," says Grace.

"Yes, and anything else?" asks Nanny.

"Well, I haven't told the other two about this yet, but when I put my hands on it, it was as if the stone was talking to me and showing me pictures of things that happened in the past," says Grace.

"Yes, yes, very good, my girl. So what did it show you?" says Nanny.

"It showed me the people who put it there – Druid-type people in long white robes, chanting and sort of levitating it into place. It seemed to be part of a bigger circle. And then it showed me the Romans tearing down the rest of the circle, but for some reason, they couldn't pull that one down. And then later, but still a long time ago, people used to gather there on special occasions, sometimes to celebrate and sometimes to have a sort of court to settle disputes. We read about that in the book, and the stone also showed me in the vision," says Grace.

"Excellent, my dear. You've seen it just as I saw it. So the name of Fairstone Court is explained – a court to settle disputes at the site of the Fair Stone, to make things 'fair.' And do you know why the Romans couldn't pull that one down? Well, I'll tell you anyway – it's on a node point, which is a crossing point of two very powerful ley lines, or Earth energy lines. If someone with bad intent tries something there, it gives them an electric shock. The Romans thought it was cursed and left it alone. So yes, you got it spot on – it is a very powerful stone."

"Wow, fascinating, Nanny!" says Archie. "And Grace, I had no idea you saw all of that!"

"And how did you come to find it, dears? Daisy, you've been very quiet," says Nanny.

"Well, we went to the Old Library, like you told us, Nanny, and we found that book about the history of Fairstone Court. Or maybe I should say someone gave us the book. We'd never have found it on our own," says Daisy.

"Oh yes, who gave it to you?" says Nanny, fixing Daisy with a penetrating stare.

"Uh, the ghost, I mean a boy, whoops," says Daisy, going red.

"Ghost, what ghost?" says Nanny.

"The ghost of Jonnie Watkins, a boy who used to go to Fairstone School," says Daisy. "Oh, I wasn't meant to say anything about that!" says Daisy quietly to herself, wringing her hands together.

"Oh really?" says Nanny, looking away. "Excuse me dears, will you for a minute – got to pay a visit to the Maharaja," and she heads out the back door towards the outside privy.

"Oh Daiz, you dimwit! We agreed not to say anything about that. Looks like your hunch was right, by her reaction," says Archie.

"I know, I know. I couldn't help it. She fixed me with one of her stares and it was like she was hypnotising the information out of me," says Daisy.

"Yes, she does that, doesn't she? I wasn't going to tell anyone what I saw at the stone because I thought you would think I was weird," says Grace.

"What, weirder than when you talked to the ghost of Jonnie Watkins, when we couldn't see him at all?!" says Archie. "We're getting used to your spooky ways, Grace. I think it's brilliant by the way – wish I had your superpowers."

"Yes, me too," says Daisy, giving Grace a warm smile. They hear Nanny blowing her nose loudly and the back door latch going, as she comes back into the kitchen.

"Well, you've done really well, finding out all that information. Thanks for coming to tell me, but if you don't mind, I've got quite a bit to do this afternoon, and I'm sure you've got better things to do than to hang round with an old lady. But here, please take these scones. I made them today – keep the hunger pangs at bay from you growing kids. Come and see me again soon, won't you?" And she ushers them out of the door with a tin of scones. "I'll be wanting that tin back when you've finished them scones."

Back at school, Daisy says, "I feel terrible. She looked really upset when I talked about Jonnie Watkins. Poor Nanny. Do you think he might have been her son?"

"He could have been. The timing is about right," says Archie.

"Yes, he definitely is. How terrible it must be to lose your son at age 16," says Grace. "I didn't tell you before, but I met him in The Spares and he told me how to find the Fair Stone. I asked him if he was Nanny Watkins' son and he said yes."

"I knew it!" says Daisy. "Did he tell you what happened?"

"No. He said he didn't want to talk about that – it's probably too painful for him to think about," says Grace.

"You're a dark horse, aren't you, Grace?! And there we were thinking how clever you were finding it all by yourself! I'm definitely going to call my Dad and ask him if he knows about Jonnie," says Archie. "I think we should do something to make it up to Nanny. How about a peace offering of chocolates and nice bath stuff, and a card with our sincerest apologies?"

"Yes, that's a lovely idea. We bought some really nice things from Ludlow that we can give her," says Daisy.

"Yes, I agree. I don't want to stop coming – I love seeing her. She's got so much wisdom. I really think we can learn a lot from her," says Grace.

Healing for Nanny

Nanny goes back out to the paddock and calls for Ahbleza. From a tree on the opposite side of the paddock, a raven speaks. "Whark! Whark!" it cries. It's Nanny's totem. Death sits on her shoulder since the loss of her son. She lives with grief every day. "I hear you, you old black croaker!" she says.

She calls out, "Where are you, my boy? I know you're not far away. I can sense you watching me." Nanny hears a blowing of air out through large nostrils and feels a nudge in her back. "Oh there you are, you rascal. Come on, this old lady needs a cwtch." She turns and puts her arms around his silky neck. Burying her face against him, she says, "Oh, I still miss him so much, Ahbleza. After all these years, it's still so painful. Talking to the kids has just brought it all back up."

Nanny hears Ahbleza's words in her heart – "I know, Love, I know. Let it all out. Soon you will be ready to let the pain go. Some of it is guilt, because you couldn't save him. When you let that go, the pain will soften and fade, so that you can just cherish the love that you have for your wonderful boy. He is still around, and helping the kids – a magical soul, just like his Mum. But he needs to properly pass over, so that he can continue on his soul's next adventure. You need to let him go so that he can do that. He sticks around because of his love for you. The kids are here to help heal you. If you can teach them – pass on the teachings that you would have given to your son, then you will have fulfilled your purpose as a mother and a wise woman."

"I know that, Blazie. Soon I will be ready to do it, I promise," says Nanny.

"Don't promise me – promise yourself and your son – do it for him."

"I will. Now I think it's finally time for you to give me that healing you offered, Ahbleza. Lord knows, I've been trying to heal on me own for all these years."

"Of course, Dear One. Put your hands either side of my neck and relax." Nanny does this. He dips his head and points his forehead towards her chest. Almost instantly, a spiral of beautiful pink light, woven with sparkles of gold, begins to radiate from the bump on his forehead and enters Nanny's heart. She feels it soothing the tightness in her chest. In her mind's eye, she sees her wounded heart beginning to heal and glow with this pink light. "There is a stone of grief that weighs on your heart," says Ahbleza. "Are you willing to let it go? I can help you remove it if you give me permission."

"Yes, it's time to let go of that burden," says Nanny. "You have my permission to do whatever you can to help." Nanny sees this stone, like a big lump of coal in her heart. Ahbleza sends an extra burst of golden light into it. It begins to lift out of her heart and as it does so, it begins to dissolve and fade, leaving only sparkles of light. The light then forms the shape of a lovely pink rose and Nanny senses that the healing is over. She gives a big sigh.

"Thank you, my dear. That was lovely. I feel the most

peaceful I've felt in years."

"It's not over yet," says Ahbleza. "Your healing will take time, and there is more you need to let go of before it is complete."

"I know, I know, but I'm not quite ready for that yet."

Nature Girl

Grace needs to be alone today. She can't bear the idea of sitting in the noisy dining room. She can't bring herself to join in with the small talk, when the hubbub of the chitter chatter grows to a deafening roar inside her head. Everything has been so full on since she started at Fairstone, so she has decided to take herself off and go somewhere quiet in nature. She has saved a boiled egg and some Ryvita from breakfast and has brought a little picnic with her.

She is sitting in The Spares, watching the sun filter through the trees, and dancing beams of light illuminate the clearing where she sits, as the leaves and branches dance in the breeze. All is well, except that her heart is aching. She is picking up on some ancient grief. Is it the grief of Nanny Watkins losing her son Jonnie, or is it a collective grief? It makes her feel melancholy.

All around her, the bird song fills her with a sense of beauty. She feels that the birds are here to heal her aching heart, to uplift her spirits. She places a hand on her heart and tunes into her surroundings, gazing into the centre of the clearing. The dancing beams of sunlight seem to be resolving into a shape in front of her eyes. A white-gold lion is looking at her from within these shapes, his shimmering eyes as blue as the sky. Regulus is here.

"Greetings, Dear One," he says. "I sense that you are sad today. Remember that I love you to the ends of the Earth. I will guide and protect you forever. There is no need to be sad."

Grace gasps – it makes her feel emotional to hear these words of comfort from him. Tears brim in her eyes.

"Hello Regulus. So nice to see you again," she manages to reply.

"Dear One, I see your tears. You are a highly sensitive being. It is both your greatest gift and your greatest burden. I am here to give you guidance on how to manage this.

"The gift is that you are able to sense and see things that others don't. You can see the truth, or lack of it, in a situation. You can sense what someone is feeling or thinking. You can feel the energy going on around you in the field of collective consciousness shared by all humans. I want to tell you that you have the power to transform energy – to raise the frequency from grief, despondency and fear into love, light and joy, once you have mastered your own energy.

"The problem lies in the fact that you are so sensitive that you don't understand what is your own energy and what is being projected onto you by others. Sometimes you feel sad, or have a sense of impending doom for no reason. But because you don't understand where this comes from, you try to make it your own and your mind makes up a story to explain it.

"So what you need to do is learn to separate it out – **this** is mine, and **that** is not. Then you can decide what to do with it. You can learn how to transform lower frequencies, such as feelings of gloom and fear coming from others, or you can choose to send it back to them (with love, of course) if it is useful for them to learn and grow from.

"As I told you in your journey, you are here on a big mission. You are a Standard Bearer for Truth and Beauty, here to uplift the world, as humankind learns to raise their consciousness, so that they can move into the next era – the Golden Age of Love, Light and Peace on Earth.

"It will not be easy. There is much darkness in the world. But you are a warrior soul, who chose to come to Earth at this time. You have done many lifetimes of training for this. It's just that you have forgotten your skills. But you are not alone. There are many like you who are beginning to awaken to their mission. Your two new friends are also part of this mission. And there are the Wise Ones like Nanny Watkins, who can help guide you on this physical realm.

"Have courage – you have the heart of a lion – and remember that I will always be here for you. So your first lesson is to transmute these feelings of grief and gloom that you feel, into love and joy."

"Yes, I would like to learn how to do that," says Grace.

"Let me help you do that and then you will know for next time…" And Regulus gives her instruction on how to clear her energy field of other people's energy. "Start by putting your feet flat on the floor," he says. "Take some deep breaths and begin to relax. Imagine you have roots coming out of your feet. Imagine these roots growing deep into the earth until you reach the centre of Earth. Here you will find a brilliant shining crystal, which is the beating heart of Mother Earth. Send your love to her and ask her to send you healing energy that rises up through the central channel of your body. Imagine it fountaining out the top of your head and cascading all around you before returning to the Earth, grounding and calming you.

"Now picture yourself making contact with the Cosmos, with God, Source, Creator of the Multiverse. Ask for God's healing energy to flow down through you, spiralling around the Earth energy that is coming up, clearing and cleaning out anything that does not belong to you. You are a glowing pillar of light and energy, spreading out from your core.

"Now picture your luminous energy field around you – it's shaped like a fat ring donut and you are standing in the centre. Imagine it like a protective bubble around you.

"Scan your energy field. Is there anything that catches your attention? Anything that feels like it shouldn't be there? Bless it with love and state that you choose for it to be removed and sent back to its source.

"Check again, are there any gaps or holes in the edge of the bubble? See your pillar of light glowing and expanding to fill the gaps and picture the edge of the bubble like a membrane that lets in what's good for you and keeps out anything harmful. There you are now; your energy is now clean and clear of anything belonging to anyone else."

Grace feels deeply comforted and energised by her visit from Regulus. She thanks him profoundly. He tells her she is welcome and begins to fade from her sight. She returns to school feeling so much lighter and ready to face the world now.

What Happened to Jonnie?

"Oh, hey guys," says Archie, "Guess what? I spoke to my Dad on the phone about Jonnie Watkins and he knew all about him. He said, 'Oh yes, he was a pupil at the school twenty years ago. One of the best swimmers this school has ever had.' Dad said he could have gone on to compete for the country if it wasn't for the accident. It's very sad – he drowned in the river trying to save his friend. Ironic really, since he was such a good swimmer. There are some photos of him in the Old Hall, getting a cup for coming first in the Inter-Schools Swimming Gala and he was in the Cross-country Team too.

"Apparently, there was some kind of whirlpool in the

river that dragged him down – he didn't stand a chance. And ironic too that his friend survived. He'd managed to get him holding onto a log which got dragged to the riverbank. The story goes that the river was in flood and Jonnie begged his friend not to get in because it was too dangerous, but the idiot friend got in anyway."

"Oh my goodness, what a sad story!" says Daisy. "Oh, poor Nanny. How terrible for her."

"I've seen the photo of him in the Cross-Country Team and he told me he was a good swimmer too. I can't imagine anything more painful than losing your child like that. He would have been our age. It's so tragic when someone dies young like that," says Grace. "It must have been such a shock for Nanny."

"Yes, you're right, Grace. He's a hero in my books – giving up his life to save his friend," says Archie.

"Hmmm, that's just like him," says Grace. "Always wanting to help people. He's helped me so much."

"And he takes after his Mum – she's always helping people too," says Daisy. The kids fall quiet, mulling over this sad news.

Friendship Reforged

"Nanny, Nanny, where are you?" Daisy calls out.

"I'm here kids, in the back garden. Come on in." They make their way down the back garden to find Nanny.

"Hi Nanny, is this a good time for a visit?" says Archie.

"Yes, dears – the perfect time to get the kettle on for a nice cuppa," and she gives them a beaming smile.

In the kitchen, Daisy says, "Nanny, we're so sorry to have upset you last time we were here. I feel awful about it."

"Yes, she can be a right klutz – always putting her foot in

it!" says Archie. Grace says nothing, but takes Nanny's hand, giving it a squeeze.

"No, no, kids, you did nothing wrong," says Nanny. "All forgotten now!"

"Well, anyhow. We've brought you a little gift, to cheer you up," says Archie, getting the present and card out of his rucksack.

"Oh my goodness, handmade chocolates and organic rose and lavender soap. My favourites – how clever of you. And what a beautiful card – so thoughtful. Let's have that cuppa in the garden, shall we?" They chat away in the garden, drinking tea and munching some of Nanny's homemade biscuits. They keep the conversation light and Archie entertains everyone, telling his best funny stories, which make Nanny chortle. The song of a blackbird creates a beautiful musical backdrop.

"Well, those biscuits were delicious, Nanny. Thank you so much. It's time we were heading back to school now," says Archie.

"Thanks for coming, kids. I've really enjoyed your company. And your stories, Archie – you have a real talent as a storyteller, my lad. You are all welcome here anytime. I hope you know that," says Nanny. "Come again soon."

"Thank you, Nanny. We will," says Grace, giving her a big hug. They set off back to school with smiles and waves. "Well done, Archie. I think you really cheered her up with all your mad stories."

"Aw, thanks, Grace. It's what I'm good at," he says.

"Yes, feels like we're back in her good books now. I'm so glad," says Daisy.

Chapter 18:
A Half-Term Adventure

A Favour to Ask

"Daiz, I've got a massive favour to ask," says Archie.

"Ask away, Arch," says Daisy.

"My parents are both away over half-term, so there's no-one to pick me up. I really don't want to stay in school, so I, uh, could I, erm, possibly..."

"Come on boy, spit it out," says Daisy. "Could you possibly come and stay at my place for half-term? Is that what you're trying to say?"

"Yes, exactly that. I love your Mum and Dad to bits and it would be so much fun staying on the farm. I'd give your Dad as much help as he wants. I'm pretty strong. I reckon I could throw a few hay bales around. Do you think they'd be up for it?"

"Oh my goodness, Archie! Of course you can come and stay. I can't bear the thought of you staying on your own in school for the whole of half-term. I'm sure Mum and Dad will be fine with it. I'll ask them tonight. There's only one thing, though – I was planning to do my Duke of Edinburgh practice expedition and I'm going to ask Grace to come along with me. We'll be away for a couple of days," says Daisy.

"Ooh, I need to do mine too, so I'd love to tag along with you, if you'd be up for it? I'll speak really nicely to your Dad and make sure he knows I'll be a proper gentleman and not try any funny business. What do you reckon?"

"Well, I think I can trust you after all these years of knowing you. Gosh, we've known each other since we were seven years old, haven't we? I'll check with Grace and put in a good word with Dad for you," says Daisy.

"Fantastic! That's settled then," says Archie.

Daisy gives a little squeal of excitement, "Eee, it's going to be so much fun!"

Camping on Vagar Hill

"There appeared a star of wonderful magnitude and brightness, darting forth a ray, at the end of which was a globe of fire in the form of a dragon, out of whose mouth issued forth two rays, one which seemed to stretch itself beyond the extent of Gaul, the other toward the Irish Sea and ended in seven lesser rays." Archie is leaning back on one elbow, with Dora the Dog curled up against him. He is reading from Brewer's *Dictionary of Phrase and Fable*, which he has brought along on the expedition despite its enormous size and weight because it is his favourite read and, according to Archie, has something wise to say on any topic you could wish to look up.

"I found this when I was looking up Pendragon, because they used to call King Arthur 'Pendragon' and I wondered why."

"Oh really?" says Daisy, whittling away at the end of her hazel staff to make a spike so that she can cook her sausage over the fire. She hasn't really been listening because Archie is always prattling on about something that he's read in Brewer's.

"That's interesting," says Grace. "Carry on – so what does Pendragon actually mean?"

"I'm glad you asked," says Archie, warming to his theme. "It means 'head of the dragon' and refers to a British chief, who would have had a symbol of a dragon on his standard, which is a kind of banner."

"Ooh, I'm getting a funny feeling when you talk about that. I think we're going to find out that piece of information is really important very soon," says Grace.

The kids have made camp on the Vagar, a hill at the edge of Sarah Evans' land, Daisy's aunt. Earlier that day, they had come across Arthur's Stone, a chambered dolmen – a huge stone slab, balanced on several other stones. It had sparked their imaginations about why it is there and who built it – hence Archie looking up Arthur in his book.

It is the May half-term holidays and they have walked from Daisy's house on their first expedition for the Duke of Edinburgh scheme. All three of them have been so excited about this. And Grace has been meticulously planning it – Daisy and Archie have come to realise she's a stickler for detail and she likes to know what she's in for. Archie has been reading and dreaming about it, and Daisy has just been in a kind of 'jumping up and down and squeaking with excitement' mood.

Grace shivers. "The wind's getting up. Let's get a fire going. I think we've gathered enough wood to last us the night," she says.

Their pitch looks onto Cefn Hill and behind it the looming bulk of The Darren. There is the occasional whinny from a herd of wild horses they can see grazing on The Cefn.

"I think something's up with those horses," says Daisy. "They seem a bit restless and jittery. I wonder what's going on?"

"There is a bit of a strange atmosphere and a kind of a tangy smell in the air," says Grace. "I looked at the weather forecast and it's not supposed to rain, but if I didn't know any better, I'd say there is thunder and lightning on the way. The air has that feeling."

"A tangy smell in the air?" says Archie, sniffing. "No, I think that might be one of Daisy's legendary farts! You better not do that tonight in the tent, Daiz, or we'll have to boot you outside to sleep with the owls. Here, have a look at the horses through these. You know much more about them than I do," he says, handing Daisy his binoculars.

"I did not fart, you meanie, Archie McBride!" says Daisy. "I know what you mean, Grace. It's not really a smell, more of a feeling in the air." She takes the binoculars from Archie and focuses on the herd. Then she lets out one of her characteristic squeals. "Oh wow, how amazing! One of them is about to foal. I'm sure she is the lead mare – I've seen that herd a few times before when I've been staying with Aunty Sarah. Her belly is really big and she's just gone off into that bit of woodland over there. She wouldn't normally go off alone without the herd like that."

"Oh, how brilliant! I hope we get to see the foal soon," says Grace.

"Probably best to leave them alone for now. But it still doesn't explain why they are so jittery though," says Daisy.

"I'll light the fire then, shall I?" says Archie. "It's going to be a two-dog night and we've only got the one, haven't we Doresy-Woresy?" he says, scratching the old black retriever behind the ear. Dora gives him an answering yelp. "I'm sure she understands everything I say. She's a very clever dog."

"Yes she is," says Daisy. "But I think she is mainly getting excited about her sausage sandwich for tea, and telling you it's about time you cooked it for her!"

"Sausage sandwich coming right up, as soon as the fire gets going, Doresy," says Archie.

"Ruff, ruff!" says Dora.

"I'm going to make the fire here, which is far enough away from the tent to not catch it on fire, but still close enough for us to sit in the tent doorway out of the wind and cook our sausages at the end of our sticks," says Archie, "Hah, see, this is for thinking (he says, patting his head) and these are for dancing," he says pointing at his feet and doing a little shuffling dance.

"Oh, you are a nutter, Archie," says Daisy, laughing.

"Can you hurry up with the fire," says Grace, unimpressed. "The sooner we have the fire going, the better. I'm getting cold and hungry."

"Yes, Ma'am," says Archie, tugging his forelock. Archie loves making fires, especially when they are to cook on. Everything is set, but for some reason, the fire just isn't taking, even though the wood is dry and he's dug a nice deep fire pit to keep the wind off. He bends low and begins to blow on the embers. All of a sudden, the wind changes direction and the fire blazes up, catching Archie's beautiful curly quiff on fire and singeing his eyebrows. He springs back, shrieking and patting at himself to put it all out, then races about in zigzags for good measure. The girls are both laughing at him.

"Aren't you supposed to 'drop and roll,' if you think you are on fire?" says Grace. Daisy dissolves into peals of laughter.

"Ha, ha, ha, very funny you two. I could have been seriously hurt then."

"Yes, but you weren't. Good job you put the fire far enough away from the tent though. Well done for that, or we'd be homeless now!" says Grace.

"And, sorry, but you did look ever so funny shrieking and flapping and doing a funny little zigzag dance."

"I suppose it wasn't very manly, was it? I can see I'm never going to hear the end of this, am I? But you've got to promise never to mention it at school. And especially never to the boys in the rugby team. I've got a certain reputation as a brave young hero to keep up!"

Grace lets out a 'phffe,' through closed lips and Daisy laughs even more, but they promise. They both know how important it is for him to think of himself as a hero.

A few minutes later and the fire is going well enough to cook on. Sausage sandwich in hand, the kids look out from the tent and admire the glowing orange ribbons of cloud that paint the luminescent blue of the sky above the Darren. The light is beginning to bleed from the land now.

Two pairs of ravens wheel across the sky in a final fly past before nightfall. "I always think their cry of, 'Conk, conk,' sounds really otherworldly. It sounds like someone hitting a metal pipe with a piece of wood," says Archie dreamily.

The last birds fly home to roost as the fading light makes grey silhouettes of the gorse bushes and trees against the skyline. The cold wind is cutting through the gathering gloom, but the three amigos feel cosy in the glow of the firelight, with their bellies full of warm sausage sandwich and hot mugs of tea, with Dora curled up by their feet.

They fall quiet and watch as bats begin their nightly forage and owls are abroad now, the sound of, 'Who, who?' bouncing from one tree to another. Lights twinkle in the few dwellings down in the valley and they can hear the odd bleating of a sheep and lowing of the cattle.

Indigo night has descended on the mountains as the first star of evening shines over the Darren. They watch as from the east a faint glow appears behind the trees, and a glorious full moon rises slowly into the sky, shedding a silver glow across the hillsides.

"Beautiful, isn't it?" breathes Daisy. "I wonder if that foal is born yet? I wonder what colour he is going to be?"

"Yes, so peaceful," whispers Archie.

"Oh my word, what on earth is that!!!" shrieks Daisy, as they watch the blazing light of a falling star descend to Earth on Cefn Hill.

"Holey moley, I have never seen anything like that before!" gasps Archie. "Just like I was reading about in Brewer's."

"I think it's a shooting star, but you're right, I've never seen one that big or land THAT close before. I hope those horses are all right. Should we go and check?" says Grace.

"It looks more like a spaceship to me. Do you think we've just seen a UFO? Hey, what if we get abducted by aliens in the night? I'm not going over there till morning," says Archie.

"Oh Archie, stop winding me up!" says Daisy, elbowing him in the ribs. "I'm too scared to go over there now too. I'm hoping the foal was born ages ago and the horses ran out of the way as soon as they saw it coming. They can sense when things aren't right ages before they actually happen. You're right, Archie – best to leave it till morning. But I'm so wound up, I don't think I can sleep now."

"Do you need me to tell you a bedtime story Daisy-Waisy?" Daisy gives him a hard stare. "I think something incredible happened just now. Don't make fun of it, Archie."

"Daisy's right, Archie. Something momentous just happened and I'm dying to find out what that was. But for now, the best thing would be if we all get a good night's sleep. So my prescription is hot chocolate, some of Aunty Sarah's homemade biscuits and a game of cards to take our minds off it," says Grace. "And if you fancy telling us a story at bedtime that would be great too, Archie, as long as it's not too spooky."

"Good idea," says Daisy and Archie together.

After hot chocolate and a game of Cack-à-tête, Archie says, "OK chaps, I'm just going to take Dora for her nightly ablutions. This is your chance to do whatever you do to get ready for bed without me around. Give a whistle when it's safe for me to come back."

"Thanks Arch, that's very gentlemanly of you. See you in a bit," says Grace.

And soon he is lulling the girls to sleep with his tales of all the funny adventures he got up to over the Easter holidays before he'd even met Grace.

In the morning, they go to gather water from the sacred spring to drink. They make toast over the fire – this time Archie makes it safely without burning anything. And there is one more sausage for Dora's breakfast.

Daisy borrows Archie's binoculars and spots a pure white foal trotting behind his pure black mother. All is well.

"Wow, he's SO beautiful," says Daisy. "His coat shines like the moon reflecting the light of the stars."

"That's very poetic, Daiz," says Archie.

"Yes, I'm feeling all poetic and inspired after what we

saw last night and seeing that beautiful foal."

"Here, give us a look then," says Archie. "Yes, he's beautiful, isn't he? Grace, have a look."

"Oh, gorgeous! Good description, Daiz. Something special really did happen last night."

"You know Nanny Watkins lives really close to here. And from there it's a really short distance to Aunty Sarah's house, and she's going to give us a lift back to my place. So shall we visit Nanny on the way back?" says Daisy.

"Yes! I'm dying to hear what she would make of what we saw last night," says Grace.

"Great idea, and I'll bet she has some delicious cake or biscuits – sausage sandwiches are all very well, but you can't beat a good fill-up on Nanny's cake," says Archie. "Are you ready then, Dora?"

"Ruff, ruff," says Dora, bouncing up and down in excitement.

"Come on then, let's go!" says Archie.

So, with Daisy leading the way, and Dora trotting alongside, they set off for Nanny's house.

The Kids Finally Meet Ahbleza

Archie calls out, "Nanny, are you here? Can we come and visit?"

"Yes dears, I'm out the back. I'll get the kettle on," she calls back to them. "And who's this little beauty?" says Nanny, as Dora leans on her leg in the kitchen and looks up at her with big puppy-dog eyes.

"This is my Dora Dog. She came with us on the adventure," says Daisy.

"Ah, adorable Dora!" says Nanny, stroking Dora's silky ears. "Well you're in luck, Miss Dora. I might have a treat for you. I've just boiled up a big beef bone for some stock. You might enjoy chewing on that." Dora gives an excited wiggle and her tail thumps on the floor. She recognises the word 'bone'.

Gathered round the kitchen table, drinking a welcome cup of tea, with Dora happily gnawing her bone on the mat by the Rayburn, Nanny asks, "So what's the news then, kids? I can tell you've got something exciting to tell me. I can feel it bubbling up."

So Archie takes the lead, describing everything that happened on the camping trip, but leaving out the bits that made him look bad, so Daisy and Grace add in the extra details.

Nanny is puzzled. By now Ahbleza is two and a half years old and their tale describes his birth exactly as she saw it in one of her visions. It's too much of a coincidence for the same thing to have happened again.

"Well, me dears, I think you've experienced a wrinkle in time. What you're describing happened two and a half years ago. Because that beautiful foal you saw born was Ahbleza and he is two and a half years old now. The lead mare that you saw, Epona, has a red roan colt now, just like his Dad."

"Ahbleza?! That's the name of the horse I dreamt about!" says Grace.

"Yes, it is me dear. I'll admit that I was quite shocked to hear you dreamt it – it's such an unusual name," says Nanny. "It means powerful and complete, intelligent and full of energy. It also means he is bold, independent, and inquisitive; he knows what he wants and why he wants it."

And then from outside they hear a deafening noise, like a great rumbling of thunder. Dora looks up from her bone chewing with a puzzled look on her face.

"What on earth was that?" says Archie.

"Oh, don't worry about that. It's just me horse, with a bit of wind. He's been a very naughty boy. He knows how to open my latch and he's very partial to my special hazelnut crunch biscuits. I had some on a cooling rack on the table yesterday, and while I was otherwise occupied, he sneaked in and scoffed the lot. He was very gentlemanly though, and closed the door after himself. It was the muddy hoofprints that gave him away. But the biscuits were a bit rich for him – which accounts for the terrible wind you just heard. They're actually very healthy – I promise they don't have the same effect on humans. And luckily for you lot, I made another batch, so you can take some home with you."

"I didn't know you have a horse, Nanny," says Daisy. "Can we meet him?"

"Yes, I think you're ready now – after hearing Grace's dream about the Radiant White Horse and your vision on Vagar Hill, I think it might be time to meet him. This is top secret, mind. Don't breathe a word to anyone else, because he's very special and I don't want word getting out about him. He is very precious and you must do everything in your power to protect him and keep him safe."

"We all promise not to tell a soul, Nanny. Don't we girls?" says Archie.

"Yes, we promise," say Grace and Daisy together.

"Let's leave Dora in the kitchen with her bone," says Nanny. "I don't want her to spook the horse," and she takes the kids out into her back garden and down the path that leads to a little gate at the bottom. Indicating the herbs and flowers that flank the path, she says, "Someday, I must teach you all about the properties of the common herbs. It's always useful to know how to heal yourself using natural remedies.

I don't hold much with these pharmaceutical medicines. In my book, they are just full of artificial chemicals that will make you sicker in the long run." She waves a hand towards the beehives and continues, "Mind you, a spoonful of honey from my bees will heal pretty much anything, as Archie found when he had that poorly tum – it works much better than Bernie's jollop!

"But anyhow, the herb lore will have to wait for another day, because I have someone very important for you to meet." She stops them before they pass through the gate to the meadow and says, "Now, I'm going to say it again – not a word of this to anyone. You must promise me that, before we go a step further. Don't even whisper it to people you think you could trust with your life, because if word gets out about this ... well, let's jus' say that it could attract the attention of them who does not have the best of intentions in their hearts. And I won't say another word on that matter."

A cloud passes in front of the sun and the kids all give a little shiver at the thought of something that is too nasty for Nanny to even spell out to them.

Archie puts his hand on his heart and says, "I give you my solemn promise that I will not breathe a word of this to anyone outside the four of us, Nanny."

"Good, good. Well said, young man," says Nanny, "And how about you girls?"

"I give you my word that I will not speak about this to anyone else," says Daisy.

"And I promise never to tell another soul," says Grace.

"Right, I believe you mean it," says Nanny. She gives a sharp whistle and calls out, "Come, my beauty. Come to meet your new friends." There is a flicker of movement from the edge of the woods that surround the meadow. The sun comes back out from behind the cloud and a shaft of sunlight falls upon a magnificent creature who stands at the bottom of the meadow. He answers Nanny's call with a whinny, raising his handsome head and cantering through the meadow flowers towards them. His long white mane is flowing from his beautifully arched neck and his white tail is held high. He seems to be at one with the wind, and sunlight gleams from his pure white coat.

The kids all feel their hearts lurch as the beautiful horse stops in front of them. He is huge, towering above them, but finely built with flowing, elegant lines.

They feel his horsey breath on their faces as he lowers his head to greet them, sniffing each child in turn, as they raise outstretched hands to touch this magical creature. He nibbles Daisy's hair and then looks at them softly from his eyes of deepest twilight blue.

"This is Ahbleza," says Nanny. "Pretty, ain't he? He's a very special boy and I believe he has a special message for each of you. Least that's what I've been hearing in my dreams, and from the big boy himself." As if he's understood Nanny's words, Ahbleza whinnies and nods towards Nanny, nuzzling her and pushing her shoulder with his muzzle. "Yes, yes, boy, I'll tell them. I'm just getting onto that.

"He wants me to tell you about his special way of communicating. See that little bump in the centre of his forehead? That's what's called his brow centre, or his third eye. We all have one too, but you just can't see ours. It's a centre of vision. He can communicate by projecting a spiral of light in a cone out of his bump." Ahbleza nickers and nudges Nanny again. "Oh yes, he's reminding me to tell you that he can use it for healing too. Would you like to see if he's got a message for you?"

"Wow, it sounds fascinating, Nanny. I'm not sure I totally understand what you mean, but I'd like to give it a go," says

Archie.

"Amazing – me too! He's SO beautiful," Daisy says in breathless awe.

"How about you, Gracie?" asks Archie.

"Oh yes," she says, shaking her head out of a deep reverie. She has been taking everything in with her deep blue eyes, absently stroking Ahbleza's velvet soft neck. "Of course I want to have a go!"

Nanny narrows her eyes, watching Grace closely and says, "I think you've been having a go already, Miss Grace. What's he been telling you?"

"Oh, no, it's hard to say, just some fuzzy impressions. Probably just my imagination," says Grace.

"You'll learn it's never 'just your imagination.' There's always a reason why you're seeing or hearing something. You just have to work out what it is," says Nanny. Archie and Daisy look at each other in bemusement. "OK, then. Archie, you were the first to volunteer. So you'll go first. So you say to Ahbleza – either out loud, or quietly inside your head is fine, 'May I step inside your field of energy?' If he nods his head, then you can stand in front of him and wait for him to lower his head. Then you touch your forehead to his, where his bump is and the same place on your forehead, so that your vision centre is touching his. Wait till you feel something coming from his bump and then see what happens. You'll find it's not exactly like hearing someone's voice – it's more like a kind of transmission, or it may come through as a feeling or a vision. I feel it as if he's dropping words in my heart. You can ask him to answer questions for you or you can just be quiet and see what he has to say. Are you ready, Archie?"

"Yes, I am." Archie stands in front of Ahbleza and says, "May I step into your field of energy?" The big horse nods his head and then lowers it until his eyes are looking directly into Archie's. They touch foreheads. An imperceptible buzz of energy passes between them and they remain like that for several minutes until finally they break contact and move slightly away from each other. "Thank you, Ahbleza," says Archie, softly stroking his muzzle.

"How was that?" asks Nanny. "Care to tell us about it?"

"It was amazing, Nanny. Like actually having a conversation with a horse, but not like a normal conversation with another human. He showed me things in pictures. And I heard words in my heart like he put them there. He said he's very pleased to meet me and we will have important work to do together. He told me that he loves my enthusiasm and my get-up-and-go attitude. But he said sometimes I need to rein myself in and think before acting because I can be too headstrong."

Daisy and Grace both laugh. "He's got you exactly right!" says Daisy, and Grace agrees.

"Let's see what he has to say to you then, Daisy," says Archie, looking a bit hurt.

Daisy steps in front of Ahbleza and asks his permission before touching foreheads with him. After a few minutes, she breaks away saying, "Wow Nanny, that was so lovely, so magical! He told me that I could get on his back and ride to magical lands in my dreams – that we can go on wonderful adventures together. I love riding anyway, so that was gorgeous. And maybe he will let me ride on his back for real one day."

Now it's Grace's turn. She steps up and makes contact. After a few minutes, Grace pulls away from Ahbleza and puts her hands over her face. Her shoulders begin to shake, and the others can see that she is sobbing.

"Oh goodness, girl! What's the matter?" Nanny asks,

putting a reassuring arm around her shoulders. "Come on, you can tell old Nanny. A problem shared is a problem halved."

"Oh Nanny, there's so much badness in the world! He showed me something he needs my help with. I want to help, but I don't know what to do about it. How can I be of any use? I'm just one single girl. I feel totally powerless."

"No, you're not!" says Archie, putting his hand on her arm. "There are five of us here – us three kids, Nanny and Ahbleza. We're all on your side. And the last two are pretty amazing and magical! And we've got Regulus, our brilliant Spirit Animal, on our side too. We're all in this together. We're a power to be reckoned with!"

Daisy draws in close and strokes Grace's hair. "We'll all take care of each other," she whispers.

"Very well said, you two," says Nanny. "Now listen, my girl. Yes, there is badness in the world. But there is so much goodness too. There is a power for good – call it God, Creator or the Universe – which is stronger than any badness. Look at the friendship you three have for a start. And this beautiful part of the world you live in, and your wonderful, kind parents, and your school is like family too. Hold on to all that. And never let your mind fall. Never let yourself be overcome by fear and darkness. Your job is to focus on the goodness, to connect with God, and to live a brave and good life. To have fun and adventure and to do what's right in the world. If everyone does that, the world will be a better place to live in. It has been shown to me how very special you kids are, and what you can achieve by working together is beyond your wildest dreams. You'll see. Dry your eyes, dear, and say thanks to Ahbleza for showing you so much." Ahbleza has come over to Grace. He softly nuzzles her hair and blows kisses in her ear, which tickle and make her laugh. She reaches up and puts her arms around his neck, pressing her face against it, breathing in his horsey smell and reassuring presence.

"Right everyone, I think we all need some of Nanny's special carrot cake. Go and put the kettle on again, you two, and the cake is in the tin on the middle shelf in the larder." Nanny continues to stroke Grace's back, whispering to her as she hugs Ahbleza.

In a few minutes, Archie and Daisy are back with more mugs of tea and slabs of scrumptious carrot cake. To everyone's relief, Grace is looking calm and relaxed again.

"I've set up the fold-out chairs and table in front of the garden gate so we can be close to Ahbleza, Nanny."

"Good lad, Archie," says Nanny. Ahbleza leans over the gate, nibbling Nanny's hair as they drink their tea and eat Nanny's lovely cake. "Cut a slice for Ahbleza, will you, Archie, or I won't have any hair left. It's safe for him to eat, there's no sugar or any nasties in it. It's just sweetened with stewed apples. And I promise it won't make 'im fart like the biscuits do. Pour 'im a cup of tea too, but no milk. He loves a drink of tea. I always think there can't be too much wrong with the world as long as you can eat cake and drink tea in your garden on a sunny day!"

"I'm on it, Nanny," says Archie, holding out a big slab of cake for Ahbleza, who gobbles it appreciatively and then raises his top lip in a toothy grin. "I think he liked the cake, Nanny. Look, he's smiling!" says Archie.

It's time for them to head back to Aunty Sarah's, and the kids begin to clear the table. Nanny takes Grace to one side and asks her if she would like to come for some lessons in herb lore. It's Nanny's way of giving Grace something practical she can do to help people.

"Oh, yes please, Nanny. I've always wanted to learn about

herbal medicine," says Grace.

Nanny puts a book in Grace's hands, and says, "You can make a good start by reading this. But there's nothing better than hands-on experience and I've got all the most useful herbs in my garden."

"Thank you, Nanny, I'd love that," says Grace, looking down at the book in her hands titled *Healing Herbs* by Margaret Parsley.

"Good, that's settled then. Come on your own next week and we'll make a start. And if you can spare some time over the summer holidays, we can really get into some good stuff."

They say their fond farewells to Ahbleza and make Nanny promise they can see him again, before collecting Dora from the kitchen and heading off to Aunty Sarah's.

Chapter 19:
The Inter-House Endurance Race

"It's going to be a warm one. We'd better take plenty of water," says Archie. He is running in the Inter-House Endurance Race in a mixed team with Grace and Daisy. They have high hopes of winning this year, as all three are good runners. It's their chance to score some big points for their house, Clifford, and they all feel honoured to have been chosen, especially Grace, as she is still relatively new and untested in these long endurance runs.

It's a Sunday morning in late May and the day has dawned bright and clear, with the forecast for it to get hot by midday. Archie, Grace and Daisy are making a last-minute check of their gear before heading to the school yard for the start of the race.

"Have we got everything? Water?" says Archie.

"Check."

"High energy snacks?"

"Check."

"First aid kit?"

"Check."

"Spare socks?"

"Check."

"Waterproof layers?"

"Check."

"Swiss army knife and emergency blanket?"

"Check."

"A length of string and some gaffer tape?"

"Huh?" says Grace.

"I know they're not on the list, but you never know when they might come in useful," says Archie.

"OK, but you can carry them."

"No problem. They don't weigh much anyway."

"As long as you haven't brought a copy of Brewer's *Dictionary of Phrase and Fable*, this time, like you did when we went camping!" says Daisy, clutching her sides laughing.

"No, not this time, Daiz!"

They make their way to the start line on the school yard outside the assembly hall, where the Long Town and Snodhill teams are already waiting.

"They're the ones to beat," whispers Archie, pointing with his nose at the Long Town team. "Burnley runs like a greyhound, and Tom and Charlie are both machines."

"Oh, don't be rude about Charlie!" says Daisy.

"Well, she is – everyone knows she's stronger and fitter than most of the boys. I couldn't believe it when I saw her chuck the javelin for the first time. It sailed about 35 metres and nearly hit Mr Aveen. He wasn't expecting anyone to throw it that far. The Snodhill team are going to be let down by Calum, who's too stocky for a distance runner. And Darius has, let's call it 'a unique running style.' It's a shame for Portia. She's the best runner in the school – like a gazelle," he says with a misty-eyed, faraway look. "But I don't like the smug look that Calum's got on his face, as if he knows something we don't."

"Good luck – you're going to need it!" shouts Calum at Archie. "You can only go as fast as the weakest link in your team."

"Don't listen to him, Daisy," says Archie.

"I meant you, McBride," says Calum.

"Oh, you cheeky git. I can outrun you any day, mate!"

"Not today, mate. Not today!" says Calum.

Mr Aveen hands out the maps and a set of questions. "Ya must all stick together and run at the pace of the slowest runner. This is a team event and for safety, no-one gets left behind. Are ya all clear on that?" asks Mr Aveen. He's met with a chorus of, "Yes Sir," from the gathered runners.

"I know you've heard this before, but just to go over this for clarity – the race is set over 22 miles as the crow flies, but it will probably be more like 26 miles depending on the route you set. Make sure ya pace yurselves. Don't tear off like idiots and burn yurselves out in the first couple of miles.

"Here is ya set of five questions, each with a map co-ordinate, to help ya find it. Ya can do the questions in any order, but ya must stop for a 15-minute brek for a wee drink and snack, and check in with a member of staff, at the halfway point. That's compulsory, not optional. Remember, it is a test of brains and initiative, as well as stamina and running ability, so make sure ya answer the questions to the best of yur ability.

"I'm going to start ya off a few minutes apart so that

yu're not running on top of each other. Snodhill, yu'll go first, followed by Clifford and then Long Town.

"Good luck everyone. May the best team win. Snodhill, On ya marks, set, go!" The Snodhill team go haring off like the clappers, and Mr Aveen shakes his head as he watches them go.

After a couple of minutes, Mr Aveen says, "Right, Clifford. Are ya ready? Set, go!" And the Clifford team set off at a more measured pace.

They lose sight of the Snodhill team until they crest a hill in a field full of sheep, where a scene unfolds in front of their eyes. Calum and Portia are in front, running briskly down the hill. Darius is a little behind and desperately trying to catch up.

The runners have startled the sheep, who begin to gallop down the hill, right in front of Darius. Darius' running style, although quite fast, is rather ungainly, on account of his very turned-out feet and bandy legs.

Suddenly, he catches his right foot on a loop of bramble, which pitches him forward down the hill. To his consternation, and that of the sheep, he lands full length on the back of the largest woolly creature, and in his instinct to save himself, grabs on round its fluffy neck, as the startled creature continues to gallop down the hill.

"He-elp!" the sheep seems to be bleating.

"Oh Nelly!" shouts Darius. "Get me off of this thing!" His fleecy top has velcroed him to the sheep's woolly coat, and for what seems like an age, but is probably only a few seconds, boy and sheep move together as one, as they hurtle down the hill. Finally, the sheep gets the idea to buck Darius off and he lands in a crumpled heap on the ground.

The Clifford team are laughing so hard they can barely run. "Are you OK, Darius?" shouts Daisy. He leaps to his feet and takes a bow. "I'm fine – here for your entertainment purposes!" And runs off after his teammates. The three disappear from view again.

The Long Town team are catching up with Clifford and they can hear Charlie saying, "Oh my God, that was so funny. I almost peed me pants!"

"Better put a bit of a spurt on if we're going to beat Long Town," says Archie. "Everyone up for it?"

"Yes, let's go – I feel amazing!" says Grace.

"Me too," says Daisy.

* * *

Although he won't admit it at first, Darius' knee was badly hurt when he fell off the sheep, bashing it on a large pointy rock. It begins to swell, as he continues to run on it. He soldiers on until it gets to the point that he can barely walk, let alone run.

"Guys – I don't know what to do here. I'm slowing you down. I think I'm going to have to bail. You carry on without me," he says.

"But we can't – the rules are really clear – the whole team has to finish the race or we'll be disqualified," Calum replies.

"What's the matter, Darius? Oh my gosh, your knee – its swollen like a grapefruit!" says Portia. "You can't run on that. You could end up doing some lasting damage. We'll have to call it a day."

"No way. I'm not giving up that easily," says Calum. "Look, I'll give you a piggyback all the way if I have to," says Calum.

"Mate, that's impossible," says Darius. "I'll flatten you."

"No you won't. You're a skinny whippet – I bet you don't weigh much. Here, stand on this tree stump, so you can get on my back." So Darius climbs onto Calum's back and the ungainly trio trot off, Calum's stocky legs pumping stoically under the added weight of Darius, and Portia slowing her racehorse gait to keep in time with Calum.

After half a mile of valiant effort, they have made it to the main road, but Calum is puce in the face and sweat is pouring off him in rivulets. "This is no good, mate – I'm killing you. Look, there's a phone box just up ahead. Let's call a taxi and get a ride back to school."

"I hate to say it, but he's right, Calum. You can't go on like that. Let's head back to school," says Portia.

"Hmmm," mutters Calum, deep in thought. "Taxi's a good idea, but how about this – we get the taxi driver to drive us round the clues and then stop at a café somewhere to hang out for a bit to make it look as if we're taking our time. Then he could drop us a little way from school and we could run in with Darius on my back, pretending the injury only just happened. What do you think?"

"Ha, ha, hilarious mate – what a great idea!" says Darius.

"No way, guys – that's cheating! It's not fair and if we get found out, we could forfeit the whole Inter-house contest, or worse!" says Portia.

"If Clifford wins the race, the whole term's contest is theirs anyway. There's not enough time to make back enough points for us to win," says Calum

"Then we haven't got anything to lose. I say we give it a go," says Darius.

"So you're out-voted two to one, Portia," says Calum. He makes the phone call and comes out of the phone booth grinning. "The taxi driver's up for it – thinks it'll be a right laugh. He was having a slow day and sounds grateful for the business. He'll be here in a few minutes."

Two minutes later, the taxi arrives and a rosy-cheeked, jolly man winds down the window – "Hop in, kids – oh I see you're only fit to hop anyway!" he says, pointing to Darius' swollen knee.

"Yes mate, very funny!" laughs Darius.

"I'm Jack, by the way," he says, sticking his hand out of the window to shake Darius' hand.

"Pleased to meet you, Jack," they all say, and they show him the set of co-ordinates and the list of questions.

"Should all be fine, except this one up at the trig point – there's no road that goes all the way up there, so you'll have to get out and give matey boy a piggyback again, or leave him in the taxi with me. Right, missy, are you any good at map reading? If so, you're in the front with me as my co-pilot," says Jack.

"I am, actually. I was the best map reader on our D of E expedition," says Portia.

"Great, I've chosen the right person for the job then. Boys, you're in the back," says Jack. "No offence, lads, but she smells sweeter than you!"

Darius climbs stiffly into the back, sticking his leg out to the side, as he can't bend his knee anymore.

"Shove over a bit, Darius. You're not giving me much room," says Calum.

"I wish I could, especially as you're so sweaty, but I can't bend my knee, so you'll just have to put up with it."

"Harrumph," says Calum.

"Right, off we go then. First stop, St Michael's Church," says Jack.

* * *

The Clifford team arrive at the main road just in time to see the Snodhill team getting into the taxi. They instinctively duck back behind a hedge so that they aren't spotted. "Oh my goodness, did you see that? The Snodhill gang just got in a taxi!" says Daisy.

"The cheating gits!" says Archie.

"Maybe, or maybe not," says Grace. "Darius looked as if he really walloped his knee when he fell off that sheep. Maybe they're calling it quits and taking him back to get some treatment."

"I bet they're not. You don't know Calum as well as I do. With him, it's winning at all costs. I bet he can smell victory for Snodhill and he won't be giving up that easily," says Archie.

"Well, whatever they decide to do, we need to crack on if we're going to beat Long Town," says Grace.

"Yes, let's do it!" Daisy and Archie chorus together, and they set off at a jog towards the first question at St Michael's Church. The sun is shining as they go through the lych gate into the pretty churchyard of St Michael's. The church is set on top of a steep mound and Grace notices that it has an unusual square tower to the left of the main door that's topped by what looks like a pointy witch's hat.

"What's the first question?" says Archie, as they make their way up the mound.

"Who is depicted in the stained-glass window and what is he doing?" Grace reads out.

"Oh, I know that already – I've been to this church before. It's Archangel Michael and he's standing on a dragon, putting a spear down its throat. I've always thought it was a bit cruel to the poor dragon," says Daisy.

"It's a metaphor though, isn't it? The dragon represents the dragon lines or ley lines – Earth energy lines," says Grace.

"Ooh, listen to you, Miss Brain Box, talking about metaphors!" says Archie.

"Yes, but why is he putting a spear down its throat?" says Daisy.

"That, I'm not sure of," says Grace.

They open the great oak door with a creak and walk down the aisle towards the stained-glass window above the altar, their footsteps echoing on the red tiled floor. The sunlight is streaming in through the window, illuminating all the colours of St Michael and the dragon, which dance on the floor in front of them.

"Ooh, I'm getting a strange feeling in my tummy. I think it must be the ley lines. I've heard that ancient churches were often built where two ley lines cross," says Grace.

"You are a sensitive one, aren't you, Grace?" says Archie, giving her a smile.

"There he is – just like I told you," says Daisy, pointing to St Michael.

"Right, let's get the answer down and crack on then," says Archie. "I expect Long Town will be hot on our heels. Sure enough, just as they are leaving the gate, the Long Town team come into view.

"Hi, guys. Gonna save us some time and give us the answer?" shouts Charlie.

"Not on your Nelly!" shouts Archie. "Come on, let's get going," and he breaks into a run.

They have worked out from the co-ordinates given to them that the next clue is the Great Hagley Standing Stone. The first part of the route is fairly flat along narrow country lanes. And then they take a cross-country hike along footpaths through pretty bluebell woods. The flowers are almost over now, but still some patches of purple cheer their way. Then it's a bit of a hot and sweaty uphill slog to a knoll, where they find a very large granite standing stone.

"What's the question here, Gracie?" says Archie.

She reads from their instructions, "Approximately how

big is the stone you will find at this map reference?"

"Well, I'm six foot tall, so if I stand next to it, how much taller is it than me?" says Archie.

"I think it looks about 4 feet bigger than you, Archie," says Daisy. "So that would make it 10 feet tall."

"And it looks about 1.5 feet wide," says Grace. "Great, we got that one. But there's a part two to the question – 'What is the name of the hill fort you can see when looking southwest from the stone?' Daisy, any clues with your local knowledge?"

"Which way is southwest?" she asks. Grace consults the compass and points to a hilltop in the distance. "Oh, that looks like Caer Caradoc," says Daisy.

Grace looks down at the OS map again. "I think you might be right, Daisy," she says, pointing to the map.

"Bingo! Another one in the bag. We're getting good at this," says Archie.

"Shame we haven't got longer here," says Grace. I'd love to find out more about this stone."

"Maybe another time. Right, let's crack on," says Archie.

Clue number three is several miles away and up a steep mountain – the Trig Point at the top of Black Hill. They are going across very rugged country now, and get into a good steady lope, matching their pace with each other.

They arrive at the car park at the bottom of the mountain and begin their ascent up a forest track, through a conifer wood. They come to a bridleway and keep running to a point south of the trig, following a yellow marker post and find that small yellow tapes stuck onto the trees direct their way.

As they gain in height, the mist comes down and they can barely see their way ahead. It's eerily quiet and the loudest noise is the sound of their own breath as they climb steadily. Grace notices that a faint route has been forced northwards through the trees and is marked by a trail of broken branches. "Hey guys, look at this. I think this might be the way. Someone has shaped the branches into arrows on the ground," she says.

"Oh yes, I think you're right, Grace. Let's follow it and see," says Archie.

They follow an old track that is slightly less impenetrable than much of the forest, which has been replanted with Sitka. But the trees are dense and planted in rows at right angles to the route. And worse – the gaps between the trees are filled with gorse. They have to break off twigs and push others aside. They are getting scratched to pieces and resort to crawling in places. Suddenly, to their utter delight, they see a small clearing off to the right with the trig point pillar in the centre. "There it is, at last! I was beginning to think we'd made a wrong choice after all," says Archie.

The column is in good condition, still with the original OS centre cap and its shallow engraved lettering. They take note of what it says and its numbers as the answer to the Endurance Race question.

"Phew, I'm glad we made it!" says Daisy. "That was a tricky one. Anyone fancy a drink and an energy bar?"

"Yes, I think we deserve it after that," says Archie. They plonk themselves down in the rough long grass that surrounds the trig point and have a well-earned breather.

"Right guys, are you ready to crack on now?" says Archie, when they have finished their drink and snack.

"Yes, rearing to go!" says Grace.

"Me too," says Daisy. "In fact, I can't wait to get off this mountain. It's a bit eerie in this mist, isn't it?"

"I agree," says Grace.

They make their way back along the overgrown track and out onto the bridleway. As they do this, Grace looks to her left and sees the Long Town team off in the distance, still going up the bridleway. "Looks like they've missed the turning and gone the wrong way," she whispers. "We'll have to be really quiet for a bit, so they don't see us and realise their mistake."

"Good plan," whispers Archie. And they sneak quietly down the other way.

The kids are back down from the mountain and making good progress. They are well ahead of Long Town since their blunder at the Trig Point and all of them feel good, loping along at a comfortable pace.

The fourth stop is at the Bluebell Café in Hopton Dando, where they are to have a mandatory 20-minute stop for a drink and something to eat. The question reads, 'Who are the owners of the café and how much is a cup of tea?'

"I think that's just to make sure that we go in and have our break," says Archie. "I bet the owner is timing how long we stay and reporting back to school."

"That's right lad. We're keeping an eye on everyone. What can I get you? Got some sandwiches ready-made and I expect you'd like a cold drink? Water or juice?"

"Apple juice and a cheese sandwich please," they all chorus together.

"Coming right up." As he brings the drinks and sandwiches over, he says, "To answer your question, my name's Ben Jones and my wife is Mandy. A cup of tea is £1.20. You're the second lot here, but one of the lads in the other team seems to have hurt his leg, so I reckon you're in with a good chance." The kids give each other a sideways glance. They were all thinking, "So the Snodhill team are still going then!"

They thank Ben and leave the café. "Feels like we're on

the homeward stretch now," says Archie, as they jog at a comfortable pace. "I think we've done the most difficult bits."

* * *

Nanny is stroking Ahbleza's neck with her forehead pressed against his. "They're coming this way soon, but something's wrong, Ahbleza," says Nanny. "They need our help. Go find 'em and bring 'em back here, my boy," she says and steps away from him. Ahbleza sets off at a canter.

* * *

The kids are back on the trail again after their break and heading for some woodland, where their last question relates to a Holy Well. "Hey, isn't this the other end of Paradise Wood? It's all starting to look familiar here. Wow, that means we'll be back at school really soon!" says Daisy.

Then disaster strikes. Daisy puts her foot down a rabbit hole, and goes tumbling forwards, shrieking in pain. Archie says, "Oh my gosh, Daiz, you've done a Darius!"

"That would be funny if it didn't hurt so much. Guys, I think I might have broken my leg!" says Daisy.

"Oh, no! Really?" says Grace.

"Yes, didn't you hear that cracking sound. I think that was my shin bone breaking," says Daisy.

"Oh, I thought that was a twig snapping!" says Archie. He and Grace look in horror at Daisy's leg, which is the strangest shape where the bone is broken. "Gosh Daiz, what are we going to do?"

"How far are we from Nanny Watkins' house? She's known as Betty the Bonesetter, isn't she? I'm sure she would be able to help," says Grace.

"It's not far at all from here," says Daisy. "But I don't think I could even walk that far – it's so painful." She's going very white and Grace worries that she might be about to faint.

"Daisy, you better sit down on this log while we sort something out. Here, let us help you. Archie, would you be up for giving Daiz a piggyback to Nanny's?"

"Absolutely – that's a brilliant idea, Grace," says Archie.

"Great! Here, give me the rucksack and let's go." Grace is about to help Daisy onto Archie's back when they hear a loud whinny. They look in that direction to see a beautiful white horse trotting their way.

"It's Ahbleza!" says Daisy. "I was just thinking about him and wishing I could get a ride from him, and here he is."

Grace laughs with relief. "You clever girl, Daisy. You called him in. Looks like you're off the hook, Archie. Ahbleza can carry Daisy to Nanny's house, if we ask him nicely."

Ahbleza arrives at Daisy's side, a look of concern in his deep blue eyes. He nuzzles Daisy's neck to comfort her and check her out. "Good lad!" says Archie, giving him a firm pat on the withers.

"Ahbleza, Daisy's broken her leg and is in terrible pain," says Grace. "Can you do anything to relieve her pain. And would you be very kind as to give her a lift to Nanny's house so she can set the bone?"

Ahbleza nods his head and nickers softly. Then he lowers his head towards Daisy's leg. A look of concentration comes into his eyes and a beam of soft pink light begins to spiral from his horn and into Daisy's leg. "Ah, that's beautiful, Blazie. The pain is just melting away. Thank you," says Daisy.

"Do you think we can get you up onto his back now the pain has gone, Daisy?" says Grace.

"Yes, I'll be fine to ride now, as long as he just walks. I think too much joggling about wouldn't be great."

"Good, come on then, Arch. Let's get her on. If you lift her, I'll support her broken leg under her thigh and then you can pop your good leg over, Daiz," says Grace.

"You ready, Daiz?" says Archie. "Here we go – one, two, three and up she goes. Ah, that was easier than I thought."

"I'm sure Ahbleza was helping," says Daisy. They set off at a steady walk with Grace and Archie walking either side of him. Ahbleza knows the way back to Nanny's house and takes them straight there.

In the wink of an eye, they are outside Nanny's cottage and she is rushing out saying, "Goodness kiddos, what's happened?"

Archie explains everything and Nanny gets straight to work. "Ahbleza, put her down gently near the door for me," says Nanny. They watch, amazed as he slowly sinks to his knees and lies down so that it is easy for Daisy to get off. "Archie, run and get a chair. Then help me get Daisy onto it. Grace, put the kettle on and make some comfrey tea like I showed you last time you were here. Don't forget a big dollop of honey."

In a flash, Archie is back with the chair and he picks Daisy up and puts her onto it. "Come on Blazie, let's get to work then," says Nanny. He stands up and shines his healing spiral of light onto Daisy's leg again. "Daisy, this won't hurt because of what Ahbleza's doing, but it will feel a bit odd, so best to grip onto the seat of the chair with your hands. And Archie, you can help by standing behind Daisy and steadying her shoulders with your hands."

"Righto," says Archie.

Nanny takes hold of Daisy's foot, concentrates her mind into Daisy's leg and applies traction to her foot. With a sharp pull and a bit of a twist, the bone goes back into place and Daisy's leg looks approximately the right shape again, although quite swollen and starting to bruise.

Grace is back with the comfrey tea. "Here's the tea, Nanny and I've brought things to make a comfrey and yarrow poultice too with a bit of lavender oil."

"Good girl, you're a fast learner. You go ahead and make that up and put it on while Ahbleza and I work the magic." She does her special action to take the shock out, using her fingers in a triangle shape, which the kids have since learned that Nanny calls 'V-spreading.' Just like last time, the kids watch in amazement as the swelling goes right down. "Daisy, take some big sips of the tea now, and Grace, put the poultice on."

A few minutes later and the colour has come back into Daisy's face. She says, "Wow, Nanny, my leg feels completely back to normal now. Thank you SO much! You are a miracle worker."

"Well, we all made a good team there. Especially Ahbleza – he's a very magical boy," says Nanny.

"Oh my goodness, yes he is. Thank you, lovely Ahbleza," says Daisy. And she pats his furry head. He lets out a big puff of air through his velvety lips and then raises his top lip in a big grin.

"That's him saying, 'You're welcome, Daisy,'" says Nanny.

"Are you still up for finishing the race now? If so, let's have a look at those questions. I might be able to help you with some of them. She scans down the list. "Ooh, I know this one," she says, pointing to the last question. It's not far from here, I can get Ahbleza to take you there. I know the Holy Well is dedicated to St Brigit, and one of the animals she's associated with is the bees. I remember that there's a beehive on the carving there. There's a lot more I could tell you about St Brigit, or should I say 'Goddess Brigit.' Very fond of Brigit, I am." She has a reverential look of awe on her face.

"And this one about the church – it's dedicated to St Michael. The church is called St Michael and All Angels. The stained-glass window has a great big picture of him standing on a dragon and putting a spear down his throat. It sounds a bit gruesome, but it has a hidden meaning. The dragon or serpent is a metaphor for ley lines, or energy lines that run through the land, and go through all the major sacred sites. The spear going down his throat is like a human putting an acupuncture needle in one of their meridians. Just like standing stones are like acupuncture needles for the Earth's meridians. Though I don't suppose they want you to put that much detail on your answer sheet! Just thought you might like to know that."

"Yes, Nanny. I love learning about things like that," says Archie. "Grace knew about the ley lines, but she didn't know why Michael had his spear down the dragon's throat or the bit about the standing stones – that is fascinating."

"But would it be cheating to go to the well with Ahbleza?" says Grace.

"I won't tell anyone if you don't," says Nanny with a naughty twinkle.

"And the Snodhill team have cheated twice as much as us already," says Archie. "They've done almost all of it in a taxi, Nanny, because Darius hurt his knee before they got to the first clue!"

"Well, what a day for it! There must be something strange happening in the stars," says Nanny. "By rights then, the prize should go to the third team, because they're the only ones who didn't cheat and ran it all properly."

"That settles it then," says Daisy. "I am going to walk the rest of the way. You've done such a brilliant job of healing me, I think I can do it if we just walk."

"Well, if you're sure, that would be the most honest thing to do," says Nanny. "Come back tomorrow through the portal for some more healing if it's still troubling you, dear."

"I will, Nanny, thank you."

"And Grace, take some more herbs to make another poultice this evening."

"Thanks Nanny," say Grace and Archie.

"Right, you better get going then, kids. Good luck."

They all hug Ahbleza and set off at a walk for the Holy Well. Once the kids are out of earshot, Nanny says, "Better follow them at a safe distance Ahbleza, to keep an eye on them. I know you're the master of camouflage and you can fade into the background so they can't see you. Good boy, off you go then." And off he trots, going silently into the woods behind the kids.

Soon the kids hear the trickling of a little stream. They follow the stream until they can see a little way ahead a small stone shrine in the shape of a beehive. They find that it is all just as Nanny told them. The crystal-clear spring water flows out from underneath the beehive shrine. The water seems to have a magical quality and emanates light.

In front of the beehive, there is a pool big enough to bathe in. And a carving on the shrine has a picture of St Brigit, which reads,

St Brigit's Well

Beloved patron saint of:

- *Babies, new mothers and midwives*
- *Healers, poets, and blacksmiths*
- *Bees and honey*
- *Livestock, cattle and dairy workers.*

"Oh how magical!" says Grace. "I think we should all fill our water bottles here. And Daisy, perhaps you should bathe your leg in it for extra healing."

"Ooh, what a lovely idea," says Daisy. "I'm going to do it!" They fill their bottles and Grace pours water over Daisy's leg. "Ah, it's so soothing," she says.

Archie notes down the final answers before they head back to school.

Just as they turn up the drive towards school, they hear running footsteps and puffing breath. They turn to see the Long Town team a couple of hundred yards behind but steaming rapidly towards them.

"Quick Daiz, get on my back, I'm going to piggyback you the rest of the way. We can still win this, but not if we walk," says Archie. Grace helps her up and they set off at a run, Daisy giggling at the absurdity of it.

Halfway up the drive, they spot the Snodhill team just ahead, Calum carrying Darius piggyback style too.

"Got any more gears, Grace?" says Archie. "Shall we give them a proper run for their money?"

"You bet, Archie. I feel all fired up, now I've seen those cheaters. Let's go!"

"Hang on Daisy!" says Archie. They quicken their pace and begin to gain on Snodhill. With the advantage of Archie's long legs and the fact that Daisy is much lighter than Darius, they draw alongside the Snodhill team.

Darius looks over, "Oh, hi guys!" he laughs. "Faster, my steed, faster!" he says, pretending to thrash Calum with a jockey's stick. Everyone is laughing now, except Calum, who is puce in the face and looks furious. He stares straight ahead and his stocky legs are pumping for all they're worth. Portia is having to curb her usual racehorse pace to match

Calum, as the rule is that they all need to cross the finish line together.

The Clifford team stretch past Snodhill just as they reach the edge of the school yard. They head for the finish line, handing their answer paper to Mr Aveen and then collapsing in a giggling heap onto the grass bank. To their delight, the Long Town team also pip Snodhill to the post, squeaking past them to cross the line just ahead. Burnley, Tom and Charlie come over to shake their hands. "Congratulations, you gev us a good run for't money. That were reet good fun!" says Burnley.

Calum dumps Darius on the floor and stomps off before Darius and Portia come over to congratulate the Clifford team. "Well done, guys, very well run," says Portia.

"Won with style," says Darius, looking sheepishly at Daisy.

"How's your knee, Darius?" says Daisy. "It looks pretty swollen."

"Oh, I'll live," he says.

"Grace has got an amazing poultice she could put on for you, if you like?" says Daisy.

"Yes, it would help to take the swelling down," says Grace.

"Well, thank you. Maybe I'll come and find you after tea," says Darius.

"Cool, see you later," says Grace.

Daisy, Archie and Grace have a big hug together before heading their separate ways. "Well, what a team we made, guys! We were all awesome," says Archie.

"Yes we were," agree Daisy and Grace.

In all the excitement, the kids have not taken in that the whole school has come out to cheer them home. Everyone is cheering and applauding. Mr Aveen comes over and says, "Well, what a finish! Congratulations, Clifford. I've just checked and yu've answered everything correctly. So I can confirm ya are the winning team. Grace, I was really impressed with yur running. We will want ya for the Cross-Country team for sure and the distance races in the Inter-Schools Athletics Meet in Birmingham later this term. Ah, here is Mr Williams to give ya the winners' cup."

Grace is glowing inside. At last, she has been recognised for being good at something sporty. Daisy gives her a little nudge and a smile.

"Well done and what a dramatic finish!" says Boss. "I have pleasure in awarding you the Inter-House Endurance Race cup and 50 points to add to your house total. I think that puts you far in the lead and you will be very hard to beat for this year's competition. So double congratulations." He hands the cup to Grace and gives her a beaming smile, as if to say, "You're coming along nicely, now."

The kids hold up the cup together. Everyone cheers and Mr Aveen takes a photo to go in the Old Hall and the yearbook.

Chapter 20:
The Swimming Gala

Looking for Volunteers

"Come on, guys, we need someone to swim, otherwise we've no chance of winning the overall team event," says Portia. "I'd do it myself, but I'm already committed to too many other races. We don't need to win that race, we just need someone to finish, so we can get a point and a chance for the team cup."

The Independent Schools Swimming Gala is coming up soon. Fairstone is hosting it this year. The swimming team captain, Portia Jenkins, has asked for someone to volunteer to swim in the Senior Girl's Butterfly race. All the other girls look away and no-one volunteers.

"I'll do it," says Grace. "I'm not very good at butterfly, but I can manage a couple of lengths if you just need a point for finishing."

"Amazing, that's the spirit! Thank you, Grace!" says Portia.

"Are you sure about this?" whispers Daisy. "Butterfly's a toughie. Just because you didn't make it into the hockey team, doesn't mean you have to volunteer for every other team."

"What, you mean just because I made an arse of myself in hockey, I shouldn't do it again in swimming?" says Grace.

"Something like that!" says Daisy and they both laugh.

Jealousy

The sun pours in through the 4th Form window. It's hot and stuffy and a lazy fly buzzes round the classroom. The end-of-term mark order is out. The English teacher, Mr Hardy, who is also their form tutor, has just announced the marks.

"And top of the mark order, winning by 10 points, is Grace Bellaport. Well done, Grace – what an excellent start you've made in your first term at Fairstone! Come up and get your medal. And you've also earned 20 points for your house, Clifford, too." Mr Hardy is beaming at her, genuinely pleased that she has won. He has a huge soft spot for her.

Grace makes her way to the front of the class to receive her medal and Mr Hardy says quietly, so that only she can hear, "Your writing, Grace, is exemplary – such imagination! Keep going like that. I see great potential for you as a writer. I predict that one day you will be a famous author."

As Grace returns to her seat, the class are whooping and cheering, the loudest cheers coming from Archie and Daisy. But one face isn't smiling. "And second place goes to Anne

Smith. Well done, Anne!" says Mr Hardy. "Third place goes to Archie McBride. Well done to both of you – some excellent work produced. Come and get your rosettes."

As they go to collect their rosettes, Archie nudges Anne in the ribs. "Cheer up, old girl – second place isn't so bad. I'm sure you'll be back on top next term." Anne tries to force a smile, but a grey cloud hovers over her.

Mr Hardy, handing a red rosette to Anne, whispers, "Your work is still of excellent quality. Don't be too disheartened. Let someone else have a moment of glory for once." He pats her on the arm and smiles at her in an encouraging way.

"And very well done to you, Mr McBride," handing him a yellow rosette. "Your writing shows huge promise – wonderfully creative and humorous. It's the physics and history that let you down a bit this time. Try to apply yourself equally to the subjects that don't interest you as much. I know you have a very smart brain box in there."

Class is over and the kids leave the classroom, heading for lunch. In the melee, Anne deliberately jostles into Grace. "That's the first and last time you come top of the mark order," she hisses at Grace. "I'm the one who always comes first. You will never beat me again. You think you're so clever, don't you, Miss Scholarship Girl? But never forget that you're only here because our parents subsidise your fees, because your parents can't afford them," poking Grace in the chest with a pointy finger, as she says this.

"Look, Anne, I never set out to beat you. I was just doing my work to the best of my ability. I'm very grateful for the scholarship – Fairstone is a great school – but if I didn't get it, someone else would take my place. I'm sorry you feel upset about not coming first, so good luck for the next one." Grace is shaking, but feels really proud of herself for standing up to Anne.

"Harrumph," says Anne, giving Grace a final poke with her elbow as she pushes past, stropping off to find her cronies.

"Whoa, that was so rude and mean!" says Daisy, coming up alongside Grace. She sees the tears welling up in Grace's eyes and taking her hand says, "Take no notice of her, Grace. She's just sore because no-one has ever beaten her in the mark order before. Not even Archie. But you deserve it – you're so clever and I know you've worked really hard. And I know Boss will be really pleased with you. Now he knows he gave the scholarship to the right person!"

"Yeah, she must be really sore to find out that the new girl is not only prettier than her, but she's smarter too! By the way, I'm very pleased for you, even if you did bump me down to third place!" says Archie. "As there's no games today, why don't we cheer ourselves up with a visit to Nanny Watkins this afternoon? I could do with a plateful of her delicious biscuits."

"Ooh, yes!" chorus Grace and Daisy together.

"Do you want me to beat her in for you?" says Charlie, arriving at the scene. "I can't stand the sour-faced cow!"

"No, don't do that! But maybe you could whack the hockey ball extra hard at her next time we have hockey practice," smiles Grace through her tears.

"You're on!" says Charlie.

Take No Notice

"Is that so, Mr Ahbleza?" says Nanny. She's in the paddock with him, gently stroking his neck, listening to the words he drops into her heart. He brings her so much comfort. The meadow flowers around her seem to sparkle in the sunlight, a glow of emerald green light shines from the grass and the trees beyond the paddock, and the sun is gleaming off Ahbleza's silver coat. There is magic in the air on this beautiful summer's day.

Ahbleza nods his head to affirm what he has just said to Nanny about asking Grace to be her apprentice, and pass on the teachings from her lineage. Jonnie would have been her choice to pass on the teachings to, but his passing put an end to that. Nanny's daughter, now grown and with kids of her own, has moved away, which makes it more difficult to share the teachings. And now she is busy with her young children, she is even less interested than before. Nanny thinks maybe one of the grandchildren will carry on the lineage, but for now they are too young for Nanny to tell.

"You're right of course, Blazie. Grace is the perfect person to carry the teachings. She has the gift and the brains. We've just got to boost her confidence a bit more. Summer holidays are coming up and she doesn't live far away. I'll see if she can come on her own for some teaching sessions. That's it, I will definitely ask her."

Ahbleza nudges her shoulder, as if to say, "And what else?" as a colourful butterfly flits past them both.

"Oh yes, I will ask her about that too and put it in the teachings. I know, I know, it's time that he passed over to the light. He's been hanging on for me. I know I need to let him go, so he can move on to new adventures. I promise I will teach Grace how to help me with that." She buries her face in Ahbleza's neck and lets out a big snotty sob. In response, he blows out a long, soothing sigh through his velvet lips, which comforts Nanny's heart.

Later... the three amigos are sitting around Nanny Watkins' table with a glass of honey-sweetened homemade lemonade and each munching one of Nanny's special hazelnut cookies – their favourites of all her baking. It's cool in the shade of Nanny's cottage, with its thick walls and small windows.

"You look a bit rattled, me dear," says Nanny, fixing Grace with one of her penetrating stares. "What's up?" Grace confides in Nanny what Anne Smith said to her earlier.

"Well, dear Gracie, I think you should take it as a compliment. A wise man once said to me, 'You ain't nobody until someone hates your guts!' It's just jealousy because she's got no imagination and you have. Grace, whether you know it or not yet, you are a very magical person, and boring people – grey sky people, as I call them – can't stand that. They feel threatened by it, because they are so competitive, and they don't understand how you do it, because you don't follow their rules. They see the light that shines from you and it hurts their eyes. She is likely destined for a boring life, always striving to get to the top, trying to get one better than the next person. And that's not the kind of life you are destined for.

"I know you hate to upset people and you want to feel that you fit in – this being your first term at Fairstone and all – but remember this, dear, 'You can't please all of the people all of the time.' And I will be very cross with you if you dim your light and your magic to try to fit in with the likes of boring old Anne.

"And that goes for all three of you. You all have your special qualities that you need to bring to the world, not hide them away to fit in with the run of the mill."

"I don't see Archie hiding much away!" laughs Daisy.

"Oh, I wouldn't be so sure," says Nanny, giving Archie a sly wink.

"Delicious biscuits – that's one of **your** superpowers, Nanny," says Archie, trying to deflect the attention away from himself, "But you're so right – what you said to Grace about Anne being jealous."

"Yes, and Gracie is very special, isn't she? I keep trying to tell her that. But it sounds better coming from you, Nanny," says Daisy.

"And she's very lucky to have good friends like you two," says Nanny, getting a bit misty-eyed. "Come on, let's go and see what Ahbleza has to say about all this. I bet he can help her in some way."

They make their way to the bottom of the garden, Archie stopping to pinch some strawberries on the way, and go through the gate at the bottom of the garden into the goat's paddock.

Nanny gives a long, loud whistle, and an answering whinny is heard. Soon the magnificent form of Ahbleza comes cantering towards them, his coat gleaming in the sunlight. He slows to a trot, then a walk and stops in front of Nanny. The kids are again in awe of this majestic being.

"Hello my beautiful boy. How are you today?" says Nanny. He blows air out through his velvet lips and tells Nanny, silently into her heart, that all is well with the world.

"Good to hear that, my lad," says Nanny. "Now I would like your help in speaking to my dear friend, Grace, here. She's had a bit of a shock today and she needs some healing and reassurance." Ahbleza nods his head in agreement. Nanny says, "He says it would be an honour and asks you to please come forward."

So Grace steps in front of Ahbleza. He dips his head in front of her and activates the flow of healing light into Grace's chest. Spirals of sparkling golden light beam from Ahbleza into Grace until her whole body looks lit up and she is glowing from within.

Nanny interjects, "If he is saying words to you, please say them out loud to us, if that feels OK, because I believe that his message would benefit Daisy and Archie too."

"OK Nanny, I will try to translate," says Grace. "He is

saying, 'Last time I saw you, I told you that I am here to help you unlock your treasure chest of skills and talents. They are greater than you can imagine and you must bring them to the world.

"You must reach deep within yourself and recognise that you are a Magnificent Divine Being – that goes for all three of you. When you are connected with your true self and with God, you are very powerful. Your task as a young person is to explore your true self and own it. Never let anyone like this Anne person knock you off that.

"When you fully understand your purpose and your mission in this life, your enthusiasm will light you up from within and it will sweep all obstacles aside to help bring about positive change in the world. Your enthusiasm and your connection with God will light up the energy field that surrounds you with a magnetism that attracts the right people and gifts into your life to help you. Archie and Daisy are really good at this already, though they don't know it fully yet. You need to build your belief in yourself and throw away anything that blocks you from tapping into this. When you master this, you will become an unstoppable force, as the Universe aligns behind you.

"But remember this, Dear Ones, with power comes responsibility, so you **must** make sure that your intention is always for the highest good of All, in service to the Divine. Always act with common sense, discernment and wisdom, and you will be able to fulfil your life purpose with joy. When you take action from this place, you can help lead others to their highest path. So all three of you, young though you are at this time, I ask you to find how to stand in your power. This is your coming of age. You all have a common purpose and that is to help bring justice, freedom and peace to the world. This is the end of my message, Grace. I ask you to take it into your heart."

Ahbleza starts to speak through Grace again, "I would like to offer a gift to Daisy. Now that her leg is healed, I would like to offer her a ride on my back. If she would like that?"

Ahbleza's beam of light fades. "Thank you, Ahbleza," says Grace, stroking his neck and stepping away from him.

"What a special message that was for all of you. Thank you, Ahbleza," says Nanny.

"Whoa, not asking much of us then?!" exclaims Archie.

"You are all very gifted in your different ways," says Nanny. "I know you will find your way to make it happen. But don't let it feel like a burden – you are far too young just yet and there are so many adventures and so much fun for you to have first. And speaking of which, Daisy, would you like that ride? Perhaps Archie could help you up."

"Oh my goodness, that's a dream come true. Thank you, Ahbleza," says Daisy.

"Come on then, Daisy, let me help you up," says Archie. He bends down next to Ahbleza's side, interlocking his fingers and making a cup of his hands for Daisy to put her foot in. She reaches up for Ahbleza's withers. "One, two, three, up she goes," says Archie, and Daisy swings her other leg up and over Ahbleza's back. There is none of her normal physical awkwardness and Ahbleza sets off with Daisy riding him very gracefully. They are cantering by the time they reach the end of the paddock and Ahbleza leaps the fence.

Archie and Grace are watching nervously for Daisy, but she sits the jump perfectly and they canter away.

"Blimey, I've never seen her so co-ordinated before," says Archie.

"Yes, that'll be a special bit of Blazie's magic. I have a feeling he's healing her in another way," says Nanny. "Right, let's have a cuppa while we wait for her. And Grace can tell us how she feels about Ahbleza's message too.

"Great idea," Archie and Grace chorus together, and they go back into the kitchen.

"So, what do you think of that message, Gracie?" says Nanny.

"Well, Nanny, so much of it feels true. I've felt different since I was a little kid and I've been trying to hide what makes me different. Meeting you and Archie and Daisy is the first time in my life that I've been able to feel that these differences might actually be a positive thing and not a burden. But I feel nervous about the responsibility of using my skills and I need to get more confidence before I can start to use them properly."

"That's only natural, me dear. You are still so young and it's good to be a bit humble. I am here to help you in whatever way I can," says Nanny. "It took me many years to master my skills. It was my Grampy who taught me at first. He is part of the lineage of Wise Ones and Healers. But after he died, I had to carry on learning on me own. But by that time, I had enough skills to listen to my intuition and my spiritual guidance. And you will find the same. I can teach you the basics, but after that, you will find your own way. And Archie, what do you think?"

"I knew from the moment I set eyes on Grace, the first day she came to school, that there was something special about her. Although I don't have the same magical skills as her, I know that I can help in my own way. I love the idea of having a special mission to do good in the world. I know it sounds corny, but I think I was born to do this!"

Nanny claps her hands together and says, "Goodness, it warms my heart to hear you say that, my lad! Yes, you were born to do this. Well done, well done! Oh, can I hear Daisy and Ahbleza coming back now?"

They hear the sound of hoofbeats and Daisy, as she says, "Whoa now boy." The three walk back out to the end of the garden to see Daisy and Ahbleza trotting up to the gate. Daisy is beaming with a smile from ear to ear.

"Here, let me help you down," says Archie, rushing out.

"Wow, that was so amazing!" says Daisy, as she bends forward to pat Ahbleza's neck. "Thank you so much, beautiful boy," she says and deftly hops off Ahbleza's back, springing lightly to the ground before Archie can get there.

"Neatly done!" says Archie. "You didn't need my help after all."

"Yes, Ahbleza has been giving me healing for my balance and co-ordination. And we've had such an adventure together – I love him SO much!"

"Wonderful, wonderful, me dear. I'm so glad you had healing and an adventure," says Nanny. "I'm very fond of you lot. Thanks for visiting an old lady. Now you better be getting back to school before anyone misses you."

Nanny Asks for Grace's Help

Nanny asks Grace to hang back. "My dear, if you are willing, I would like your help with something. I know you have the skill and natural ability. You've shown time and again how sensitive you are. Your vision and intuition are the best I've come across in anyone except me! But if you don't mind me saying, you need some direction in how to handle these abilities, so that you can put them to best use. And not to feel overwhelmed by them."

"Yes, Nanny – that would be SO helpful. I really do want to learn how to work with my abilities. Regulus told me I need to do this too. But so far, I haven't understood how."

"I'm very happy to help with that. I have a selfish reason

for it too. There is something that I can't do on my own and I need some help with. It's not something to be taken lightly, but I feel it is part of your calling."

Grace looks questioningly at Nanny. "What are you talking about, Nanny? I'd really like to help you, but I'd like to know what I'm letting myself in for first."

"Fair do's – well, my dear, you have an ability that others don't. Namely, you see into the Spirit World and you hear the messages very clearly. You've also seen and spoken with the spirit of someone who's passed away. Sometimes these spirits need some help to cross over to the other side. Some people find it difficult – they might be hanging on to be close to a loved one who is still living. Or they might just be confused about where to go. So people like you and me have the ability to help them cross over and be at peace."

"You're talking about Jonnie, aren't you?"

"Well, yes. It's high time he let go of this old lady and moved on to new adventures."

"I can see how hard that is for you, Nanny, and I'd love to help, if I can. But I wouldn't be telling the truth if I didn't say it really scares me."

"Oh, I'm sure it does. First time I did it, I nearly wet me pants, I was so nervous! But honestly, when you know how and you have called in your guides, there is nothing to worry about."

"Okay Nanny. I will help you."

Competition Day

"What on earth was I thinking?!" Grace asks herself. "I should have listened to Daisy. I should stick to running – that's my sport."

It's the day of the Swimming Gala, and her nerves

have been building, as the coaches with the other school's competitors arrive. It's a warm June day and she's got that sweaty, clammy feeling about what's to come. And the smell of the chlorine as the sun shines on the outdoor pool is making her feel nauseous.

She has had a few practices at the butterfly and finds it really hard. The main issue is that she can't get both her arms to come over her head at the same time. Try as she might, her left arm always lags slightly behind her right one. She desperately wants to back out. In fact, she wants to run as far away as possible and hide until this is all over. But she's given her word to Portia that she will swim and she doesn't want to let the team down – they won't be eligible for the team cup unless they have a competitor in every race.

"Someone help her, she's drowning!" Tom is taking off his changing robe ready to jump in and rescue her. Archie holds him back. "No mate, she's going to be embarrassed enough about her performance. Imagine how much worse she'll feel if you jump in there and hoick her out so she doesn't even get the team point?"

"Seriously – you're just going to let her flounder like that?!" says Tom.

"Yep and then give her loads of, 'Well done, you did so well,' afterwards. Believe me, it's the best way."

After an excruciatingly long time, full of splashing and thrashing, Grace reaches the end of the pool. Grabbing onto the side, she pants for breath. There's a weird hush, as no-one knows how to react. All the other competitors finished ages ago – they're all out of the pool with their robes back on. Then Archie starts the clapping and cheering, motioning everyone else to do the same. Grace looks around in confusion, but breaks out into a smile when she realises the applause is for her. Archie goes over to help her out of the pool.

"Goodness, that was harder than I realised," she wheezes.

"I know, but you did SO well. You were outstanding! So brave of you to do it just for the team point. We're really proud of you."

Daisy rushes over. "My goodness, Grace, you are a brave one. I could never have done that. Swimming's not my thing, but I didn't have the courage to just do it for the good of the team like you did." The two of them usher her past Anne Smith, doing their best to shield her from the ugly sneer that Anne is sending in Grace's direction. The look on her face says that she is disgusted by the spectacle created by Grace's performance, thinking it reflects badly on Fairstone's reputation as having the best swimming team. Archie motions silently to Anne to zip it, indicating that she will be in big trouble if she says anything to Grace.

The results are in. Archie, Tom and Calum all won their races, as did several of the 5th and 6th Formers. Portia and Charlie both came first in all their races and the senior girls relay came first too. Grace watches as they all go up to collect their medals, feeling sheepish about her dismal performance and sad that she doesn't qualify for anything.

The points for the team competition are totted up. Fairstone are only one point ahead of their arch rivals Upton, but it's enough to win the cup for the team event. A huge cheer goes up round the swimming pool. Portia goes to collect the cup and then motions for all the other team members to come up and help her celebrate. Grace hangs back until Portia beckons her over too. "You deserve this as much as anyone," she says to Grace. "You might not have won your race, but we wouldn't have got the cup without you. Now smile for the team photo!"

Chapter 21:
The End of Term

A Midsummer Night's Dream

The summer term is drawing to a close. What an amazing adventure-filled first term Grace has had since she started at Fairstone. She's made some wonderful new friends, especially Daisy and Archie, and including a magical horse, a spirit lion, a ghost and of course, last but not least, Nanny Watkins. She's discovered what she previously thought of as her 'weirdness' is actually a set of magical skills not shared by everyone, but highly valuable when channelled in the right direction and given structure by the teachings of Nanny Watkins. She has even found a sport that she excels at – something she never thought would happen – and played a big part in helping her house, Clifford, win the House Cup, with the big win of the Inter-House Endurance Race. She feels proud of herself for making such a good start, despite her initial insecurities. She looks back at how scared and inferior she felt at the beginning of term, when she compared herself to what she thought of as all the rich posh kids, and realises how much her confidence has grown since then.

Grace ponders all these things as she sits on the bus next to Daisy and across the aisle from Archie, who is sitting next to Tom. The old jalopy is bouncing and spluttering its way to Ludlow, where the senior classes are going to watch *A Midsummer Night's Dream*, set in the grounds of Ludlow Castle. It's the evening before the last day of term and there's a palpable buzz of excitement in the air as the kids head for their end-of-term treat.

"We're lucky with the weather this year," says Daisy. "Last year was a washout when we went to see the Scottish play that begins with 'M' and ends in 'beth' – they told us it was bad luck to say the real name."

"But don't you think it added to the atmosphere?" says Archie.

"Oh, definitely," says Daisy. "But the thunder and lightning were pretty scary. I was worried it was going to strike the top of my umbrella."

"Yes, there was a risk of that," says Archie. "Wasn't it cool that the actors applauded the audience at the end, for sticking it out in the pouring rain?"

"They didn't realise we had no choice because we weren't getting picked up by the bus till the end. We had nowhere else to go!" says Daisy.

"Do you think it had anything to do with the bad spirits there? I got a really weird feeling the first time I saw it when we went past in the bus," says Grace.

"I think you're probably right, but Nanny's fixed that now, hasn't she?" says Archie.

"Yes, she has, and I think that's probably why we have beautiful weather tonight and hopefully a peaceful atmosphere," says Grace.

"What on earth are you talking about – bad spirits? You guys spend far too much time with that funny old stick, Nanny Watkins," says Tom.

"She's amazing, Tom. So clever and interesting, and she's a brilliant healer. If you ever break your leg, she's the person to go to, to heal it in super quick time," says Archie.

"I'll take your word for it, but I'm not going round there for a visit," says Tom.

The bus is just pulling into the car park and all the kids get off and wait for the teacher to lead them to their seats.

"Wow, how beautiful!" says Daisy. The castle has been decorated to resemble a fairy grotto, with twinkling lights, beautiful flowers, real trees and gauzy fabrics fluttering in the breeze.

They take their seats and the play begins. A magical atmosphere descends on the castle and the kids are enchanted and amused by the play. They hardly notice the time go by. And suddenly, the play is at an end and the actors are taking a bow.

The Form 4 kids all gather in a little huddle while they wait to go back to the bus. "That was splendid!" says Archie. "I thoroughly enjoyed it."

"Give over, you big softie," says Tom, giving him an elbow in the ribs. "It was quite good, and funny in places, but a bit airy-fairy for my liking."

"You didn't feel the magic then, eh Tom?" says Archie.

"Well, maybe a bit," whispers Tom. "But I'm not going to admit that in front of so many of the rugby team."

"Ay-up, that were reet nice," says Burnley, joining their conversation. "Don't you think, Arch? I luvved them fairies – so pretty!"

"Yes, Burnley, I thought it was great. There you go, Tom – I'm not the only manly bloke who liked it!"

"Oh, you're so cute, Burnley," says Charlie, putting her arm around his shoulder and giving him a rib-crushing squeeze. His eyes nearly pop out of his head and he looks pleadingly at the other kids.

"Put him down, Charlie, before you squeeze all the life out of him!" says Archie.

"Ooh, sorry mate. I don't know me own strength," says Charlie, releasing him from her grip. He takes a big gasp of air and the colour in his face returns to normal.

Darius bounds over. "Hey Daisy, how did you enjoy that? A tale where true love triumphs in the end. Just like you and me, eh?" He lifts her hand to his mouth and kisses it, before walking back to his 5th Form buddies with his best swagger, saying over his shoulder, "I'll wear you down and one day you'll realise how much you love me!"

Daisy blushes crimson, as everyone laughs with good humour at Darius' boldness about his feelings for her. Daisy says nothing, but does Grace detect the tiniest of wistful sighs?

They all bundle onto the bus and head back to school, at first chattering excitedly about the play and then calming down. And soothed by the rocking and farting of the bus, many fall asleep.

Prize Giving Day

There's an hour to go before all the parents start to arrive for Prize Giving Day. The girls are in their dorm, packing the last of their belongings before they go home for the long summer holidays.

"I hate to admit it, but I'm going to miss you guys," says Charlie.

"It's perfectly understandable, because we're really nice!" says Daisy, winking at Grace.

"It's been great getting to know you this term," says Grace, "And a lot of fun."

"Likewise, Grace – you're a good egg. I wasn't sure at first, but you've grown on me! And you've had a stormer of a first term," says Charlie.

"Maybe we can meet up in the holidays? You don't live a million miles from us," says Daisy.

"I'd like that," says Charlie. "We could go to a show together. Keep in touch and we'll sort something out." She looks at her watch and says, "Right ladies, I think it's about time we went down to school for Prize Giving. The parents will be starting to arrive now."

They make their way down to their Form Room and wait for Mr Hardy to lead them to the Assembly Hall.

Sunlight pours in through the large side windows, illuminating motes of dust that swirl in the air currents of three hundred children and their parents, shuffling about in their seats. The atmosphere is charged with excitement – not only from the prize winners, but also the high emotions of finishing the school year and going home for the long summer holidays. For some of the 5th Formers and the Upper 6th, this will be their final ever day of school.

Seated between Daisy and Archie in her house block, Grace's tummy is doing little flips of excitement. The parents are all filing in at the back and she is about to go up on stage to collect her prize. It's getting uncomfortably warm in the hall and Grace is glad that she is wearing the cooler option of the school uniform summer dress.

It's almost a relief when she hears Boss say, "And the English prize this year goes to our newcomer, Grace Bellaport. Grace, if you'd like to come up and collect your prize from Mr Hardy, the English teacher."

Grace makes her way up to the stage, her heart beating fast and her knees trembling. Mr Hardy is saying, "I chose Grace for the English prize because, although she's only been here for a short time, she has achieved top marks in all her work. She's an outstanding storyteller and I always can't wait to read the next instalment of her homework. Her piece on The Wedding was exceptional. She captured the magic and the emotions of the day beautifully. She's also a talented poet. I hope one day to be reading a book with her name on the cover.

"She has chosen as her prize a book called The Mystery of the White Lions: Children of the Sun God, by Linda Tucker – a very intriguing title! Here you are, Grace. Very well done. I hope you enjoy your book and I look forward to reading more of your stories next term."

"Thank you so much, Mr Hardy. You have been a wonderful teacher to me – so encouraging and supportive," says Grace.

"Oh, thank you, my dear," says Mr Hardy, looking very touched by her comment.

Mr Williams leans towards Grace and whispers, "You've done very well and I am so glad that I chose you for the scholarship." She smiles and thanks him, feeling a warm glow of pride and confidence kindle in her heart.

She returns to her seat as Boss says, "And the science prize this year goes to another of our outstanding students, Anne Smith. Anne, please come and collect your prize from

Mrs Crystal, the Science teacher." Grace is too busy looking at her book and reading the inscription from Mr Hardy to pay much attention to Anne.

"And finally, the House Cup this year goes to Clifford House. It was a close-run thing and Snodhill were only a couple of points behind. We teachers feel that the House Competition is a wonderful way to encourage excellence in our students.

"I have great pleasure in inviting Archie McBride to come and collect the cup on behalf of Clifford House. We chose Archie because the biggest factor in securing the win for Clifford was the outstanding performance put in by their Inter-House Endurance Race team, comprising of Archie, Grace Bellaport and Daisy Davies. And Archie was the hero of the day, with the strength and endurance to carry his injured teammate, Daisy, over the finish line on his back. It was a brilliant show of teamwork and stamina, which sealed the deal for them to get the winning team points."

Archie looks utterly taken by surprise, but leaps up with enthusiasm to go and receive the cup. On stage, Boss hands him the cup, saying, "Very well done, young man. You are a credit to the school."

Archie accepts the cup, saying, "I feel very honoured to receive the cup on behalf of Clifford House. We all did this. We all deserve this. We made a brilliant team and I have to say that my house is full of the best people – they are all ... erm ... good eggs. Commiserations to Long Town and Snodhill, who also have many good eggs in them. Great competition, guys." He raises the cup above his head and a huge cheer goes up from the kids and parents of Clifford House.

Mr Wilson finishes by saying, "And so I declare this term and indeed this school year, over. You are all free to go home now. Have a wonderful summer and we look forward to welcoming you back in September. Do please stay for refreshments. There will be tea and sandwiches on the lawn outside the hall. Thank you, everyone, for attending."

"Well, guys, that's it till September. Really going to miss you. Give us a call sometime, will you? Here's my number," says Archie and he hands Grace a piece of paper with his number on it. "Daisy, I know you've already got my number. Give us a goodbye hug." And he hugs first Daisy, then Grace. They make their way out to where the parents are chatting and drinking tea. Grace's parents have found Daisy's parents and Archie's parents are nearby too.

"Well, it was lovely chatting to you, Mr and Mrs Davies, but we really must get going now," says Grace's Dad.

"Congratulations on getting the English prize, Grace," says Mr Davies.

"Yes, and very well done to all of you for getting the House Cup and winning the Inter-House Endurance Race – sounds like it was full of drama!" says Mrs Davies. "I am sure we will see you over the holidays, Grace." Daisy and Grace have a big hug and Daisy says, "I'll be in touch soon. Till then, have a good one."

"See you soon, Daisy, and thanks for everything this term. You've really made me feel part of the Fairstone family," says Grace.

"You are family now," she says.

And with that, they make their way to their cars. "We've picked up your trunk and your holdall from the dorm, Love. So unless there's anything else you need, we're free to go," says Grace's Mum.

"No, that's everything. Let's go – I hate long goodbyes," says Grace.

"That's my girl," says Grace's Dad. And they set off for home, chatting all the way about the events of the term and congratulations from her parents for the English prize and her part in winning the House Cup.

"Sounds like you've made a fantastic start to your time at Fairstone, my dear," says her Mum. "I'm so pleased that you're happy there."

"Yes, I am Mum. So very, very happy," and she relaxes back onto the car seat, remembering back to the first time she came up the drive at the beginning of term, feeling awkward and nervous in her stiff new uniform. So much has changed since then!

Chapter 22:
Summer Holidays

Over the course of the Summer Holidays, Grace takes to riding her bike to see Nanny Watkins for her lessons in herb lore and the magical teachings of her lineage. Grace's Mum thinks that Grace is going to see her friend Daisy. Grace's Mum loves Daisy and is so pleased that Grace has made such a good friend in her first term at Fairstone.

Grace and Daisy visit each other regularly over the holidays. Grace's Dad is looking after two horses for a woman who can no longer afford their keep. So the two girls love to ride out across the fields and through the woods of the beautiful estate of farms that Grace's Dad manages.

Daisy is riding Miss Pebbles, a chestnut mare who came to Grace's Dad in a very skinny and out-of-condition state.

Under Mr Bellaport's care, she is now gleaming with health and bouncing with vigour.

Grace is riding Buccaneer – the complete opposite of Miss Pebbles, a grey roan New Forest gelding. He is young and stocky, with a tendency to put on weight if the grass is too rich, with the danger of getting laminitis. He's a naughty boy – headstrong with a great thick neck and wanting to just go all the time.

After tacking up in the lovely old-fashioned farmyard in front of Grace's house, surrounded by old stone barns with a stream-fed pond at the centre, the girls mount up and ride out up the hill behind the farmhouse. After a bit of a warm-up, they get to a wide open field that stretches uphill to some woodland on the crown of the hill.

"Shall we have a canter?" says Grace. "Bucky is raring to go and I'm having difficulty keeping him back."

"Yes, great. Let's go!" says Daisy. And they urge their steeds on – both are excited about getting to stretch their legs.

Grace sits down into the rocking motion of Bucky's canter and feels exhilaration flowing through her. With the wind in her hair, the scent of the grass and herbs in her nostrils, and Bucky eating up the ground in front of her, she has one of those moments when it feels utterly good to be alive.

Bucky soon stretches out into a gallop – he can't bear to be behind when he thinks a race is on, and Pebbles responds too, the girls laughing with the thrill of it.

They manage to slow their horses as they reach the top of the hill, ready to go into the woodland.

When everyone has their breath back, Daisy says, "Hey, Grace, do you miss Archie? Because I do. Do you think there's a way we could get to meet up with him in the hols?"

"Yes, I do miss him. We've had such adventures together,

especially going to see Nanny Watkins. Where does he live?"

"Oh, in a little village in darkest Somerset, I think," says Daisy.

"Well, my older sister, Jane, lives in Bath, which is in North Somerset. I was planning to go and stay with her soon. Would you like to come? Then maybe we could get Archie to meet up with us in Bath."

"That's a great idea! We could catch the train down from Hereford together."

"Yes, perfect! I'll talk to Jane. I'm sure she'd love to meet you."

"Brilliant. Can't wait to go. I'll get on the blower to Archie. Eee, exciting!" squeaked Daisy.

And so the following week, the two girls are on the train headed for Bath. "I have to warn you about my little niece. She's two years old and absolutely gorgeous. She's so funny, but she's a naughty little pickle – she runs rings round Jane," says Grace. "If my sis tries to tell her off, Emily just wags her chubby little finger at her and says, "No, No! I naughty!" and laughs her head off. Then everyone laughs and she totally gets away with it."

"Great, I can't wait to meet her. I love naughty little pickles!" says Daisy, and they both laugh.

The train finally pulls in to Bath Station. "My brother-in-law, Mike, should be here to meet us and take us back to their house," says Grace.

"Oh, that's kind of him," says Daisy.

"Look there he is," says Grace, indicating a big bear of a man, with a magnificent head of dark, curly hair and a neat beard. Grace waves and calls out, "Hi Mike!"

They make their way towards each other. "Hi ladies, did you have a good trip?" says Mike in a deep booming voice,

"Yes, pretty smooth. No delays for once," says Grace. "Mike, this is my friend Daisy."

"Very pleased to meet you, Daisy. I hear you go to Fairstone with Grace?" and he grasps her hand in an eye-watering handshake.

"That's right and we live quite close to each other at home, which is so cool because we get to see each other outside school too. It's been so great getting to know Grace. She's such a lovely girl," says Daisy.

"Yes, we're very fond of our Gracie," says Mike. "Thanks for showing her the ropes at the new school."

"Oh, you two are making me blush!" says Grace.

"Sorry to embarrass you, little Sis," says Mike. "Here, let me help you with your bags," and he picks them both up, as if they are as light as matchsticks. "Come on, let's get you back to our place. Jane and Emmie are looking forward to seeing you. In fact, Emmie has talked of nothing else for days now!"

They make their way out of the station to the short-stay car park out front. "Such a beautiful city," says Daisy, looking around her, as the afternoon sun bathes the golden sandstone of the houses that stretch up the hills in all directions. "Thank you so much for having me to stay. I have always wanted to visit Bath."

"You are very welcome. I hope you have a brilliant time here," says Mike as they get in the car. He dons his mirrored Ray Ban sunglasses and looks like a singer from the Bee Gees.

It's a short journey along the Bristol Road to Oldfield Park, where Mike, Jane and Emily live. Mike drives up a steep hill and parks outside a pretty terraced house made of the same golden sandstone, with a neat hedge to the front garden and colourful hanging baskets on either side of the door. He gets the luggage out of the car and they make their way to the front door, which opens just as they get to it.

Jane is there, holding Emily on her hip, waiting to greet them. Mike kisses Jane and Emily as he goes in with the bags. "Gwacie!" exclaims Emily. "Down, down!" she implores her Mum and then rushes out to clasp Grace around the knees. "I wuv you, I wuv you!" she says.

Grace strokes her curly head and says, "I wuv you too, Emmie."

Jane, laughing, says, "Hiya, Sis, and lovely to meet you, Daisy. Come on in, you're very welcome."

"Wow, you two are SO different!" says Daisy. "I wouldn't have known you are sisters." Dark-haired, dark-eyed and petite, at first glance Jane doesn't resemble Grace at all. It's not until later that Daisy begins to notice similarities in their mannerisms, their voices and a certain look around their eyes.

As they follow Emily back into the house, Jane says in a quiet, pleading voice, "We're trying to potty train her. Whatever she does, do NOT laugh at her. She needs to know it is serious business and not a toy."

Now she has an audience, Emily goes straight to the cupboard and gets out her bright red, shiny potty. She puts it on her head, and then starts singing, "The piggies are waiting. They're waiting for you. Down at the NatWest, they say, 'How do you do?' They say, 'How do you do?'" It's a song she has learned from an advert on the TV. She dances around in a circle, her fat shiny ringlet curls bouncing up and down as she bobs at the knees.

Daisy says, "Well, aren't you the most adorable little girl I've ever met?! And I love your song and dance. But you know, missy, it's probably best not to put that potty on your head. We don't want any accidents when you've done your business in it, do we?!"

Emily giggles and takes the potty off her head. Then she rushes up to Daisy and throws her arms around her. "You're nice. I wuv you!"

"Oh, you're nice and I wuv you too," says Daisy.

"Well done, Daisy. I was really struggling not to laugh. You've obviously got a knack with little ones," says Grace.

"Oh, I've had plenty of practice. I've got lots of little nieces and nephews – all naughty little pickles too. My brother and sister are both older than me with five kids between them. Aunty Daisy often has to babysit."

"Oh great," says Jane. "Can we book you to babysit this little bundle of mischief sometime? Oh, now where's she gone?"

From the kitchen, they can hear the crinkling of wrappers and contented sounds of munching and Emily saying to herself, "Ooh, lucky girl!" They all rush in to see Emily sitting on the floor in front of the fridge, just polishing off the last in a pack of five KitKats, her chubby cheeks all smeared with chocolate.

"Oh my goodness, have you eaten all of those? You won't have any room for your tea," says Jane.

"Yes, yummy. Lucky girl!" she beams at them with twinkling brown eyes. Again, Daisy and Grace both put their hands over their mouths to stop themselves laughing.

"I hid those in the fridge, thinking she wouldn't find them in there. Looks like I'll have to find another hiding place!" says Jane.

"Wow, she is a bundle of mischief, isn't she?" says Daisy.

"Yes, she is!" says Jane.

The next morning after breakfast, Jane says, "Anyhow, I expect you girls want to get into town to meet your friend – Archie, isn't it?"

"Yes, we're going to meet him at the bus station," says Grace.

"You know which bus to get into town, don't you, Gracie?" says Jane.

"Yes, see you later, Sis," The two girls say their goodbyes to little Emily and walk down to Moreland Road, past rows of quaint terraced houses, with neat little front gardens, many with hanging baskets full of colourful flowers, just like Jane and Mike's.

From there, they catch a bus into town to meet Archie at the bus station. "Gosh, I just can't get over what a beautiful city it is," says Daisy. "I love how all the houses are made of the same golden stone. It seems to glow in the sunshine."

"I suppose I've been coming here for so long that I kind of take it for granted. But yes, as cities go, it's very beautiful. I'm glad my sister lives here and I get to stay regularly in the school holidays. I miss my Somerset friends, so this means I get a chance to meet up with them again."

"That's cool, but I hope you feel at home at Fairstone now. You're like family already," says Daisy.

"I'm loving it. You and Archie have made my first term so much fun. And Charlie, in her own way, too. Hopefully, I'll get a bit better at hockey next term and maybe even make the First Team," says Grace.

"Yes, I'm sure you will. We've all been playing since we were little squibs, but you seem to be picking it up really quickly. And you've got so much stamina and fitness. You'd make a really good winger. If you'd like, I can ask Charlie if she could put in a word to Mr Aveen. He listens to her – she's his star player," says Daisy.

"Oh gosh, would you? That would be so brilliant, thank you!" says Grace.

The bus is now pulling into the bus station. "Look, there he is!" squeaks Daisy. Grace looks out of the bus to see Archie leaning casually against the bus station wall. She thinks somehow he looks extra tall in his faded blue jeans and desert boots, with an aqua coloured surfer's t-shirt. Perhaps he's grown over the holidays? The sun is glowing off his unruly curls, which now have streaks of gold in them from the summer sun.

The girls jump off the bus and go to meet him. "Hey, Arch, how's it going?" says Daisy.

"Oh, hey girls! Great to see you. Where shall we head first?"

"I know a lovely café on Pulteney Bridge with a terrace that overlooks the weir," says Grace.

"Sounds perfect. Lead the way," says Archie.

At the café, they find a table outside, which overlooks the Parade Gardens and the river. The sound of the water rushing over the weir percolates up to their ears and gives a fresh feeling to the air, a bit like the ocean breeze at the coast.

"Perfect spot. Well-chosen, Gracie," says Archie. And they order coffee and pain au chocolat. "What's the news then, girls? Have you seen anything of Nanny Watkins over the hols? I have to say, I'm dying to see her again – what a character she is! And Ahbleza too."

"Grace has been going to her for lessons in herbal medicine, haven't you, Grace?" says Daisy.

"Ooh, tell me more!" says Archie.

"Yes, I cycle over on my bike once a week and she teaches me all about the healing properties of the different plants and herbs," says Grace.

Archie gives Grace a sideways look. "You're not telling us everything, are you Grace? There's something else, isn't there? Come on, spill!" he says.

Putting her cappuccino down, Grace shifts uncomfortably

in her seat and says, "Well, yes, there is more, but I'm not sure how to tell you. It sounds a bit weird when I try to put it into words."

"We already know you're the nicest kind of weirdo, Grace," says Archie. "Wow, we've all seen and done some pretty weird things this last term. It comes with the territory when you're talking about Nanny Watkins. So don't be shy, you won't shock us."

There's a pause while Grace thinks about this. The sound of children's laughter rises up from the gardens below. "OK, I'll tell you. I guess I've been busy hiding it from my parents, because it would definitely weird them out – I think it's probably against their religious beliefs. So, we've been doing lots of journeying and she's been teaching me a thing called psychopomp."

"Psychopomp? What on earth's that?" says Daisy. "You haven't told me about this before, you naughty!"

"Well, you know sometimes when someone dies, their soul doesn't pass over? It could be because they're staying to be near someone they love who is still here, or sometimes they can get lost if their death is very sudden and a shock, like in a car accident, and they weren't ready to go. So psychopomp is a way of helping their soul to pass over, so they can go back to heaven ready for the next part of their soul's journey," says Grace.

"Oh, I get it – she wants you to help Jonnie pass over. And she can't do it herself because she's too emotionally attached to him," says Archie.

"Yes, bingo! That's exactly right," says Grace."

Archie blows out a big sigh of air and says, "Wow, that's a big responsibility for you! Are you up for it?"

"Goodness Gracie, that sounds terrifying!" says Daisy.

"Yes, it is scary, Daisy. Nanny admits that she nearly wet

her pants the first time she did it. But that was because no-one showed her what to do and she had to figure it out for herself. But we've run through it lots of times. I know exactly what to do and it feels like the right thing. After all, it's lovely Jonnie – who's always been so kind to me – and not some stranger."

"You're right, Grace. It sounds like the kindest thing for Jonnie, and for Nanny. They both need to let go of each other," says Daisy. "But wow, it's going to be hard for them. We saw how upset she got when we talked about Jonnie."

"Yes, but she's been getting a lot of healing from Ahbleza. I think she's ready now."

"Well, good on you, Grace. You're the girl for the job," says Archie, clapping her on the back of her shoulder. "Wow, that is big news," he mutters half to himself. "Well, come on guys, let's lighten things up a bit. What else you got?"

"Oh well, if you want to lighten things up, I've got to tell you about Grace's cute little niece, Emily. What a little rascal she is..." and Daisy tells Archie about the potty on the head dance and how she munched all the KitKats.

He laughs his head off, saying, "Well, she sounds like a character. Hope I get to meet her sometime!"

They spend the rest of the day shopping, wandering in the Parade Gardens, where they have an ice cream, and visiting the Roman Baths.

"OK, time to go," says Archie, looking at his watch. "My Dad is going to pick me up at the bus station, so we can wander back that way together and you can catch the bus back to your sister's."

At the bus station, it's hugs all round. "What a brilliant day. Going to miss you guys for the rest of the hols. Give us a phone call soon," says Archie. "Here's my Dad."

An even taller man than Archie gets out of a beaten-up

old Mercedes and greets the girls. "Hello Daisy. And you must be Grace – pleased to meet you," he says, holding out his hand. "I've heard so much about you! Well done for beating that stinker, Anne Smith, in the mark order! It's about time someone took her down a peg. I know Archie's been trying. Anyhow Arch, we better make a move. Your mother's got the supper on."

They wave him off and head back to Jane's for supper before heading home the following day on the train.

Autumn Term

Image based on an original pen and ink of Bedstone College by J Hibbs

Chapter 23:
Friends Reunited

"Hey guys, isn't it cool we're sharing a dorm again?" says Charlie, as she begins to unpack her luggage.

"Yes, so cool – and we're back in the same dorm too. I love this room," says Daisy, also unpacking.

"I'm really happy to be back with you two. Don't we make a great team?!" says Grace.

"Talking of teams, Grace, shall we try and get you in the First Team for hockey? You have amazing stamina – you did so well in the Inter-House Endurance Race. I'd love to have you as my right wing girl. The three of us could practise some set moves with Daisy passing you the ball, you running it up the wing and then I'd be ready just to pop it in the goal.

We can practice your ball control skills whenever you've got some free time," says Charlie.

"I'd like that very much," says Grace, laughing. Daisy is laughing too.

"What's so funny?" says Charlie.

"It's so kind of you, Charlie, but it sounds like you've spent your whole hols thinking about hockey and planning how we can win more games!" says Daisy.

"Well, yes, quite a bit of it. Apart from the time I spent helping me Dad on the farm and the day we all met up at Long Town Show – which was ace by the way. Right then, enough taking the mickey out of me. Let's go and see what the lads have been up to."

"Yes, let's," says Daisy. They make their ways down to the school yard, to find Archie, Tom, Burnley and Calum standing in a huddle, hands in trouser pockets, all trying to out do each other with the best stories of their holiday adventures.

"Hey fellas, what's new?" Charlie calls out in a booming voice. They all look round as the girls join them.

"Wotcha Charlie! Hello Daisy and Grace," says Burnley.

"Oh great, my favourite girls are all here! Give us a hug," says Archie, starting with Daisy, then Charlie, then Grace.

The other boys look a bit sheepish at the hug fest. Calum's muttering about Archie being a big nancy, but Tom manages to say, "Great to see you again, girls. Hope you all had good hols?"

"Yes, thanks, Tom," says Grace, giving him a shy smile. "We went to stay with my sister in Bath, didn't we, Daisy. And we met up with Archie too."

"Did you? Why haven't you told us about that then, Archie?" says Calum.

"Oh, just hadn't got onto that yet," says Archie.

"Well, I can't believe we're all in 5th Form now!" says

Daisy, sensing some discomfort and quickly changing the subject. "'O' Levels this year. Do we all feel ready for them?"

"Yes, can't wait!" says Archie with a note of sarcasm.

"Hey, shall we check out our new form room?" says Charlie. "Bagsy a desk by the window."

"Oh yeah, me too," says Calum. They all make their way to the form room at the end of the corridor, formerly occupied by Darius, James and Phil's class. Walking past their old Form 4 room feels very strange.

"Isn't it weird they're not here anymore?" says Daisy.

"Your lover boy's come back in 6th Form now," says Charlie, and they all laugh, to Daisy's great embarrassment.

"I remember my first day, last term. I came down here to check out our form room and heard Darius, James and Phil singing 'Ghost Town'. They were brilliant – it was really eerie," says Grace.

"Yes, they were brilliant – those boys should form a band," says Tom.

"Aye, they were reet good," says Burnley. "I luvved it when Darius did Freddie Mercury. 'Ee 'ad all the moves." They all agree with Burnley.

"Anyone up for a spot of tea?" says Archie, looking at his watch.

As they join the tea queue, who should come out to greet them but Darius. It was as if he had been waiting for Daisy.

"Hi guys, 5th Formers now, eh?" says Darius.

"Yes mate, we were just talking about you singing 'Ghost Town' with James and Phil, and how good your Freddie Mercury impressions were," says Tom.

"Aw, thanks guys, but I've lost my band mates now. They didn't come back for 6th Form. Hey, there's my beautiful Daisy! How are you my love?" he says, putting his arm round her shoulders. "I remember you've got a lovely singing voice.

Fancy forming a duo together?"

All the others chime in with, "Yes Daisy – go on!" "You'd make a lovely couple." "We'd love to hear you sing together!" etc, etc.

"I'll think about it, Darius," says Daisy.

"OK, I'll wait eagerly for your reply," says Darius, winking at her and then doing his best swagger back to the 6th Form studies.

There were murmurs of, "Whey hey, you're in there, Daisy!"

And she quickly changes the subject again, saying, "Come on guys, let's get some tea. I'm starving!"

"Yes, but don't get too excited," says Archie. "Have you forgotten how dire the food is here? Looks like it might be cardboard lasagne tonight, served by the lovely Rhino Woman and Mouse Woman. But on the positive side, the lovely Ethel may have saved some bottoms for her favourite Tom." It is Tom's turn to blush, as they all laugh at his expense.

"Time you found another girlfriend," jibes Calum, elbowing Tom in the ribs, "One your own age!" Archie and Daisy both clock Tom's swift glance at Grace and then away as he realises he's been spotted.

After tea, Archie suggests they all go and reacquaint themselves with the Rec. "Anyone for a game of pool and a lukewarm 'hot' chocolate from the MaxPax machine?" he says.

"Yes, why not? It's a tradition now," says Tom.

"Yeah, can't wait to thrash you at pool!" says Charlie.

On the way to the Rec, Archie leans in towards Grace and Daisy and says quietly, "We should plan a visit to see Nanny Watkins soon."

"Yes, defo! Can't wait to see her again," says Daisy and she whispers, "I'm dying to give Ahbleza a big hug too."

"I've seen quite a bit of her over the hols, but it would be great for the three amigos to go together again. I feel there's more adventure brewing," says Grace. "I'll bet we start getting more crazy dreams again, now that we're back together."

"Yes, sounds about right," says Archie. "How about Saturday afternoon? Don't think we have any matches then. If the weather's nice, we could go the long way round and walk through Paradise Wood, to make a change from using the portal."

"Yes, that sounds like a great idea," says Daisy.

"I'll send a message to Nanny to let her know we're coming. Maybe she'll make us a cake if she knows," says Grace.

"Oh, how are you going to do that then?" says Archie.

Grace taps the side of her nose and says cryptically, "Oh, I have my ways."

Daisy blurts, "I bet she's going to send her Owl messenger. Nanny speaks fluent Owl!"

"Thanks, Daiz – now my secret's out!" says Grace.

"Oops, sorry, Grace. I didn't realise it was a secret."

By now, they are nearing the Rec, so they go in and have a raucous evening of pool and hot chocolate. As she predicted, Charlie beats everyone at pool and the boys are miffed to be beaten by a girl.

Chapter 24:
The Day Cook Fell Down the Stairs

The bell for the lunch break rings and Archie and Grace make their way into the main corridor to get in the lunch queue. At the other end of the corridor, they can see Simon Foster, the new Head Boy, standing at the bottom of the stairs looking up. Simon is one of life's natural heroes. You couldn't wish to meet a kinder, more noble sort of person. He would help anybody. This personality trait, coupled with the fact that he is the Captain of the rugby team, has been a big factor in his being made Head Boy.

But today, something looks odd about him to Grace and Archie. It dawns on Grace that usually this area is well lit by the light which streams in from the landing window, but for some reason, he is in shadow. They can both sense something is wrong. Grace has that feeling in the pit of her stomach that she gets when something bad is about to happen. And Simon is staring intently up with a look of concern on his face.

Earlier, at break time, Daisy had told her that she'd seen Cook lumbering up the stairs to the first floor. It is a rare occurrence to see Cook out of the kitchen. Her gargantuan size means that walking anywhere is very taxing for her and no-one has ever seen her attempting the stairs before. Daisy assumed that there was something important that she had to speak to Boss about. They couldn't think why else she would have bothered to drag herself up there.

As Archie and Grace walk down the corridor, it soon becomes obvious why Simon is in shadow. Cook is making her slow, breathy return journey down the stairs. A sudden look of horror comes over Simon's face. It must have taxed all of Cook's energy to haul herself up the stairs because now she stumbles and falls. Down she comes like a tsunami of billowing floral cotton and surgical support stockings, whipping up a great wind around her as she gains speed and momentum.

Simon's first instinct is to hold out his arms to try and save her. As she hurtles towards him, Grace can see the realisation dawn on him that there is nothing he can do to save her and that it would be much better for his own health to get out of the way. But it is too late to take evasive action and her mammoth bulk hits him, like no rugby tackle he has ever experienced before, toppling him to the ground. A sickening snapping sound ricochets around the corridor walls as his outstretched arm is broken.

Archie and Grace are on the scene in moments and trying to help Cook up off Simon. But they can't budge her. "Are you OK, Cook?" Grace asks.

"Oh, yes, dear. My fall was broken by this lovely, helpful

young man. I'm not hurt at all, apart from my pride!" A muffled sob of pain comes from beneath the voluminous drapes of fabric of Cook's dress.

"Quick, Archie, run to the 6th Form studies and get all the strongest people down here as fast as you can. We've got to get Cook up before Simon suffocates," Grace says. "It's OK, Cook, we'll help you back on your feet. And Simon, we'll have you out of there in no time," says Grace, trying to sound convincing. He sees her surrounded in golden sunlight and in his oxygen-deprived state, he thinks an angel has come to save him.

A herd of 6th Formers comes stampeding down the corridor. Lead out by the strapping frame of Curly Jones (named for his shock of auburn curls), all of the rugby team and several other able-bodied people come running when they hear of their hero's plight. They soon have Cook back on her feet again and heading for the kitchen for a restorative cup of tea. She is miraculously unscathed. Simon, on the other hand, has had better days. "Let's get him to Nurse Bernie's room," says his friend Pete.

"Oh please, no! She'll only try to rub Bonjela on my arm. That's her answer to everything. Call an ambulance. I need to go to Casualty to get my arm in plaster. And they should probably check Cook out too."

"Oh, you're right mate, it is hanging at a strange angle!" says Pete. "You're never going to live this one down. What were you thinking? I'd have run the other way! This puts an end to you leading the team for the Inter-Schools Under 19s rugby final. How are we going to manage without our captain?"

"I don't know. I was just trying to do the right thing. I acted on impulse. But it's a disaster – I've only been Head Boy for a day and now I've got a broken arm. How am I going to captain anything?"

"Yeah, you're just too nice, mate!" says Curly.

"I have an idea," says Grace. "Curly, do you think you could carry Simon to Nanny Watkins' house in the woods? It's just past Farmer Morgan's land. They call her the bone setter. She's brilliant at setting broken bones and healing things like this in double quick time. You might still have a chance of captaining the team in the tournament. And she makes really good pies too," this directed at Curly, who looks like he enjoys a good pie.

"I've heard the locals talk about Betty the Bonesetter. She sounds a bit of a miracle worker," says Pete. "Simon, are you up for it?"

"I'll give it a go, as long as you promise to get me to Casualty if it doesn't work."

"What d'you reckon Pete? Can we carry him between us?" says Curly.

"Yeah, if we can rig up some kind of a stretcher, we could do it. But we better get him out of sight before the teachers notice the commotion. They'll want to take him to Casualty straight away. Grace, meet us at the back of the studies in five minutes to show us the way to Nanny Watkins' place."

"OK, will do," says Grace.

"I'm coming too," says Archie. "They may need some help carrying Simon."

The boys reappear from the back of the studies with an old army blanket wrapped around two brooms to make a stretcher, with a very quiet and white-faced Simon lying on it.

"Gosh, he looks as if he's going into shock," says Grace. "Mind if I do a quick thing to help him out of it?" she says to Pete and Curly.

"Not sure what you mean, but if it's quick and will help

him, go ahead," says Pete.

Grace does the V-spread technique on Simon's arm, just as she has seen Nanny do. He lets out a whimper and some tears roll down his face, but the colour and life seem to come back into him too.

"Whoa, look at that! You brought him back to life," says Curly.

"Let's get going then," says Pete.

"We'll have to go across Morgan's land – it's the quickest way, but we'll need to set our intention not to get caught, or we're in big trouble," says Grace. "OK everyone, I want you to picture a shield of invisibility around us, so we aren't seen."

Archie sees the look of puzzlement on the boys faces and says, "I know it sounds a bit weird, but just pretend you're in Lord of the Rings or something and do what she says – always seems to work."

"OK, we'll give it a try," says Pete and they set off for Nanny Watkins' cottage, holding the blanket tightly to the brooms.

With a lot of wincing from Simon and a few calls of, "Slow down a bit, lads – all this bumping up and down is agony on my arm," they arrive at Nanny's cottage.

Archie calls out, "Nanny, are you there? We have an injured man who needs help."

"I'll be right there!" shouts Nanny from the back. Grace gets the impression she's with Ahbleza, and is telling him to go hide.

Nanny bustles out of her front door, saying, "Oh my goodness, gentlemen! What's happened here?"

Archie relates the tale of the fall of Cook and how Simon tried to save her, which led to his arm being broken.

Nanny says, "Well, what a misadventure!" She gives Grace and Archie one of her looks that has them stifling back giggles, but says kindly to Simon, "You're a brave young man, and you're lucky it's just your arm. You're sure your ribs are OK?"

"Yes, Mrs Watkins. It's only my arm that's in pain."

"OK, let's have a look then, shall we?" as she begins to gently examine Simon's arm. "Grace, you know the drill – comfrey tea and a poultice, but I also think he needs some white willow bark for the pain. Oh, and some lavender oil for calming. Archie, get a chair for Simon. And you can be my assistant – he's a big lad and it'll take a bit of force to reset that bone."

Archie comes back with a chair and Pete and Curly get him onto it. First, Nanny does some V-spreading to take more of the shock and pain out of Simon's arm. Grace comes back with the willow bark tea, which Simon drinks gratefully, and the lavender oil, which Nanny drops gently onto his arm and wafts under his nose.

"Oh my goodness, Mrs W, I'm feeling better already. The pain's almost gone," says Simon.

"Good, good lad. But you're going to have to be brave when we re-set the bone. The willow bark and lavender will help, but it will still be..." Nanny searches for the right word, "...uncomfortable." She carries on with the V-spreading for a few minutes to let the willow bark take effect. She's concentrating hard and to Grace's mind, it looks as if she is sending sparkling light into Simon's arm and taking out a big lump of pain, which she is alchemising with the light. "Right, are you ready now, lad?" she says.

"Ready as I'll ever be. Just carry on, Mrs W," says Simon.

"Right, you two come and hold onto his shoulders," Nanny says to Pete and Curly. Archie, you're going to help me pull the arm into place. I'll direct the force, but if you can grab my forearms and put extra oomph into the pull, that'll help," says Nanny.

"Righto Nanny. Like this?" says Archie and stands behind Nanny, gripping her forearms just below the elbows."

"Perfect," says Nanny, taking hold of Simon's arm. "Right, on the count of three – one, two, three, pull!" Nanny gives a yank and a twist and Simon's arm seems to magically snap back into place.

He yells out an expletive and then says, "Sorry for my language, Mrs W."

"No need to apologise, lad – totally understandable!" Grace comes back with the comfrey tea and a poultice.

"We'll put the poultice on and then splint it. You should be OK in a couple of days," says Nanny.

Curly asks the burning question, "Can he still play rugby, Miss? He's captain of our team."

"Well, maybe just coach from the sidelines for the next couple of matches and just go easy with it for a couple of weeks – no going in for hard tackles!" says Nanny. "Grace can give you some more healing. I'll give you some comfrey tea to take back with you. It's called knit-bone and it's marvellous for healing breaks up quickly."

"Wow, you're a star, Mrs W," says Simon. "I can't believe how quickly it's healing. How can I thank you?"

"You're very welcome, my lad. It's my gift and I love to help out," says Nanny. "Right, you better get back to school before anyone misses you."

They set off back to school with a reminder from Grace to put their invisibility shields up. The lads are all a bit stunned by Nanny's magic healing skills. They arrive back to school without getting caught by Morgan.

Chapter 25:
Studded on the Rugby Field

It's Wednesday afternoon and it's Match Day – the first rugby match of the new term. It's a home game against Fairstone's arch rivals, the Uptonians.

Fairstone is at a disadvantage. They are without their captain, Simon Foster, on the field. He is coaching from the sidelines, having told Nurse Bernie that he sprained his arm in the practice session yesterday. She has put his arm in a sling and signed him off games for two weeks, which is exactly what he wanted. That way, he will be back fully in action with plenty of the term's matches still to play for.

The girls don't have a match today, so they've been asked to go and watch the boys play and cheer them on from the sidelines.

It's a cooler day today. There's a sharp wind and heavy clouds are scudding across the sky. "Looks like rain," says Charlie to Simon.

"I hope it will hold off till the end of the match," says Simon.

"How's that arm now?" she asks. He gives her a look, as if trying to gauge how much she knows about the healing from Nanny Watkins.

"It's OK, Simon. Charlie knows about Nanny and she won't blab about it," says Daisy, smiling up at him.

"Oh cool. Yes, it's actually really good now. The sling is just for show. But Nanny advised me to stay out of the first couple of matches just to be double sure it's healed OK. I should be back in action soon. But now we have to count on Darius and the lads to win this one. They're a really good team even without me. And it's great to see lads like Archie, Tom and Burnley have grown so much over the holidays. I think we've got this one. But keep cheering them on, girls."

Daisy says, "You'll be absolutely fine, Simon. Nanny mended my broken leg in the Inter-House Endurance Race. It felt a bit weird for the first couple of days, but after a week it was completely back to normal – good enough to play netball."

"Is that so?" says Simon. "Very good to know. Thank you, Daisy. I always wondered why Archie had to carry you over the finish line. Well, well, she is an amazing healer, isn't she?"

The match is about to start. The referee flips a coin and Fairstone win the toss. Burnley kicks the ball beautifully from the halfway line, which is skilfully caught by Archie. Archie passes the ball to Calum, who passes to Tom and now to Darius in a move they have practised many times. Darius surges forward, fending off a tackle from a large Uptonian and dives over the try line. He's scored the first try for

Fairstone and everyone is cheering.

Burnley converts the try with a perfect kick over the bar and Fairstone now have 7 points on the board.

But the Uptonians are seething and Darius is a marked man. They're known to play dirty and now their ire is up. In the first scrum of the game, one of the Uptonians stamps on Darius and one of his boot studs goes right through the fleshy part of the side of Darius' nose.

Poor Darius staggers out with blood pouring down his face. "Ref, they're playing dirty. Look what they've done to me," shouts Darius. The referee blows the whistle for injury time. Darius runs past Daisy to get to the first aider. "Hey Daiz, do I look macho enough for you now?" he says.

"Oh my goodness, Darius, you poor sausage. We must get you to Nanny Watkins for some treatment," says Daisy.

"No, my love, I'm going to play on. These guys are going down after that! We're already short of our hero, Simon. We can't let them win now."

"That's the spirit, Darius," says Simon. "But don't do anything stupid. Just win the game fair and square, eh?"

"You got it, boss," says Darius and he goes to get patched up by the first aider before returning to the field. They see Darius gesturing at the guy that he thinks studded him, telling him in sign language, "I've got my eye on you!"

The referee awards a penalty to Fairstone, which Burnley deftly kicks over the bar again. Three more points on the board for Fairstone and cheers all round.

"Ahem, 'poor sausage'? What kind of a hero's name is that, Daisy?" says Simon.

"Oh, sorry. Perhaps I should have said 'brave soldier' or something instead?" says Daisy, mortified to be told off by the Head Boy.

And then he laughs. "I was only joking, Daisy," he says.

In the second half, the Fairstone lads are tiring, having played their hearts out in the first half against brutal opposition from Upton. Darius is not the only one to be injured by their dirty play, but the Uptonians are very clever at hiding it and the referee hasn't actually seen any of it first-hand.

Fairstone concede a try and a conversion to Upton. "Come on lads, dig deep. You're still in the lead. Let's keep it that way," shouts Simon.

Play goes back and forth between the two teams with no further score until a few minutes before full time. Tom gets possession of the ball and in a stroke of genius, gives it a massive kick to Archie at the far end of the pitch. Archie skilfully catches the ball and within a few strides, he dives over the try line for another score. Once again, Burnley does his magic and converts the try.

The whistle goes for full time and Fairstone are the winners with 17 points to 7. A huge cheer goes up. The Fairstone team gallantly go to shake hands with the sullen-faced Uptonians.

As Burnley comes off the pitch, Charlie grabs him in a big squeeze, tousling his curly hair and saying, "Ooh, you're me little hero!" Burnley looks terrified and everyone laughs.

Grace calls Darius over, "If you won't go to Nanny Watkins, I can help you with that injury. Come and find me after your shower and I'll give you some treatment."

"But won't I look more macho for Daisy with a nice scar?" says Darius.

"No, you idiot. I'm sure she'll fancy you more without a scar," says Simon. "And this girl's good. She gave me some treatment before I got to Mrs. Watkins' house. It completely took the pain away. So my advice, as your captain, is to take her up on her offer, and get yourself fit and injury-free for the next match."

"Yes, Darius. He's right. I think you should come and see Grace later. I can help too if it'll encourage you to come," says Daisy.

"Oh, how can I resist now, Daisy? Will you hold my hand while she's doing the painful stuff?"

"Of course," says Daisy. And Darius gets that dreamy look on his face.

"Come on lads. Can you please get Darius down to school and through the showers, ready for his treatment? You all played magnificently today. I'm really proud of you – what a win, under difficult circumstances!" says Simon. Curly Jones, Ramesh and Pete escort Darius away. And everyone walks back to school.

Later, there's a knock at the girls' common room window, downstairs at Fairstone House. It's Darius. Grace and Daisy check that no-one else is around, then let him in quietly through the back door.

"Hi Darius. Come on in," says Daisy.

"Hey Darius. How are you feeling?" says Grace.

"Evening ladies – a bit sore, but I'll live. I'm a brave soldier."

"Yes, you are a brave soldier. But now let Grace work her magic on you and get you better," says Daisy.

Grace invites Darius to sit in an old vinyl padded chair with wooden arms. The common room is cosy but scruffy with a midge-modge of different second-hand furniture – old velour-covered armchairs, taller wing-backed chairs and cushions everywhere, including some floor cushions and a large orange bean bag. The girls have put up posters of their favourite pop heroes on the walls. An inviting smell of coffee and slightly burnt toast fills the air.

Grace pours boiling water over the herbs she has

prepared to bathe Darius' wound. The scents of lavender, chamomile, sage and calendula begin to edge out the burnt toast smell.

"We'll let that cool while I do some healing on your wound, Darius. I'll be bringing out the shock and pain, so be prepared for it to get a bit worse before it gets better. This is the bit where you might want to hold Daisy's hand," says Grace.

"Yes, please," says Darius. Daisy pulls up a floor cushion and sits next to the chair. She takes Darius' hand and he lets out a big sigh. Grace notices that around the stud hole, Darius' face has begun to swell and bruise. She begins to V-spread his wound.

Darius lets out an "aargh!" and a tear rolls down his face. "Oh, sorry to be a nancy," he says.

"Don't worry. It's a natural reaction to let the pain out. I'd be more worried that the treatment wasn't working if you didn't react," says Grace. "There, look Daisy – the swelling's going right down."

"Oh yes. She's working her magic, Darius. It looks so much better already," says Daisy.

"OK, I think we're done here. Let's bathe the wound and I've got some of Nanny's special healing ointment to put on afterwards."

Grace pours half the liquid into a cleaned-out jam jar and uses the rest to bathe the wound, swabbing it with clean cotton wool balls. "Sorry if this stings a bit," she says.

"Actually, it doesn't. You've worked some kind of miracle and the pain has gone," says Darius.

"Great, then I can stop worrying about hurting you when I put the ointment on," says Grace. "It's very mild – calendula, chamomile, lavender, beeswax and honey. All from Nanny's garden." She scoops a bit out of a little jar and smears it over the wound.

"Oh my gosh, thank you so much, Grace, and Daisy too," says Darius. "I feel much better."

"You are so welcome," says Grace. "Here, take this jar of the herb infusion. Use it to bathe the wound twice a day and put a little ointment on it until it's healed. And here, take some cotton wool balls to bathe it." She hands him a little bag with everything in.

"Right, I better get going before I get caught in here," says Darius. "Thank you again." And he kisses Daisy's hand, before leaping out of the chair and dashing away.

Chapter 26:
Lion Roars a Warning

It's Friday morning and Archie, Daisy and Grace are sitting at breakfast together.

"I so love these farty eggs and sweaty toast," says Archie. "I've missed them SO much over the holidays."

"You lie, Archie McBride!" says Daisy.

"Yes, I was joking, of course!" says Archie.

"Guys, on a more serious note, I had a really disturbing dream last night and I was wondering if either of you did? And whether we should bring our trip to see Nanny forward to today?" says Grace.

"Well, let's hear the dream then," says Archie. "We can do the Lightning Dreamwork on it and decide after that. So tell us the dream. Make it into a juicy story and give us the title for it."

"My title for the dream is *Ahbleza is in Grave Danger*," says Grace.

"Oh my gosh!" says Daisy, putting her hand over her mouth. "Sorry to interrupt – just a bit of a shock – carry on."

"So I was just coming half-awake this morning and Regulus' giant head is right there in my face. He's saying, 'Ahbleza is in great danger. He needs your help right away.' And he shows me some images. I saw the three of us in the woods somewhere, watching from the sidelines as something unfolded. Ahbleza came into a clearing and we noticed some men crouching in the bushes, watching him. I got a really bad feeling from them and saw that they had rifles. Ahbleza seemed totally unaware of the men who were about to shoot him. Then I see awful images of hunting trophies – stuffed animal heads – mounted on a wall, including lions and a beautiful white horse, just like Ahbleza," says Grace.

"Oh my gosh! Tell us how you felt after the dream?" says Daisy.

"I felt awful – shocked and sick to the pit of my stomach, and a feeling that we need to do something fast," says Grace.

"Tell us what you recognise from this dream in your everyday life, and do you think this could possibly come true in the future?" says Archie.

"Well, obviously I recognise Regulus as the animal guide that has come to me many times before. And Ahbleza, the beautiful horse – we've all met him. The clearing in the forest seemed familiar. It could be somewhere in Paradise Wood. The men with rifles – one of them I didn't recognise, but the other one could have been Farmer Morgan. And I hate to say that I recognised the white horse trophy as Ahbleza. I'm afraid that this could definitely come true in the future, if we don't do something quickly," says Grace.

"Look back inside the dream. Are there any other details

that could help us work out the time or place when this could happen?" says Archie.

"It was misty and cold and felt very early in the morning – just as dawn was breaking. And as I said, it felt like somewhere in Paradise Wood."

"What would you like to know about this dream?" says Daisy.

"How we can stop it happening!" says Grace.

"Would you like some feedback on your dream?" says Archie.

"Yes please!" says Grace.

"If this were my dream – and I think it is because as you were telling us about it, I had flashes about a half-remembered dream from this morning that had faded," says Archie.

"Yes, me too!" says Daisy.

"Well, if it were my dream, I would go to Nanny Watkins as soon as possible and ask her advice about how to stop this from happening," says Archie.

"Yes, that's what I would do too," says Daisy. "We could do a quick trip through the portal this afternoon when everyone's in Ludlow."

"Yes, let's do that," says Grace.

The hours drag by until they get a chance to use the portal. They wait till no-one is around and then stand in front of the Calendar Window, calling in Regulus and waking up Old Father Time.

"Please take us to Nanny Watkins' cottage in Paradise Woods. And when we're done, please bring us back in the blink of an eye, so that no-one notices that we've been gone," says Archie.

"We ask this with the humblest of hearts, with pure

intention and for the highest good of all," adds Grace.

"Oh, definitely that too," says Archie.

Regulus is with them and Old Father Time comes to life and winks at them. "It is granted. Let's go, Dear Ones," says Regulus.

"Let's hold hands," says Daisy. They clasp hands and step into the sparkling tunnel which has appeared in front of them. And whoosh! They are in Nanny's garden.

Nanny is picking some herbs. She looks up and says, "Oh, you're a day early! Good job I made a cake this morning – I think I knew it in me bones."

"Sorry Nanny. Something urgent has come up," says Grace.

"Yes, yes. It feels like that," she says. "Right, someone get the kettle on and let's have some of that cake, while you tell me all about it."

The weather is still good at this time of early September, so they have their tea and cake in the garden.

"Well, come on then. Tell me what's up?" says Nanny.

"Grace has had one of her dreams," says Archie. "It's a pretty upsetting one and we want to know what we can do to stop it from happening."

"OK Grace, go ahead and tell me the dream, with its title," says Nanny. Grace tells her the dream just as she told Archie and Daisy, including the 'reality check' and her feeling that it was imminently about to happen in real life.

"I see, I see," says Nanny. "I think you're right. I think there's a strong chance that this is likely to happen. And I think you've seen these bad men before, haven't you? What is good to know is that you didn't actually see the bad men shoot and kill Ahbleza. So that gives me hope that it can be avoided.

My advice would be for us all to picture Ahbleza in our

minds – to see him protected and well. To see the bad men stopped in their tracks and running away with their tails between their legs. We can do some drumming and journey to ask Regulus for his advice on what to do too."

"That sounds like a great idea," says Archie.

"OK, has everyone finished their tea and cake? Right, let's get on with it then. I'll go and get me drum." Nanny sets up her drumming circle and begins to drum. They sit and set their intention to call in Regulus and ask his advice on how to protect Ahbleza from the danger of being shot by the trophy hunters.

In a blaze of light, Regulus appears in the centre of the circle. He is huge and magnificent. "You called, and I am here," he says in his deep, resonant voice. "Find the place that Grace saw in her dream. Call me in when this scene begins to unfold. Give me permission to assist you and Ahbleza. I know what to do. I only need to be asked and I will get to work. Have no fear. I will ensure no harm comes to Ahbleza. And now, do what Nanny suggested – to see Ahbleza protected and well, and see the bad men walking away, while she keeps drumming. Create a bubble of love with your vision at its centre, then send it off into the world. You are loved, you are blessed, you are safe. All is well. Now create your vision." And he fades from their sight.

They all project their vision of Ahbleza, seeing him safe, well and protected. And the men dropping their guns and walking away, never to commit any such atrocity again. They surround their vision in love and send it off to the Universe.

Nanny calls them back with the drum. "Coming fully back into your bodies now. We are safe, we are well. Our work, for now, is done!" she says. "OK kids, I think we've done a good job. We've done what we can, and now we need to wait for the next part of the story to unfold. Keep a look out for this place you saw, Grace. So I think it's time for you to head back to school again. You can still come back tomorrow, as you had planned, and perhaps we'll have a bit more news then."

"Nanny, can I ask you something?" says Archie.

"Yes lad, go ahead," says Nanny.

"Where is Ahbleza now and why aren't we talking to him and warning him about this?" says Archie.

"Very good question, my lad. Truth is, I ain't seen Ahbleza in a couple of days now. I've called for him a few times and no response. He does this from time to time – goes off on his own horsey business, so I hadn't been too worried before you gave me your news. I still don't think it's a terrible sign. Maybe he's gone into hiding. He is a magical creature, as you know, and he may have already sensed this coming or seen it in a vision."

"So we're planning to walk through Paradise Wood tomorrow when we come, to see if we can find the place I saw in my dream," says Grace. "We can keep an eye out for him too."

"That's a really good idea, Gracie. And fits right in with what Regulus said. Righto, time for you to go back now. Remember not to be afraid. Do not put your fears into the world, it will only attract bad things to happen. The work we've done today was very powerful. I have faith that he will be OK. Keep remembering that Regulus said 'All is Well' and he knows what to do. See you tomorrow, my Dears."

Thanks Nanny. See you tomorrow," they all say and head for the portal to be beamed back to school.

Chapter 27:
A Strange Land Rover

The following day, the kids are on their way back to see Nanny and keeping an eye out for Ahbleza. It's a beautiful autumn day, and as there are no matches this afternoon, they have decided to walk the long way round through Paradise Wood. As they walk through the field, which gives access to the forest, they think it is strange to see a Land Rover parked there.

"Hey, I wonder who that belongs to?" says Archie. "Shall we have a little nosey inside?"

"We'll be in trouble if we get caught!" says Daisy.

"Oh, you just need to bat those brown eyes and sweet-talk your way out of it, if we do. You're pretty good at that, Daiz," says Archie.

"He's right, Daiz. I think we should have a look. I've got a feeling these are the people who are up to no good, and I want to know who they are. Archie, you and I will have a look and Daiz will keep an eye out for anyone coming. Look at the tracks in the grass. They've gone into the forest, so that's the way they'll most likely come back."

"Alright, I'll keep a look out, but be quick, will you?"

"Hey, we're in luck, they didn't lock the passenger door," says Archie opening it and searching through the glove compartment. "Nothing interesting here."

"Let me have a look," says Grace. She spots a folder stuffed under the passenger seat and looking around to check that no-one is coming, says, "Let's have a look at this, it might have a name on it." She pulls out a sheaf of paper titled, 'Game Hunting Contract.'

"Oh my goodness, what's this?!" She has a skim-read and says to the others. "It seems to be a contract between Farmer Morgan and some guy called 'A. Hunter' to let him shoot game on his land. There's also a section about the hunter paying a huge bonus for bringing down the 'prize specimen' and turning it into a wall-mounted trophy."

"Euw, how disgusting!" says Daisy. "I hate those trophies you see hanging on the wall. They give me the creeps. I didn't know people still did that these days. But it fits right in with your dream."

"Yeah, there are some weirdos that think it makes them some kind of a macho man to do that," says Archie. "And yeah, it looks like we've found the bad men from your dream, Grace."

"I wonder what it means by the 'prize specimen'?" says Grace. "Does Morgan have any stags on his land?"

"Not that I've ever heard of," says Daisy. "I'm afraid I think they're talking about Ahbleza."

"Oh gosh, yes, I think you may be right. Hey, shall we follow the tracks and see if we can find out what they're up to?" says Archie.

"Yes, we can always pretend we were just out for a walk and got lost, if they see us. It's safer than hanging around here," says Grace, putting the folder back and closing the door as quietly as she can.

They follow the tracks through the long grass to the edge of the woods. "The tracks seem to be heading for Nanny Watkins' house," says Archie. They creep as quietly as they can until almost upon a sun-dappled clearing. Archie holds the girls back and puts a finger to his lips. He points to the undergrowth at the edge of the clearing. Two men with rifles are hiding there.

"This is where he often comes to graze," says Morgan. "If we wait quietly, we might be lucky today. But if not, we'll come back earlier another day. Just after dawn would be a good time to score a unicorn," and he gives a nasty, sneering laugh.

"Oh my goodness, he is talking about Ahbleza!" whispers Grace. "You're right, Daiz. That is what the contract meant by the 'prize specimen.'"

"Damn! We have to find a way to warn Ahbleza," says Archie. "Looks like your dream is coming true right in front of our eyes, Grace."

"Oh, how horrifying! I can't believe they're really planning to do that!" says Daisy. As she is saying this, she feels a warm waft of horsey breath blowing down her neck. She turns to see Ahbleza standing behind her. He's been watching the scene over their shoulders. "Oh Ahbleza, you've got to get out of here – you're in such danger!" He peels back his lips from his teeth in a huge grin.

"He doesn't seem too worried," says Archie.

"He doesn't understand – he thinks all people are nice like us," says Daisy.

"How are we going to get him out of here, without making a huge racket and giving ourselves away?" asks Grace.

"I think you're underestimating him. He managed to sneak up on us without us noticing. Daisy, why don't you have a word with him – see if you can send him quietly back to Nanny's house the long way round and we'll follow him and make sure those two idiots aren't coming after us," says Archie.

"Yes, you could do that thing with putting your forehead against his to communicate," says Grace.

"OK, I'll have a go," says Daisy. She whispers, "May I come into your field of energy?" and Ahbleza obligingly lowers his forehead towards hers. "Blazie, you're in terrible danger from those two men over there. They want to shoot you with their rifles. We must go the long way round – very quietly – to Nanny Watkins, so that they don't see us."

He nods silently and turns to walk the way Daisy showed him in his head. The kids follow, hardly daring to breathe. In a couple of minutes, they are safely out of sight and earshot of the hunters. Soon they are outside Nanny's cottage and they call out to her. She comes rushing out.

"There you are, my Blazie. They found you!" Nanny says and throws her arms around him. "Oh kids, what's happened? You all look so shocked," she says.

"Oh my gosh, Nanny, Grace's dream is coming true. We saw the bad men with rifles, and heard them talking about shooting Ahbleza," gushes Daisy. And Archie fills Nanny in with the rest of the details.

"Umm, umm, I see," says Nanny, listening intently and thinking fast about how to remedy this.

"OK kids, here's the plan," she says. "Reckon they'll be

back again, just after dawn, like they said tomorrow morning. I expect this hunter fella is keen to get on and snag his prize. I will have a word with Ahbleza and try to keep him here. You can go back to the clearing and call in Regulus. He's told you that he knows what to do and only needs permission from you calling him in. Remember, the intention is to get them to drop their guns and walk away. Keep holding that in your minds. Stay safe and out of sight. I will be sending my protection around you and asking Ahbleza and Regulus to do the same."

"That sounds like a great plan, Nanny. This is our mission guys. We were born to do this – we're Guardians of the Wild!" says Archie.

"Yes, we're going to save you, boy. We'll keep you safe," says Daisy, putting her arms around Ahbleza's neck. He nods his head up and down and gives them one of his best toothy grins.

The kids use the portal back to school. When they're back, Daisy says, "I'm going to call Mum and ask her not to pick me up today. We can stay over so that we can sneak out very early tomorrow morning."

"Yes, I'll do the same," says Grace. "We can get out via the coal scuttle and Archie, you could let us in through the 6th Form studies window like Darius did, then we can use the portal to get straight to the clearing."

Chapter 28:
The Final Showdown

It's Sunday morning, just before dawn. It's still dark, but a glimmer of light is starting on the horizon. The girls negotiated the coal scuttle and the entrance through the window without a hitch. Regulus is already with them, as they called him in to help with the portal. This time, they asked the portal to take them straight to the clearing, and they are hiding in the bushes, knowing where the men will arrive.

To their horror, they find Ahbleza is already grazing there. And then, before they can warn him, they spot the trophy hunter and Farmer Morgan arrive and crouch in the bushes ready to take aim and fire – just as Grace has seen in her dream. Morgan's two sons are also hanging around in the background.

The three kids are in shock, but they manage to ask Regulus for his help. He seems to grow to twice his normal size – his huge being shining with radiant light, his great thick mane shimmering and the star on his forehead blazing. "You called and I am at your service. What is your will?" They state their intention to Regulus to protect Ahbleza and get the men to drop their guns and walk away.

"Regulus, please do all you can to protect Ahbleza," says Archie.

"And tell us if we can do anything to help," adds Grace.

"Hold your intention that all will be well and let your love form a shield of light around him," says Regulus. The kids concentrate as hard as they can on this intention, seeing Ahbleza cocooned in a big bubble of love.

Regulus races around the boundaries of the clearing and an eerie swirling mist appears behind him. The hunter and Morgan can no longer see where Ahbleza is. They are confused and fear creeps into their hearts. A crack of thunder and lightning splits the sky, illuminating the hunter who, still hiding in the bushes, has raised his gun ready to shoot Ahbleza. And in the centre of the clearing, a horse rears up, beating its front hooves against the air. Its spiral horn of light suddenly illuminates. And then, Regulus's great white head with its magnificent mane materialises out of the mist right in front of the hunter. His confusion turns into terror.

In his deep, commanding voice, Regulus tells him to stand up and show himself. Still holding the gun, but now by his side, he does so.

"Hunter, it is not your choice to take this life – to decide whether this precious creature lives or dies. What you are truly hunting cannot be found here. Killing this being will not bring you power or glory as you believe it will. It cannot mend the hole in your withered heart. It cannot make you feel more of a man. It will only bring you disaster. It will bring you death and destruction. Karma will bring justice for this evil deed. Put down your gun!

"It is not too late for redemption. It is not too late to repent and ask for forgiveness for your evil ways. If you do this, you will be shown mercy. You will be offered the chance for healing."

Shaking at the knees, the hunter drops his gun and drops his head in shame. Regulus steps to one side ... and there is Ahbleza, blazing with light and rearing up. His hooves beating the air in front of him, he lets out an earsplitting scream.

"Don't hurt me, I beg of you," says the hunter. Ahbleza drops to his feet, dipping his head and pointing his horn at the hunter's heart. Everyone gasps – will Ahbleza be merciful? What is his intention? His horn begins to pulse with brilliant white light, which penetrates the hunter's chest like an X-ray. It illuminates his black and withered heart within his chest. The beam of light turns golden and begins to pulse within the hunter's heart. His heart begins to swell and crackle. Bits of charred black flesh – old and wizened – begin to crack loose and fall to the ground. The hunter clutches his chest in pain. His life is still in the balance.

But slowly, slowly, a miracle begins to happen. Soft pink flesh, glowing with radiant light, starts to form where the blackened flesh has fallen off. Before long, the hunter's heart is perfect – just as it was when he was young, before the traumas of life hardened his heart. His face begins to soften, losing its frown lines and the look of pain behind his eyes.

"I am so sorry. Please forgive me for ever thinking that killing you would make me more of a man." He begins to sob.

A beautiful sonorous voice seems to beam out of Ahbleza,

"You are forgiven. Go in peace and find ways to do good in the world, to make amends for your wrongdoing."

"I will, I will," he sobs.

"Call yourself a man?! If you're not going to do it, I'll finish the job," shouts Morgan as a look of bitter twistedness comes over his face and he raises his gun at point blank range towards Ahbleza's chest.

"No!!! Dad, don't do that!" His eldest son, Gareth, rushes forward and gets between his Dad and Ahbleza, pushing the barrel of the gun down to the side. "I will never let you do this. You'll have to kill me first. I've had my doubts about this all along, and now I see how terrible it is. It would be so wrong to kill this beautiful animal. Can't you see how special he is?

"It's not like shooting squirrels and rabbits, like you tried to tell me. Something really bad will happen to you if you kill him. I will never forgive you if you hurt him."

Morgan's shoulders slump and he lets go of the gun. "You'll turn me soft in my old age, Son," he says, shaking his head.

As Gareth speaks, Ahbleza walks up behind him, nuzzling his back and sending his golden light into Gareth's heart area. His heart chakra begins to glow and then it shines into his father's heart. Father and son are connected at the heart, as they have always been, but this time the father gives way to the son's will. "I could never do something that made me lose respect in your eyes, Son. I'm sorry I got you involved in all this," says Morgan.

"It's not too late to change your ways, Old Man. We can find other ways to make money round here. Like teaching people about the beautiful nature and wildlife we have all around us. They can take shots in other ways – we could run photography retreats. We live in such a beautiful place Dad

– we're so lucky."

The mood has changed completely now. Everyone's smiling. The mist disappears and the sun appears over the horizon, sending a shaft of golden light into the clearing.

Regulus and Ahbleza stand side by side. How magnificent they are! "That's the spirit, Gareth. There are always ways to bring in abundance when you connect with your heart and align with your life's purpose. For you lad, it looks as if that purpose is in showing people the beauty of nature. And what better purpose could there be?" says Regulus.

Ahbleza blows softly through his lips and nods his proud head. Now the three kids feel brave enough to step out of the shadows. "Good one, man!" says Archie, slapping Gareth on the back. "That's a brilliant idea!"

Grace says, "We can help you set up your business. I know lots of families who would love to get out in nature and learn to take beautiful photos of the wildlife."

The hunter chimes in, "Yes man. I'll be your first customer. And now I've seen the error of my ways, I will pledge to convert others to taking their shots with a lens instead of a gun."

Regulus speaks once more, "Hunter, we know you are a wealthy man and I have a request to make. You have pledged to make amends for past wrongdoing. There are three young people here whose greatest wish is to go to South Africa and to meet the White Lions of Timbavati, my living counterparts. I have a mission for them there. Would you fund a trip for them to go there?"

"Oh yes, it would be my honour to show them my country," he says.

"Oh wow, that would be amazing! Thank you, thank you, thank you," says Daisy, running forward and taking his hands. "You SO did the right thing. We are so relieved that you saw the light!"

"Please do come and visit me when you are in South Africa. I will get my PA onto it right away."

Archie and Grace come forward to shake his hand and thank him too.

"Thank you, you will receive your reward in heaven," says Regulus, as he fades into the bright sunshine and is gone.

"Ahbleza nudges Daisy. She turns and wraps her arms around him. "I'm so glad you are safe, my beautiful boy," she says. "He's telling me that he wants us to get on his back and he'll take us home."

The three friends climb onto Ahbleza's shining white back. Suddenly, he has great feathery wings. With a few soft beats of his wings, they lift off from the clearing and are gone, up into the blue sky.

Chapter 29:
Letting Jonnie Go

It is heading towards dusk on All Hallow's Eve, as the kids arrive at Nanny Watkins' cottage – a time when the veils are thin between this world and the next. As they step out of the portal, bats are flitting and an owl hoots from the crab apple tree. A full moon is already rising.

"Oh, hello Owl," says Grace. "I was wondering if you would show up today." Owl has been making her appearance as one of Grace's guides when she worked with Nanny over the summer holidays. Nanny has said that Grace carries Owl Medicine and explained that people with Owl Medicine are very wise and intuitive.

"They can see and hear things that others can't – owls can see in the dark and have very good hearing. Owl Medicine people often have the second sight and are drawn to magic.

No-one can deceive them about their motives, because they can see right through them. Many people are frightened of this, because they can sense that the Owl Medicine person can tell exactly what's going on in their heads and hearts," Nanny had said.

Grace had replied that it fitted very well and it explains people's reactions to her 'magical skills.'

Grace looks down as they cross the threshold into Nanny's cottage to see that Owl has left her a feather on the doormat. She picks it up with a smile and says, "Thank you for the gift, Owl." An answering hoot comes from the crab apple tree.

"Wow, it's as if the Owl understood what you said!" says Archie.

"I'm sure she did," says Grace.

"That's a beautiful feather," says Daisy. "Come on Archie, let's make ourselves scarce so that Nanny and Grace can get on with what they need to do."

"Yes, good idea," says Archie.

"Are you ready, Nanny?" says Grace.

"Hmph, ready as I'll ever be. Come on then, let's get on with it."

"It's time. I know how hard this is for you, Nanny, but it's time," says Grace.

"Yes, I know," says Nanny, giving a little sniff and dabbing her eyes.

Daisy and Archie go back outside to Nanny's garden. They don't want to intrude on her grief. So Archie makes a fire and they heat some soup and cook thick pancakes on the griddle.

"So if you're ready then, I'll begin," says Grace. She lights a candle, saying, "I light this candle to invite our loving, helping spirit guides to come and be with us today. Then she takes her rattle and, standing in each of the directions, first facing the east, then south, then west, then north, she calls in the powers of the directions, just as Nanny has taught her. And then the powers of below, Mother Earth, and the powers of above, Great Spirit, God Source, the Universe.

The room feels alive with the presence of the bright loving beings here to help and witness what is about to happen.

"I call the presence of Jonnie Watkins, beloved son of Nanny Watkins, to be here present in this circle." Nanny's face is contorted by grief. And she twists her hands together, waiting, waiting.

A faint glimmer begins to appear in the centre of the circle. It gradually materialises into the shape of Jonnie. Nanny gasps. "Oh my boy, oh my lovely boy!" she says. "How I love you. How I wish I could hug you one last time. I am so sorry that I couldn't protect you, that I couldn't save you."

"Mum, there is nothing to say sorry for, nothing to forgive. It wasn't your fault – it was my choice and my fate. I love you with all my heart, but it's time to let me go, for both our sakes. My spirit needs to pass over. My soul has a new adventure waiting. And I know one day, we'll see each other on the other side. But you must promise that you won't come too soon. You've still got plenty to do here before it's your time. But for now, let's have that last hug." He smiles and holds his arms out to her.

They hug for a long time, until Nanny feels complete. "It's time for me to go now, Mum. I can feel the angels calling me and Granny is here to help me to the other side." The glimmering shape of a radiant, smiling older woman stands beside Jonnie.

"Is that you, Mother?" says Nanny.

"Yes, it is me, dear. So good to see you. I've come to help your boy cross over. We'll take good care of him."

"Thanks Mother, I love you. Goodbye Son. I love you so much. Till we meet again," and she blows him a kiss.

"Go in peace to be with God. May your soul be guided by angels. Blessings on your soul's next journey," says Grace. The two figures fade away and are gone.

Outside in the garden, Archie and Daisy see a shooting star streak across the sky. "Did you see that, Archie? I think that was Jonnie on his way to heaven."

"Yes, I think you're right," says Archie.

Inside, Grace closes the circle, thanking God and the helping spirits, and blowing out the candle. There is a loud tooting sound as Nanny gets out her hankie and blows her nose. Grace hugs her and says, "Well done, Nanny!"

"Thank you, Gracie. You did it perfectly. I think I would like to be alone with my thoughts now," says Nanny.

"Of course. I'll tell the others. I think they've made you some soup and pancakes for your supper. We'll leave it on the table.

Archie comes in with the food and gives Nanny a big bear hug. Daisy kisses her on the cheek. And then they leave, heading back to school.

"Poor Nanny," says Daisy

"Brave Nanny," says Archie.

"Had to be done," says Grace. "It's for the best. But perhaps it won't be the last we see of the soul we know as Jonnie Watkins."

"We saw his star pass overhead, as he left," says Daisy.

"Did you? Wow, how wonderful!" says Grace.

Epilogue

Ahbleza flies across the countryside and high into the mountains. They can see the landscape spread out below them like a quilt. "Wow, it's so beautiful!" says Daisy. "You can see everything from up here."

"Hey guys, I hate to tell you this, but I can't stand heights and I'm feeling a bit queasy," says Archie.

"Don't you dare puke up on me, Archie McBride," says Daisy.

"Oh Archie, you'll be fine," says Grace. "Try pressing the acupressure point on your wrist for motion sickness."

"Number one, I don't have the foggiest where that might be, and number two, if I let go of Daisy's waist, I'll fall off. Anyhow, thanks for your sympathy, girls!" says Archie.

"Oh, well, just try to stay calm then. I wonder where he's taking us?" says Grace.

"He says we're going to a mountain called the Dragon's Back," says Daisy. "There's a stone circle he wants us to visit. Then he'll take us home."

The Dragon's Back comes into view and they touch down near the stone circle. The three kids dismount, thanking Ahbleza for a safe ride. Archie's legs are still wobbly and he almost falls off, getting hoots of laughter from Daisy. "It's usually me doing the falling over," she laughs.

"That's right, have a good laugh at my expense, Daiz. You don't get the opportunity very often!"

"Exactly," says Daisy.

They walk into the stone circle, marvelling at the height

of the stones. "Wow, they're massive!" says Archie.

Inside the stone circle are three more stones, arranged in a half circle at the centre. "Have you noticed that the inner stones have very distinct shapes?" says Grace. "The one on the left looks like a horse's head and the one in the middle looks like a male lion's head. The one on the right reminds me of something, but I can't quite get it yet."

"It looks like the head of a humpbacked whale breaching the surface of the sea and coming up to feed. Look, the stripes and circular markings made by the lichen are just like the markings you see on their throats," says Archie.

"I'll take your word for it, Archie – you are the marine biology nerd after all," says Daisy.

"Hey guys, have you noticed anything else?" says Grace. "The energy here is incredible. It's almost sizzling. It's making the hairs on my arms stand on end."

"Oh yes, so it is! At first, I thought that was just the after-effects of the thrilling ride here," says Archie.

"Maybe it's another portal?" says Grace. "What would Nanny Watkins tell us about this place? Why did Ahbleza bring us here?"

"I'll tune in with him and find out," says Daisy. "Ahbleza says we're to stand in the centre and meditate, then to just see what happens."

They stand in a semi-circle, each facing one of the stones. Daisy faces the horse's head, Grace faces the lion and Archie faces the whale. Just as Nanny has taught them, they tune into this place and imagine silver roots of energy growing down from their feet deep into the ground, and breathing into their hearts.

Suddenly, Regulus is with them. "The three of you have three important missions to complete. Your first mission, saving Ahbleza, represented by the horse's head, is now complete. Without your willingness to learn the ways of sacred magic and to call me in, I would not have had permission to intervene. Ahbleza is a magical being and could always have saved himself – you probably didn't realise that. But without your courage to be there, we could not have worked the magic that caused the change of heart for the hunter and Morgan and his sons.

"Now at this time in Earth's evolution, it is necessary to raise the consciousness – the mindset, and for that matter, the heartset of all humanity. Where there are pockets of darkness – like the selfish and cruel behaviour of the hunter and Farmer Morgan – if we can get them to change their hearts, it will have a ripple effect out to all of the world. Look what has happened already – the hunter has vowed to work on speaking to all his trophy hunting friends, to get them to see the error of their ways. He will need much assistance with this, but it's a start.

"You are the catalyst and the bridge that allows us to come in and work with physical human beings. For that, I thank you with all my heart.

"And what of these other two stones – the lion and the whale? Your next task is to go to South Africa to meet the White Lions." As he says this, the stone seems to light up and images start to form on the stone's surface. "Your mission will unfold when you get there.

"And then there's the whale ... and that's another story." Images of great humpback whales and other whale-like creatures with spiral horns like narwhals, singing and making sounds, move across the stone.

"Are you ready for your next challenge?" says Regulus.

"Well, yes, well, maybe, almost. But how about some tea and cake back at Nanny Watkins' house first? I'm sure she would love to hear all about it," says Archie.

"That sounds like a great idea," says Grace. "I've had about as much excitement as I can manage in one day."

"How about it, Ahbleza? Are you up for taking us back to Nanny Watkins' cottage?" says Daisy. He nods his head and nudges Archie so hard in the back that he almost lifts him off his feet. Then he lifts his beautiful head up, pulls his lips back from his teeth and gives them the biggest, toothiest horse grin they've ever seen, neighing and nodding his head up and down, to peals of laughter from all three of them.

* * *

This is Book One of a three-part series, so hold tight for more magical adventures with Grace, Archie and Daisy.

Ackowledgements

My heartfelt thanks in helping me write and publish this book go to:

My daughter, Phoebe, who helped me dream up the story concept and whose love of horses inspired the character of Ahbleza. And for her enthusiastic laughter when I read scenes out to her.

To all my friends from Bedstone, especially Rachel and Monty, and to the wonderful Bedstone staff, for all the cherished memories of our time there.

To Robert Moss, Active Dream Teacher extraordinaire and bestselling author of many books, including *Active Dreaming: Journeying Beyond Self-Limitation to a Life of Wild Freedom* and *Dreamways of the Iroquois: Honoring the Secret Wishes of the Soul*. Thank you, Robert, for always praising and championing my writing – it has been such a confidence boost to hear from someone with such brilliant writing skills and many successful published books. Your course on *Writing and Creating as a State of Conscious Dreaming* helped me to gather the bones for this story and dream them alive.

And to the brave band of dreamers who met in the Czech Republic under Robert's wonderful tutelage to write and dream, and even helped me by acting out some of the scenes from the book. Including Jennifer Linse Bichanich, Richelle Dassin, Eva Dostalova, Ricky Goodman, Monica Kenton, Jana Lamurai, Janne Loekkeberg, Zbyněk Merhaut, Patty Miller, and Petr Nemcansky.

To Nicola Humber, who re-inspired me many times, when my creative flow was flagging, through her writing sprees and virtual writing retreats; and to all the team at the Unbound Press, including Emma Mulholland, Jesse Lynn Smart and Lynda Mangoro, who kept me on track to complete and publish this book.

To my Beta Readers, Tracy Thursfield, Eimear Stassin and Jennifer Muldoon, for giving me such kind and enthusiastic feedback, for helping me to iron out the kinks and for spotting things that I had missed. And especially to Isla Halls for being my first teenage beta reader.

And to my beloved husband, Bill – always a source of enthusiasm and encouragement, helping to create space for me to write and boosting my confidence about my writing.

About the Author

Anna is a Shamanic Teacher and Healer, an Active Dreamer, a Journeyer between the Worlds, a Writer, a Wordsmith, a Writing Coach and an Editor.

Just like Nanny Watkins, she is experienced in all the core techniques of shamanism, and her power animals have inspired some of the characters in this book.

Anna uses her shamanic journeying skills to help inspire her writing and brings these techniques into her work as a writing coach to help you draw on inspiration from the magical realms and your dreams.

In a healing session with Anna, she will use her shamanic journeying skills to go with her guides to find information to help you on your soul's journey. She can connect you with your own guides and power animals. She can help you recover parts of your soul that may have gone away through trauma. She can help you with extracting energy intrusions, with house healing and with psychopomp. And she can teach you how to journey for yourself.

Anna has wide-ranging experience of many alternative healing modalities, including a diploma in Shiatsu, Reiki, Kinesiology, Homeopathy and Herbs. She brings this wisdom into her shamanic healing work.

She is an Active Dreamwork Teacher, trained with Robert Moss. She can help you to make sense of your dreams and to use what comes through in your dreams for your healing and inspiration.

Anna lives in the beautiful Black Mountains of Herefordshire in the UK, with her husband Bill, her daughter, her cat – Mr Reggie Bonbons (aka Agent Fluff) – and her Springador, Holly.

This is Anna's third book, her first being *Wild Animals and Wedding Outfits: A voyage of self-discovery around the world* with Bill, her husband. And her second book is *A Wild Adventure on the Big C: My Journey of Natural Healing for Cancer.*

Contact Details
You can reach Anna in the following ways:
Email: anna@anna-bromley.com
Website – https://anna-bromley.com
Facebook – https://www.facebook.com/anna.bromley.7
Substack – https://annabromley.substack.com